Wyatt Earp was the stuff of legend. Nowhere is this more evident than in the array of books and motion pictures devoted to "The Gunfight at the O.K. Corral." Through the decades, from that autumn day in 1881, the O.K. Corral shootout has become the most widely celebrated incident in the mythology of the Old West.

Yet there was far more to Wyatt Earp than a gunfight that lasted barely thirty seconds. A westering man, Earp roamed the frontier for the majority of his life. And the usual accounts portray him as nothing more than a lawman with a fast gun. The reality, in fact, proves to be far more absorbing.

The portrait rendered here of Wyatt Earp is neither history nor myth. This is a fictional account based upon chronicles, court records, and certain recollections of those who lived through that deadly autumn of 1881. Literary license has been taken with time, place and various characters who people the story. What emerges is a Wyatt Earp not so much larger than life as true to life. Not literal truth, but the personal story of a lawman who aspired to more than a badge. The untold story of a Western myth.

# WYATT EARP

# WYATT EARP

## MATT BRAUN

St. Martin's Paperbacks

WYATT EARP

Copyright © 1994 by Matt Braun.

ISBN: 0-312-95325-9

Printed in the United States of America

St. Martin's Paperbacks edition / June 1994

10 9 8 7 6 5 4 3

# AUTHOR'S NOTE

Wyatt Earp was the stuff of legend. Nowhere is this more evident than in the array of books and motion pictures devoted to "The Gunfight at the O.K. Corral." Through the decades, from that autumn day in 1881, the O.K. Corral shootout has become the most widely celebrated incident in the mythology of the Old West.

Yet there was far more to Wyatt Earp than a gunfight that lasted barely thirty seconds. A westering man, Earp roamed the frontier for the majority of his life. His career as a peace officer was relatively brief, encompassing the years 1875–1881. The Kansas cowtowns of Wichita and Dodge City were where he first gained notoriety as a lawman. There, policing the riotous Texas cowhands, he acquired a reputation for tough law enforcement. But it was in Tombstone, an Arizona mining town, where the man and the myth became one. Three men died at the O.K. Corral, and a legend was born.

History, as well as myth, often proves to be oddly selective. The Gunfight at the O.K. Corral was swift and deadly, a face-to-face, kill-or-get-killed confrontation. For sheer drama, however, the aftermath of the O.K. Corral was far more compelling. Men were ambushed and assassinated, others were killed in gunfights, and the impact on those who survived was little short of tragic. Yet these events have been largely overlooked, particularly in the creation of the myth. Nor do the usual accounts portray Wyatt Earp as anything more than a lawman with a fast gun. The reality, once again, proves to be far more absorbing.

The portrait rendered here of Wyatt Earp is neither history nor myth. This is a fictional account based upon chronicles, court records, and certain recollections of those who lived through that deadly autumn of 1881. Literary license has been taken with time, place and various characters who people the story. What emerges is a Wyatt Earp not so much larger than life as true to life. Not literal truth, but the personal story of a lawman who aspired to more than a badge. The untold story of a Western myth.

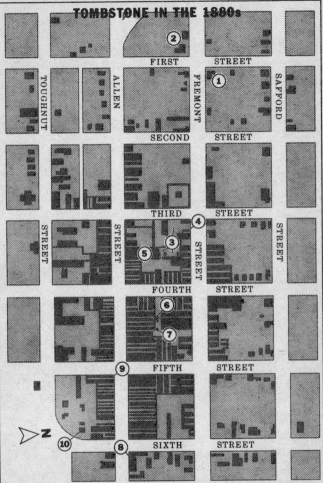

**TOMBSTONE IN THE 1880s**

1. Earp Brothers' House 2. Homes of Virgil, James Earp (to March '82); Morgan & Wyatt lived here July '81 to Oct. 26 '81 3. Vacant property; open stalls used in connection with O.K. Corral 4. New building; former-ly part of O.K. Corral, yard scene of battle, Oct. 26 '81 5. O.K. Corral stable 6. Occidental Saloon 7. Alhambra Saloon 8. Cribs, rooms of Big Nose Kate and Doc Holliday 9. Jacob Meyers' Clothing Store; Virgil Earp was shot here 1881 10. Cabin where Wyatt & Morgan lived from 1879 to 1881.

# Chapter One

THE RIDERS ENTERED TOWN IN A DUSTY WEDGE. They slowed their horses to a walk as they passed the blacksmith's shop. The smith paused at his anvil and watched with open curiosity as they proceeded upstreet. A group of Mexicans, mounted on fiery ponies with Spanish rigging, was an unusual sight in Charleston.

Located in southern Arizona, the town was less than a day's ride from the border with Old Mexico. Yet there was little interchange, whether in commerce or custom, between the Anglos of Charleston and Mexicans from below the border. Stores were closing along the street as the sun dipped westward toward the horizon. On the boardwalks, townspeople stared as the men rode past.

The one out front, an older man, was clearly the *patrón*. Though he wore range clothes, his bearing set him apart, and he was mounted on a prancing black stallion. His hair and beard were flecked with gray, and he ignored the stares of passersby with an imperious expression. The four men strung out behind him were vaqueros, easily tagged by their saddle trappings and the style of their clothing. All of them were armed, and like their leader, they stared straight ahead.

Halfway through town, the older Mexican reined to a halt before Walsh's Cafe. The vaqueros spread out on either side of him, halting their horses at the hitch rack. Lolling in chairs outside the cafe were six men whose manner of dress identified them as cowhands. Having just finished supper, some were picking their teeth and others were in the process of lighting roll-your-own cigarettes.

They inspected the horsemen, noting the wide-brimmed sombreros and heavy rowled spurs.

A moment passed as the Mexican *patrón* examined the men on the boardwalk. Then he nodded quizzically, looking from one to the other. His English was thickly accented. "Senor Brocius?"

One of the men straightened in his chair. "That's me."

"You are William Brocius?" the Mexican asked. "*Jefe* of the Clanton Ranch?"

Bill Brocius rose to his feet. A large man, tall and wide through the shoulders, he had thick curly hair and full mustaches. He arched one eyebrow in question. "I run the Clanton outfit," he said. "Who's askin'?"

"Senor, I am Don Gonzalo Ortega, of Sonora. You are familiar with that name?"

"Ortega." Brocius repeated it, rubbing his whiskery jaw as though puzzled. "No, can't say as I recollect hearin' the name."

Ortega smiled. "Perhaps I can refresh your memory, senor. My ranchero lies eighty kilometers south of Nogales, on the Rio de la Concepcion River."

The men seated around Brocius exchanged sideways glances. They slowly unfolded from their chairs and stood, positioning themselves on either side of Brocius. The Mexicans stiffened, suddenly tense, and there was a moment of silence as the two groups stared at one another.

Brocius shook his head. "Don't recollect you or your spread. Why d'ya ask?"

"Think back to six nights ago, senor. You and your men visited my ranchero, and the next morning I found myself poorer by almost two hundred steers."

"Mister, do I understand you're accusing me of rustlin' your cattle?"

Despite his aggrieved tone, Brocius looked anything but innocent. To the townspeople of Charleston, he and his men were known cattle rustlers. They stole cows in Mexico, trailed them to Arizona, and sold them to ranchers who turned a blind eye to brands from below the border. Everyone, including the townspeople, benefited by the trade.

The practice had originally started under the leadership of a rancher outside Charleston, known universally as Old Man Clanton. His chief lieutenant was Bill Brocius, and the principal members of the gang were his two sons, Ike and Billy, the McLaury brothers, Tom and Frank, and Johnny Ringo. A year ago, when Old Man Clanton had been killed in a raid south of the border, Brocius had assumed leadership of the gang.

Don Ortega took his time answering Brocius. He calculated the odds, six guns to five, and found them less than favorable. At length, he waved his hand in a dismissive gesture.

"Please, senor," he said, "let us not speak harshly of such things. I merely state that my steers were thoughtless enough to follow you across the border."

Brocius grunted. "You'll play hell provin' it."

"I regret to say that is so. The trail was difficult to follow at times, and when we arrived at your ranch, my steers had once again disappeared."

"You've been to our place?"

"Si," Ortega informed him. "We have just come from there. Your cook—I believe his name is Clyde—told us you were taking dinner in town tonight."

"Sorry sonovabitch," Brocius said gruffly. "He's gonna be lookin' for a new job."

"Your men are your concern, senor. I am concerned only with the return of my steers."

"Goddamn, Bill!" Ike Clanton pushed forward, his voice raised to a strident pitch. "Are you gonna let this greaser stand up in front of the whole town and make us out to be rustlers?"

Johnny Ringo, who appreciated unintended irony, chuckled aloud. Everyone in Charleston, not to mention southern Arizona, was all too aware of their occupation. Brocius gave him a dirty look, then turned back to Ortega.

"Senor, it appears to me your cows have got some mighty bad habits. Now just supposin' them cows did follow us across the border. Exactly what'd you have in mind doing about it?" Brocius paused, swept the town with a broad motion. "I mean, this here's the United States, not Mexico."

Ortega nodded agreement. "A point well taken, Senor Brocius. But then, men like ourselves have no use for legal technicalities, is it not so?"

When Brocius seemed to ponder the question, the *patrón* decided to elaborate. "Clearly, you can understand that as a man who protects what is his own, I have no choice but to demand payment for my steers."

"And if I'm not of a mind to see it your way?"

"We are reasonable men, senor. Rather than spill blood, is it not better to choose some less costly way?"

Brocius hooted laughter. "Godalmighty!" he said, glancing around at his men. "Boys, here's a man after my own heart. Willin' to go whole hog and let you call your own tune!"

The gang watched Brocius closely, waiting for a cue. His moods were mercurial and they were never certain what his laughter meant. Still grinning, his gaze shifted back to Ortega.

"Why don't you and your men climb down off of them horses? We'll walk across to the saloon and get ourselves a bottle. Settle this thing like—what was it you called it—like *reasonable* men."

Ortega studied him for a long moment. Brocius's face was twisted in an amiable smile, and the rest of the gang stared at the Mexicans with neutral expressions. At last the *patrón* nodded and shifted in his saddle to dismount. The youngest of the Mexican riders spurred his horse forward, blocking Ortega from stepping down.

"*Mi padre,* he said hotly, "*no haces cuento delos perros gringo! Ellos sueiren tomar tragos para matar les.*"

Ortega brushed aside the warning. He looked at Brocius with an apologetic shrug. "Pardon, senor, my son is young and mistrustful of americanos. He believes you wish to cloud our minds with liquor, so that you might more easily kill us."

Brocius appeared wounded. "Well, I don't know how it is in Mexico, but hereabouts it's an insult to refuse a man's drink. I reckoned you'd accept the offer the way it was meant."

There was a beat of hesitation, then Ortega motioned to his men. "*No hablan mas! Nos vamos con estos hombres para tomar.*" He nodded to Brocius. "We will accept your offer, senor."

Ortega started to dismount, and the vaqueros reluctantly followed his lead. Brocius waited until the Mexicans were trapped with one leg over the saddle and suddenly jerked his pistol. He stepped off the boardwalk and shot Ortega from a distance of only a few feet. The *patrón* went rigid, the front of his jacket aflame from the powder flash of the pistol. He slumped sideways, losing the stirrup, and tumbled to the ground.

Only an instant behind Brocius, the rest of the gang drew their guns and poured a volley into the Mexicans. The McLaury brothers, positioned to the left, fired simultaneously, wounding one vaquero and killing another. Ike and Billy Clanton fired too quickly, their snap shots hitting the *patrón*'s son in the left arm and creasing his hairline. Johnny Ringo, always a deliberate killer, blasted the last vaquero from his saddle.

The wounded vaquero and young Ortega were now in the street, backing away from the pitching horses. They managed to pull their pistols, but the shots went wild, thudding into the cafe wall and shattering the window. Brocius yelled, scattering the horses, and brought his gun arm level. He took careful aim and shot the Ortega boy in the head. As though struck by lightning, the youngster stood bolt upright, then fell dead in the street.

Ringo and Billy Clanton fired on the wounded vaquero. One shot struck him in the shoulder and the other punched into his chest. He stumbled backward from the impact of the slugs, then dropped to his knees and tried to bring his gun to bear. Ringo calmly thumbed the hammer on his Colt, centered the sights on the Mexican's breastbone and touched the trigger. The vaquero's arms windmilled as a dark splotch of blood spread over his shirtfront. He toppled face forward onto the ground.

An abrupt stillness settled over the street. Brocius waved the gang forward, watching while they nudged each of the bodies with booted toes. Townspeople began edging onto the boardwalks, reappearing from where they had taken cover when the shooting commenced. They were drawn by morbid curiosity and a certain sense of admiration for their own. While none of them knew the cause of the gunfight, they found nothing to criticize in the killing of Mexicans who rode so boldly into their town.

Don Gonzalo Ortega lay crumpled at Brocius's feet. The dead man's clothing continued to smolder as the sun vanished westward and dusk slowly fell over the grisly scene. The gang members gathered around Brocius, holstering their guns, and followed his gaze to the fallen *patrón*. Finally, unable to contain himself, Ike Clanton broke the silence.

"What you lookin' at, Bill?"

"Damn fool," Brocius said, staring at the body. "Should've known a white man wouldn't drink with a greaser."

"Bought it, though!" Clanton crowed. "You fooled him slicker'n spit!"

Brocius traded a look with Ringo. Neither of them held the Clanton boys in high regard. But business was business, and the Clanton Ranch, now owned by the brothers, was well-situated for their forays into Mexico. After a mo-

ment Brocius shook his head, gesturing as though to an
overly excited schoolboy.

"Ike, go fetch the undertaker. Tell him to come collect
hisself a spade flush. Get this trash off the street."

# Chapter Two

HOLLIDAY AWOKE FULLY ALERT. HE LAY PERFECTLY still, listening. His pistol was on the nightstand, beside the bed, within easy reach. A noise had penetrated his sleep, and he wouldn't move until he'd identified the source. Then, out in the hall, he heard the voices of two men fading toward the stairway. He relaxed, let the tension melt away.

Often as not, Holliday was awakened by noise. Drunks on the street, voices outside, the footstep of a maid on creaky floorboards in the hallway. Whenever he'd camped at trailside on a trip, surrounded by wilderness noise, he hadn't slept at all. But he never chided himself for being easily spooked, too cautious to sleep. On more than one occasion his ingrained wariness had saved his life.

Tossing the covers aside, he sat up on the edge of the bed. He took his pocket watch from the nightstand and checked the time. Going on noon, and he'd got to bed sometime after five in the morning. An all-night poker game had been suitably profitable, but routinely boring. Lately it seemed there were no challenges, for the other players were too predictable, too easily read. Perhaps, in the end, that was the curse of a professional gambler. No one to pit himself against, put him to the test.

A sudden spasm wracked him with a fit of coughing. He reached for a bottle on the nightstand, popped the cork and took a long pull. The whiskey was raw, almost molten when it hit his stomach. But on the way down it stopped the coughing, and he was able to collect himself without a second drink. He rose, quickly dressing against the chill of the room, and moved to the washstand. Since arriving in Tombstone, he'd discovered that autumn nights in October could be uncomfortably cold. All the more so for a man with consumption.

Ten minutes later, freshly shaved and his mustache neatly trimmed, he walked from the room. Today he wore a swallowtail coat and a black cravat, with a gold watch chain looped across his vest. Along the hallway he stopped at a room and rapped lightly on the door. He waited a moment, listening for a response, then proceeded downstairs. The lobby of the Occidental was appointed with a grouping of leather chairs that looked out through a broad window onto the street. As he passed the desk clerk, he saw that the town was bustling with activity. He noted, not for the first time, that people could be drawn anywhere, even the desert wastes of Arizona, by the scent of money.

In early 1878 a bedraggled, footsore prospector struggled along the jagged mountain slopes east of San Pedro Valley. His name was Ed Schieffelin, and quite literally, he stumbled upon one of the richest silver strikes in frontier history. With ore assaying at twenty thousand dollars a ton, the discovery sparked the greatest mining boom ever recorded in the southwest. Schieffelin named his strike Tombstone, and within a matter of months the mile-high camp had mushroomed into a carnival of speculation. A stagecoach line was established across the seventy-mile stretch of desert to Tucson. Men and machinery began pouring in, followed closely by merchants and tradesmen, gamblers and saloonkeepers, and the finest assemblage of whores ever gathered in the Arizona barrens. From a few hundred whiskery desert rats, huddled in tents and squalid shacks, Tombstone burst upon the map as a riproaring boomtown. Within three years the population leaped to six thousand, and still growing. A town, complete with all the civilized vices, was spawned in a land previously thought inhabitable only by Apaches and scorpions. It was a dusty helldorado, vitalized by the mother lode, and it ran wide-open day and night.

Holliday wouldn't have changed a thing. As he entered the hotel dining room, it occurred to him that he'd made a life for himself in the mining camps and cowtowns of the West. Not the life his genteel ancestors would have envisioned, but one that admirably suited his own needs. He crossed to a table where Earp was seated alone, eating breakfast.

"Good morning, Wyatt."

"Mornin', Doc." Earp speared a bite of ham on his fork. "All set for another day?"

Holliday took a chair at the table. "One day's like any other. I take 'em as they come."

"Don't be so cynical. The way folks here play poker, you're on the gravy train."

"I'd sooner have some competition. Dulls a man's edge when there's no one to play but greenhorns."

A waiter appeared, pouring a mug of coffee for Holliday. He took a flask from inside his coat and dosed the coffee with a liberal shot of whiskey. After a long sip, he produced a cheroot and lit up in a cloud of smoke. He smiled, waving the thin, black cigar.

"A good smoke, a cup of java, and a dose of the devil's own. What more could a man ask?"

Earp frowned, smearing jam on a biscuit. Though they occupied hotel rooms close together, he never awakened Holliday in the morning. He figured the gambler needed all the rest he could get, and then some. He also had no qualms about expressing his opinion.

"You ought to try food for a change, Doc. You're damn near a bag of bones."

"I make it a practice to eat only when I'm hungry. Meanwhile, whiskey keeps my gears oiled."

Holliday was a southerner, a man of breeding and education. Incurable tuberculosis had brought him West, seeking a drier climate. Even on the frontier, however, there was small demand for a dentist who coughed blood. Circumstance, and physical frailty, had led him into the life of an itinerant gambler. An ungovernable temper, coupled with that same physical frailty, had transformed him into a man-killer. In the truest sense, the Colt six-gun was for him the equalizer. He killed men simply because it was his sole means of defending himself. Then, too, he enjoyed the sport of wagering life against life. It gave a certain tang to an otherwise bleak existence.

Tall and emaciated, with ash-blond hair and a brushy mustache, Holliday was somewhere in his thirties. His visage was that of an undertaker; sober but not really sad. His attitude toward his fellow man was an inimical union of gruff sufferance and thinly disguised contempt. Speculation had it that he had killed twenty-six men, and his manner left no question that he was equal to the task. He impressed the people in Tombstone as someone who could walk into an empty room and start a fight.

By contrast, Wyatt Earp was of medium height, powerfully built, with close-cropped hair and a handlebar mustache. His slate-colored eyes and taciturn manner were striking, leaving the impression of a serious man who found little time for laughter. A Yankee whose family had joined the westward migration, he began as a drifter with a yearning to better himself. His upward climb had taken him from buffalo hunter, to a lawman in the Kansas cowtowns, to a mining entrepreneur in Tombstone. He possessed a near infallible insight into the actions and motives of other men. Like Holliday, he had killed men, but never out of some quirky sense of contest. He killed to uphold the law, or to protect himself and what he found of value.

Their friendship, from the start, had been a subject of wide speculation. A lawman and a stone-cold killer made for a curious match. Yet Holliday, despite his sullen manner, was not altogether misanthropic. No man ever completely purges himself of the need for human contact.

Several years ago, in Dodge City, he had saved Earp's life in a showdown with Texan cowhands intent on killing a Yankee marshal. From that point onward, Earp had accepted him as he was, seemingly unconcerned with his racking cough or his cynical outlook. At the time, Holliday thought it was perhaps his last chance to throw in with someone worthy of his respect. He was of the same opinion even now.

"What's on for today?" Holliday asked, swigging his laced coffee. "Out to make yourself another fortune?"

Earp chuckled. "Haven't made the first one yet. Still looking for the end of the rainbow."

"Don't kid an old kidder. By now, I'd calculate you own half of Tombstone."

"You're mighty optimistic for a dyed-in-the-wool pessimist. Anybody hear you talk, they'd think I was one of those Wall Street robber barons."

"Perish the thought," Holliday deadpanned. " 'Course, those business pals of yours aren't exactly small potatoes."

"No, I reckon not." Earp finished his breakfast, shoved the plate away. "Trouble is, they've got theirs in the bank and I'm still trying to cash my chips."

"By last count"—Holliday ticked it off on his fingers—"you owned a couple of houses, three storefronts, and a piece of three mining properties. Did I miss anything?"

"There's the Oriental."

"How'd I overlook that? A piece of the biggest gaming den in the town. And Virgil's town marshal and you're running for sheriff. I'd say you've got a finger in just about every paint pot in the county."

Holliday had a point. But Earp was of the firm belief that a man's reach should always exceed his grasp. "Doc, it's not what you've got," he allowed, "it's what's on the table to be won. The game's not over till it's over."

"Lord love us!" Holliday grinned, the cheroot wedged in the corner of his mouth. "A trailhead lawdog turned business mogul. Wyatt, you've been bit by the ambition bug."

"Think so, huh?"

"Don't think it," Holliday said jocularly. "I know it for a fact. You've got the itch to be rich. Tell me it's not so."

There was no denying the statement. Earp and his brothers, Virgil and Morgan, along with Doc Holliday, had arrived in Tombstone the latter part of 1879. Virgil wore the badge of deputy U.S. Marshal, and Wyatt, out to make his mark, had sought appointment as sheriff of Cochise County. Instead, the territorial governor appointed his chief rival, John Behan. But politics was only one of the games in town. Wyatt turned his attention to the business arena.

Fame as a cowtown marshal had followed him from Kansas. Now, with his sights set on fortune, he'd gone after a bigger prize. One of his first allies in Tombstone was John Clum, editor of the *Epitaph* newspaper. Through Clum, he had been introduced to several mine owners and influential businessmen. To a man, they opposed Sheriff Behan, and Tombstone's other newspaper, the *Nugget*, owned by Harry Woods. So they had aligned themselves behind their newest political champion, Wyatt Earp.

Part of their support was in counseling Earp on business matters. He'd slowly acquired an interest in mining properties, town real estate, and the Oriental Saloon. Hardly six months past, John Clum had been elected mayor, and one of his first acts was to appoint Virgil to the post of town marshal. Sheriff Behan, widely thought to be in cahoots with the Clanton gang, still controlled the county. But with Virgil as town marshal and federal deputy marshal, the Earps dominated law enforcement in Tombstone. And Wyatt intended to take all the apples during the election for sheriff next spring.

As autumn spread over the countryside, October of 1881, the Earps had been in Tombstone not quite two years. Whether the topic was politics or business, no one questioned that their fortunes had indeed risen. Wyatt Earp, in particular, was seen as a leader, a man who would bring Cochise County into a new era. The enemies he'd made brought him even greater respect from his business associates and a large segment of the townspeople. He was known as a man who wouldn't quit, whatever the odds.

Today, as he emerged from the hotel with Holliday, he had reason to be pleased with his world. Fortune had smiled on him, and he'd taken advantage of opportunity at every turn. While he would never admit as much to Holliday, for he enjoyed bantering with his old friend, he had ample reason to say grace. Things were going his way, on a downhill slide.

"I'm headed over to see Virg," he said. "You want to come along?"

Holliday shaded his eyes from the noonday sun. "Maybe I'll check out the Oriental. Someone might be looking for a game of chance."

"The way you play," Earp said amiably, "it's no game of chance. I wonder that people still take a seat at your table."

"Just goes to show, Wyatt. Fools and their gold are soon parted."

Holliday stepped off the veranda and angled across to the saloon. Earp turned upstreet, nodding to the men he passed, tipping his hat to the ladies. The crisp October air put a spring in his step.

He tried not to look too pleased with himself.

# Chapter Three

EARP CROSSED TOWN AT A BRISK PACE. AS HE walked, he was struck again by the rapid growth of what had started as a raw mining camp. There was now a sense of permanence about the community, and with it, a strong scent of money.

Tombstone was laid out in a grid pattern, with the business district centralized in the heart of town. The main thoroughfares were Allen Street and Fremont Street, both crossing the grid east to west. North and west of downtown were the better residential areas. To the south were warehouses and the less desirable residential quarter. Vice, in the form of cribs and parlor houses, was restricted to the eastern section of the community.

Allen Street boasted most of the saloons and gambling establishments, along with three additional hotels and the Birdcage Theater. One block north, on Fremont Street, was the main commercial district. City Hall and a couple of banks were flanked by several blocks of cafes, shops, and general business concerns. At night, when Tombstone's sporting element awakened, Allen Street came alive. But during the day, Fremont Street was the busiest part of town. Here the hustle and bustle of everyday affairs was conducted in a more sedate atmosphere.

Tombstone, by light of day, revealed itself as a veritable money tree. The outlying mines were processing millions of dollars of silver every year. Unlike most mining camps, the influx of people and a stable economy had created a sense of something built to last. Whoever controlled the political apparatus of Cochise County would have access

to a fortune in taxes and patronage. Whoever wore the
sheriff's badge would play a key role in the distribution of
that largesse. In tax fees alone, the sheriff pulled down
upwards of thirty thousand dollars a year. That was a veritable fortune, particularly at a time when men labored in
mine shafts for six dollars a day. Moreover, the sheriff's
office provided a legitimate front for certain hidden forms
of skulduggery. It was small wonder that John Behan
fought so hard to hold the post of the county's chief
lawman. Some people believed that his share of the
Clanton gang's rustling operation was, at the very least,
equal to what he hauled in as sheriff.

Uptown, Earp turned west on Fremont Street. The office
of town marshal was located beside a frame building that
served as City Hall. Attached to the marshal's office was
the city jail, with eight cells off a central corridor. Meals
for prisoners, mostly drunk miners, were provided by a
nearby cafe.

With the mines operating on double shift, and loose
money there for the taking, Tombstone attracted grifters
and bunco men from across the West. Regulars on the
gambler's circuit, noteworthy among them Luke Short and
Bat Masterson, routinely drifted in by stagecoach. Yet, despite its reputation as the "town too tough to die," only a
small segment of the citizens ran afoul of the law. Miners
spent ten hours a day, six days a week, in the underground shafts. For the most part, they were rough, unedu-
cated men whose chief diversion was a drunken spree on
Saturday nights. Their differences, usually in the form of
saloon brawls, were settled with fists rather than guns.

Entering the marshal's office, Earp was reminded of an
enforcement technique he had developed in the Kansas
cowtowns. There, when he encountered drunken Texans
spoiling for a fight, he had "buffaloed" them with a pistol
barrel across the head. The idea was to move quickly,
while they were still talking themselves into a fight, and
lay them out with what amounted to a steel blackjack.

Virgil had perfected the technique as well, and employed it with great effect in policing the dives in Tombstone. A pistol barrel laid across the skull of a burly miner was a persuasive deterrent. Troublemakers soon got the message.

Virgil looked up from his desk. "Glad you stopped by," he said, leaning back in a creaky chair. "Saves me a trip down to the Oriental."

"Morning, Virg." Earp seated himself on the edge of the desk. "What's so important it would bring you downtown?"

Virgil Earp was a lean man, with hard eyes and a slow smile. The family resemblance was immediately apparent, and like his brother, his upper lip was covered with a brushy mustache. He knuckled the mustache back now, his expression somber.

"Word came over the telegraph this morning. There was a shooting in Charleston last night. Some folks might call it a massacre."

"Brocius and the Clantons?"

"Who else?"

Charleston was located some fifteen miles southwest of Tombstone. A part of Cochise County, it was nonetheless considered the enclave of Curly Bill Brocius, so named for his wavy hair, and the Clantons. Any bad news from Charleston was immediately associated with the gang of rustlers.

Earp looked concerned. "Who'd they tangle with?"

"Five Mexicans," Virgil replied. "A big rancher from Sonora, name of Ortega. Brought along his son and three vaqueros for good measure."

"How many were killed?"

"All of them."

Virgil's features twisted in a scowl. He was a calm man, seldom given to temper. But he had a general aversion to outlaws, and a personal loathing of killers. He was known for his rough treatment of those who resorted to the gun.

"Way I get the story," Virgil said, "Brocius and his boys

rustled a herd off Ortega's spread. Ortega somehow tracked them into Charleston and demanded payment."

"Bad move." Earp shook his head. "Brocius wouldn't back down on his own homeground."

Virgil nodded. "Ortega learned that the hard way. Brocius pulled some sort of dodge and took'em by surprise."

"He started the fight?"

"Not much of a fight," Virgil remarked. "More along the lines of cold-blooded murder. Brocius and his bunch opened fire and shot'em to ribbons. The Mexicans never had a chance."

"How about Brocius, the Clantons?" Earp asked. "Any of them hit?"

"No, more's the pity. Bastards came through without a scratch."

"Just doesn't stop, does it? And damn small likelihood they'll ever face charges."

"None a'tall," Virgil amended. "Not while Johnny Behan's the sheriff. Even if there was a hearing, he'd rig it and clear them on justifiable homicide."

"Always comes back to same song, second verse."

Earp's observation stemmed from bitter experience with the law in Cochise County. Almost from their arrival in Tombstone, he and his brothers had been at odds with N. H. "Old Man" Clanton and his gang of cutthroats. The Clantons were a rowdy, unsavory lot who acted as if they were a law unto themselves. Their contempt for sworn lawmen was expressed with open defiance.

A year past, in October 1880, the gang had gone on a drunken spree, firing shots and smashing windows in the vice district. The town marshal at the time, Fred White, had called on Virgil, as a federal marshal, to assist him in jailing the gang. When the arrest attempt was made, White had been killed by a shot fired from Brocius's gun. Virgil, Wyatt, and Morgan Earp then performed the arrests and tossed the gang in jail. But Fred White, on his deathbed, admitted the shooting was accidental, thereby absolving Brocius. The incident nonetheless ignited a spark of animosity between the Earps and the Clantons.

Some while later Old Man Clanton had been killed, when he and his rustlers were ambushed by Mexicans below the border. For a brief time it was thought that his death would write an end to the simmering feud with the Earps. But Curly Bill Brocius took over the gang and soon thereafter struck his pact with the Cochise County sheriff, John Behan. The antagonism between Behan and Wyatt Earp merely added fuel to the fire. Editorials lambasting the gang in the *Epitaph,* which openly supported Earp, further aggravated the hostility. The gang let it be known that the Earps would be wise to avoid Charleston.

To compound matters, Sheriff Behan then attempted to smear the Earps through Doc Holliday. Following a stagecoach holdup, he took into custody Holliday's lady friend, Kate Elder. Behan got her drunk, playing on the emotional abuse she suffered when Holliday drank too much, and convinced her to sign a statement accusing him of the robbery. She later repudiated her accusation, and Holliday was cleared of all charges. Kate Elder, fearing his wrath, promptly boarded the next stage out of Tombstone. The scheme backfired on Behan, but not before the damage was done. His actions had rubbed a raw spot and set it to festering.

"What do you think?" Virgil said now. "Should we arrest the whole lot? Bring charges of murder?"

"For openers," Earp commented, "we'd need an army to back our play. I'm not sure we could raise a posse that big."

"Yeah, you're probably right."

"Then there's Behan to consider. He'd sandbag any evidence brought before a grand jury. Odds are we would never get an indictment."

"How about federal charges?" Virgil persisted. "The

Mexicans crossed an international boundary into Arizona. As a deputy marshal, that ought to give me jurisdiction."

"Never work," Earp advised him. "Murder is a state offense, not federal. Even with the Mexicans being foreigners, we'd never get it to hold water."

"Goddammit!" Virgil exploded. "There's got to be some way we can nail those sonsabitches."

"Not unless you've got another trick up your sleeve. Behan's county sheriff and that makes it his bailiwick. You being town marshal, or even a federal marshal, doesn't cut hot butter."

"All the more reason to get you elected sheriff. Then we'd have 'em by the short hairs no matter what the jurisdiction."

"No argument there," Earp agreed. "Come next spring, I'll play all this up in my election speeches. Folks might get the idea it's time to put Johnny Behan out to pasture."

"That's the ticket!" Virgil chortled. "Show him up for what he is. A cheap crook who runs with outlaws."

"Who's a cheap crook?"

Startled, they looked around to find Morgan Earp standing in the doorway. The youngest of the brothers, he was a strapping six-footer, ruggedly handsome, with sandy hair and a full mustache. He closed the door, moving into the office.

"Lemme guess," he said. "You're talking about our bosom buddy and all-around Christian gentleman—Johnny Behan."

"Actually," Virgil amended, "we're talking about how to get Wyatt elected sheriff. Behan's just the fly in the ointment."

"I second the motion," Morgan said jovially. "Our election slogan ought to be, 'Boot Behan out on his ass!' "

Earp laughed. "Morg, we'll make a politician out of you yet. Hell, I might just sign you on as my campaign manager."

"That'd suit me real fine. I'm plumb tired of bustin' my butt riding shotgun."

Morgan worked as an express guard for Wells Fargo. Between runs to Tucson on the stagecoach, he served under Virgil as a deputy town marshal. Like his brothers, he was handy with his fists as well as a pistol. He had just returned on the backleg trip from Tucson to Tombstone.

"How's tricks?" Earp inquired, straight-faced. "Anybody rob you on the way home?"

"Small chance!" Morgan hooted. "Toughnuts steer clear whenever I'm sittin' on the strongbox."

"Don't get too cocky," Earp warned him. "Overconfidence has got lots of good men killed."

Morgan pulled a face. "You're a worrywart, big brother. Everybody knows I'm gonna live forever."

Earp punched him on the arm. Morgan went into a fighting stance, bobbing and weaving as he dodged imaginary blows. Exchanging an amused look with Virgil, Earp crossed to the door.

"See you boys later," he said. "Time to move something off the back burner."

"What's that?" Virgil asked.

"The Clantons." Earp paused in the door, grinning. "And Johnny Behan."

He left them to ponder the riddle.

# Chapter Four

OUTSIDE, EARP TURNED DOWN FREMONT STREET. A few minutes later he approached the *Epitaph*, which was located beside the Mining Exchange Building. Directly across the street was the *Nugget*.

The proximity of the two newspapers never failed to amuse Earp. John Clum, publisher of the *Epitaph*, and Harry Woods, publisher of the *Nugget*, were bitter rivals. Clum was a staunch Republican, and Woods was an equally staunch Democrat. Their views on any subject were as though filtered through prisms of starkly different colors.

Their greatest difference was in the matter of local politics. Clum supported town growth, expansion of the mines, and Wyatt Earp. Woods supported the mine workers, the farmers and ranchers throughout the county, and John Behan. Clum was particularly outraged that Woods had chosen to locate his newspaper directly across the street. He often referred to Woods as the "spy in our midst." The two men had never been known to exchange greetings.

The interior of the *Epitaph* was strong with the smell of printer's ink. The presses were situated at the rear of the building, operated by a printer who forever looked as though he had just crawled from a coal bin. Toward the front were filing cabinets, bundles of old newspapers, and the desk of John Clum. He served as publisher, editor, star reporter, and advertising salesman. His desktop was covered by mounds of neatly stacked writing paper, separated by subject matter.

When Earp came through the door, Clum glanced up from studying an invoice. He was a stout man with hair receding into a widow's peak and inquisitive eyes magnified behind reading spectacles. Highly intelligent, and a brute for work, he often put in twenty hours a day between the newspaper and his position as mayor. His features widened in a warm smile at the sight of Earp.

"Good morning, Wyatt," he said. "Or is it afternoon? I tend to lose track."

"You once told me that a busy man has no need of a clock. Since you're never on time, I took you at your word."

"Only the idle watch the hourglass. A great American journalist—Horace Greeley—made that observation before his untimely passing."

Earp nodded absently. "That's real interesting, John. But today I was thinking more along the lines of 'time and tide wait on no man.'"

"Hmmm." Clum peered over the rims of his glasses. "Do I detect a somber note in that remark?"

"Guess it all depends on whose ox got gored. I take it you haven't heard the news out of Charleston."

"No, I haven't. What happened?"

"Last night, Brocius and his gang killed five Mexicans. According to the report Virg got, it was cold-blooded murder."

Clum leaned forward, suddenly intent. "Who were the Mexicans? Why were they killed?"

Earp related the details of the shooting. He stuck to the salient points, trying to recount the story in Virgil's words. As he talked, Clum took paper and pen and began scribbling furiously. Earp concluded with a sober look of disgust.

"Way I see it, there's little or no chance of preferring charges. Leastways, not so it would stick."

"Dirty scoundrels!" Clum fumed. "They have no regard for the laws of man or God."

Earp thought the remark typical of the man. John Clum was a strict law-and-order advocate, with a bent toward the codes of the Old Testament. An Easterner, with a college education and compassion for the downtrodden, he had volunteered for the Indian Bureau in 1871. Assigned as the agent at San Carlos, the Apache reservation on the Gila River, he had set about establishing civilian control over his wards. To circumvent army rule, he enlisted Apache warriors as policemen to help him control nearly a thousand tribesmen under his charge. Shortly, he had secured the consent of Washington to remove all military troops from San Carlos.

Clum's progressive measures so impressed the Indian Bureau that the reservations at Rio Verde and Camp Apache were closed, and over two thousand tribe members were relocated to San Carlos. By 1876 the Chiricahua Apache had been placed under his charge as well. A year later he staged the most celebrated feat of any Indian agent, the arrest of Geronimo. Ordered to the Southern Apache reservation in New Mexico, he and his tribal police, in a bloodless coup, took Geronimo prisoner. The infamous warrior and his band were peacefully relocated to San Carlos, in Arizona.

Later that year, his mission completed among the Apache, he resigned from the Indian Bureau in search of greater challenge. For the next three years, after an apprenticeship at law, he practiced as an attorney in Tucson. Then, with the silver strike in Tombstone, he found his true calling. Operating on the principle that "the pen is mightier than the sword," he published the first edition of the *Epitaph* in 1880. His penchant for law and order, along with a gift for expressing himself in print, made him something of a reformer in Tombstone. He joined Wyatt Earp and others in a campaign to rid Cochise County of its criminal element. His efforts ultimately resulted in his election as mayor.

"Sorry to see anybody got killed," Earp said now. "Especially a bunch of Mexicans a long way from home. But the situation might just be turned to advantage."

"Advantage?" Clum appeared doubtful. "How so?"

"Let's suppose you cranked up a series of editorials. Laid it on hot and thick about honest citizens being shot down in the street. You reckon anybody would take exception to the fact that the deceased were Mexican?"

"Well . . ." Clum considered a moment. "People normally aren't all that sympathetic to Mexicans. I mean, most folks tend to think of them as one step above an Apache." He paused, thinking it through. "But if I took the tack that Ortega was a rancher, albeit a Mexican . . . a God-fearing, hardworking cattleman—"

"—shot down," Earp interjected, "for trying to protect his own, the sweat of his labors."

"Yes, that's it!" Clum said excitedly. "And his son, an innocent young boy, killed trying to defend his father. That's certain to elicit sympathy. People simply will not condone the murder of youngsters, Mexican or otherwise."

Earp nodded. "You ought to play on the fact that it could happen to anybody. Today a Mexican, tomorrow an American. Unless it's stopped, nobody's safe."

"Eureka!" Clum clapped his hands. "I see where you're headed."

"Where's that?"

"Our noble sheriff, John Behan. Paragon of virtue, defender of liberty and justice. Assuming, of course, that your vocation happens to be rustling cows and killing people."

Earp smiled. "You hit the mark dead center. Tie him to Brocius and the Clantons, tag him with the same label. A man no better than the men he protects."

"Worse!" Clum intoned. "Worse, because he wears a badge. I can see the headline now." He painted broad strokes in the air. "Sheriff Allows Killers to Go Free. Murder Condoned by Our Officials."

"You've got it," Earp said. "And keep hammering it

home until election time rolls around. One editorial after another. No letup."

"Oh, don't worry," Clum assured him. "I'll play every variation on the theme. The voters won't be allowed to forget."

"John, I think we're on to something here. It might just win me the election."

"Old friend, it *will* win the election. You are the next sheriff of Cochise County. No question of it!"

Politics was the foundation of their friendship. Their shared belief was that, with the right men in office, they could shape the future to fit their vision. Yet, politics aside, Earp and Clum were kindred spirits in many ways. They thought of themselves as westering men, in the vanguard of those who were bringing settlement and growth to a raw and untamed land. Clum particularly admired Earp for the venturesome life he'd led as a plainsman and law officer.

A native of Illinois, Earp had been instrumental in leading his family ever westward. From 1864 to 1868 he had worked as a teamster in California and a section hand for the railroad in Wyoming. Two years later, in Missouri, he'd married his childhood sweetheart and been elected town constable. Then tragedy struck, claiming the life of his new bride in a typhoid epidemic. A widower at twenty-two, he once again turned west.

Earp spent the next several years as a buffalo hunter, drifting with the herds throughout Kansas and Indian Territory. In Wichita, one of the great Kansas cowtowns, he was hired as a peace officer in 1875. A year later he became deputy marshal of Dodge City, where he served with distinction until late 1879. As railroads expanded into Texas, and the Kansas cowtowns died out, his westering instinct turned to a new and fabulous boomtown in Arizona. He'd led his brothers and their wives to Tombstone, settling there in time to celebrate Christmas.

A few months later John Clum arrived in town, establishing the *Epitaph*. A lawyer by trade and a newspaper-man by preference, Clum had a wide assortment of friends and political associates among wealthy mine owners and influential businessmen. When he met Earp, they immediately recognized one another as birds of a feather. As well, Clum recognized in Earp the stuff of leadership and drive, unfettered ambition. He introduced Earp to his friends and associates, and opened the door to lucrative investments. On the one hand, he merely wanted to assist a newfound friend. On the other, he saw the start of a far-reaching political partnership. One that would become a power in the growth and prosperity of Cochise County.

Earp was of a similar view. Together, operating as a team, they would secure mutual goals, to their mutual benefit. Today, he thought they had engineered a significant step in the right direction.

"I'll leave you with it," he said, turning toward the door. "Put all the hellfire and brimstone you've got in that first editorial."

"Never fear, Wyatt." Clum was busily checking his notes. "I'll blast them clear into perdition."

Earp was almost at the door when Clum's voice brought him around. "Oh, by the way," he said, in a sudden afterthought. "I have some news about Behan, myself."

"What's he done now?"

"According to the town gossips, he has a new lady love. A theatrical performer, no less."

Earp looked at him quizzically. "An actress?"

"Nooo," Clum said slowly, an evil glint in his eye. "A songbird with a healthy set of lungs. From what I hear, she's a real show stopper."

"How is it I haven't heard about her?"

"She only arrived on the morning stage. I understand Behan imported her from Tucson. Convinced her that Tombstone would do wonders for her stage career."

Earp wagged his head. "You reckon Behan's turned into a ladies' man?"

"Check it out for yourself," Clum said. "I understand she starts at the Birdcage Theater tonight."

"Maybe I'll put it on my list. Not that I'd trust Behan's taste in women."

Outside, Earp turned downtown. He reminded himself to check with Morg, who had ridden shotgun on the morning stage. It wasn't like Morg to overlook a new lady in town.

Unless, of course, she sang better than she looked.

# Chapter Five

HARRY WOODS SELDOM LOST HIS TEMPER. HE prided himself on never losing control, never allowing emotion to overcome reason. A newspaperman must, in his view, remain objective and removed, personally separated from the story. Today was an exception.

Woods stormed into the sheriff's office. He slammed the door, relieved to see that the deputies were out. No witnesses were needed, for this was a private matter between Behan and himself. One that had already made him appear the fool.

Behan was tallying figures from tax assessments. He glanced up from the paperwork, surprised to see the expression on Woods's face. The *Nugget* editor looked anything but sociable.

Woods halted in front of the desk. He unfolded the latest issue of the *Epitaph,* released only that morning, and flung it down in front of Behan. His eyes blazed with anger.

"Have you read that?" he demanded. "And don't tell me it's another one of Clum's fairy tales!"

Behan casually scanned the headline. "Yeah, I read it this morning. Spoiled my breakfast."

"Good!" Woods shouted. "I hope it spoils your whole damn day."

"Simmer down, Harry. What's your problem?"

"The problem, Sheriff Behan," Woods said with heavy sarcasm, "is that I had to hear about it through the *Epitaph*. Why is that?"

"Beats me." Behan spread his hands in a bland gesture. "Everybody in town knew about it."

"No, not everyone," Woods corrected him. "You knew, and quite obviously Clum heard about it from Earp. But I never heard so much as a peep. And do you know why?"

"I think I'm about to find out."

"Damn right you are! I don't know because you didn't tell me. A shootout like that and you didn't say a word. Not a word!"

"Well, hell, Harry." Behan dismissed it with an elaborate shrug. "What's to tell? Some Mexicans got themselves killed. So what?"

"So what?" Woods croaked. "Five men killed by Brocius and his gang of merry men. One of them hardly more than a boy! And you have the gall to ask me 'So what?'"

"For your information, that 'boy' was pretty near full-grown. He wasn't exactly wearin' knee pants."

"So what?" Woods threw back at him. "According to the *Epitaph,* he and his father and three vaqueros were summarily executed. Shot down in cold blood."

"C'mon, Harry," Behan scolded. "Don't believe everything you read. Especially in Clum's rag."

"Are you denying Clum's version of the story? Is that why you haven't called for an inquest?"

The question hung between them. Their relationship was more of a political alliance than one of personal friendship. Behan was a product of politics, his adult life devoted to serving the Democratic party. Originally from Tennessee, he had drifted westward, arriving in Arizona in the early 1870s. Afterward, he had held positions in various county governments, notably as a deputy sheriff and a tax assessor. When Cochise County had been created, carved out of an overly large Pima County, he had called in his political markers. Influence had been brought to bear on the governor, resulting in his appointment as sheriff. However long the job lasted, he fully intended to retire a wealthy man.

Harry Woods, on the other hand, was an idealist. A southerner by birth, shaped by the Civil War into a die-hard Democrat, he had come west with a utopian dream. He'd hoped to find a land where the underdog could prevail, and Tombstone had seemed to him fertile ground. His avowed enemies, northern Republicans, were there in force. Large mine owners and bankers, in particular, controlled the economic lifeblood of the town. But he was a scrapper, committed to defending the working man and small landowners. By necessity, since there was little choice, he'd cast his lot with Behan and the local Democrats. Still, from the outset he had been uncomfortable with the arrangement.

Johnny Behan, though a lawman, seemed too cozy with a certain element. Woods had never met the Clantons, or Curly Bill Brocius, and he had no desire to do so. Their reputation as rustlers was commonly accepted, and so long as their raids were confined to Old Mexico, no one took them to task. The prevalent view was that rustling cows south of the border was more sport than theft. Other ranchers, and small landowners, looked upon them as a devil-may-care if somewhat rowdy lot. Yet these were by and large the Democratic voters of Cochise County, and therefore the natural constituency of Johnny Behan. Woods, looking to the greater good, saw no recourse but to oppose the Republicans and support the sheriff.

A thin, reedy man, Woods placed more value on intellect than physical stature. He generally took the measure of Behan, who was a stocky bulldog of a man, with a square, tough face and humorless eyes. Yet today he sensed that Behan was skirting the truth, trying to fob him off with only half the story. He refused to be played for the fool.

"Answer me," he insisted now. "Has Clum printed the straight of it? Were those Mexicans murdered?"

"I don't know," Behan said. "And what the hell does it

matter, anyway? They had no business crossing the border and looking for a fight."

Woods stared at him, astounded. "Are you saying that you intend to do nothing about it? Just ignore it?"

"Have you got a better suggestion, Harry?"

"At the very least, you could question Brocius and the Clantons. Maybe you'd find there is reasonable cause for an inquest."

Behan frowned. "You oughta remember who your friends are. Brocius and his boys will turn out lots of votes when Earp tries to unseat me as sheriff. I don't intend to get crosswise of them."

"For the sake of argument," Woods said, "suppose they had killed a local rancher? Would you have gone after them then?"

"Well, they didn't, did they? So that's not something we've got to worry our heads about."

Woods was silent a moment. "You know," he said at last, "I'm forced to agree with Clum. You're not much of a lawman."

"Maybe not," Behan conceded. "But I know how to win an election and I look after my friends. You ought to think on that, Harry."

"And what am I supposed to write in the meantime? Should I quote the sheriff to the effect that Mexicans don't count?"

"No," Behan said bluntly. "You write that after an investigation, the official finding is that the Mexicans started the fight. You can quote me as saying that Brocius and his boys acted in self-defense."

"And what about the stolen cows? Any quote on that, John?"

"Nobody gives a good goddamn about the cows. Earp and Clum are just trying to stir up trouble before the election. Truth is, they don't give a damn about the Mexicans, either."

"I do," Woods said morosely. "But then, I still have a conscience. Not much, but enough to bother me."

"Good for you," Behan said without conviction. "Go down to the church and light a candle for the dead. That'll square things nice and proper."

Woods suddenly looked whipped, all his resolve depleted. He turned, his shoulders slumped, and trudged toward the door. When it closed behind him, Behan sat lost in thought. He was disturbed by this sudden display of conscience.

Harry Woods would have to be watched closely.

Early that evening, Behan left his office. He had a solitary supper at the Bon Ton Cafe and then started uptown toward his home. Though he was a bachelor, he refused to live in a boardinghouse or a hotel. He believed that appearances counted, and voters liked to believe that their sheriff was a man of substance. He played the part expected of him.

On the way uptown he planned the evening ahead. He would wash away the day's grime, then shave again and splash himself with bay rum. After donning a suit and vest, with a string tie, he would time it to arrive at the Birdcage Theater just as the first show began. His evening would be spent at a front row table, applauding as Sadie entertained the crowd. Then, after a late supper, he might at last be invited to her room. She was something of a coquette, and so far that hope had gone unrealized. Tonight might be his night.

Dim starlight cloaked the street in shadow. As he neared the front door, he caught movement from the corner of the house. A voice brought him around, suddenly wary.

"Don't get antsy. It's me."

"Ringo?"

"You expecting someone else?"

Behan moved deeper into the shadows. Johnny Ringo was his source of contact with the Brocius gang. Though

their unscheduled meetings occurred with some fre-
quency, Behan's nerves were always on edge. The gunman
was whipcord lean, with sharp, penetrating eyes, and he
wore crossed gun belts, with a pistol on either hip. His
white teeth, bared in a smile, shone brightly in the starlight.

"Spooked you, did I, Sheriff?"

"Just surprised me," Behan said lamely. "What's up?"

"Not much," Ringo said in a soft drawl. "We got wind of
that piece in the *Epitaph* today. Curly Bill sent me to have
a word with you."

"Word about what?"

"Well, you know how Bill frets about things. He got to
thinking you might do something dumb."

"Dumb?" Behan parroted. "What's that supposed to
mean?"

Ringo grinned. "Bill figured you might try to cover your
backside. Convene a coroner's inquest, or some such nonsense."

"Hell of a note," Behan mumbled. "He ought to know
me better than that."

"I told him the same thing. Said you're true blue and
good as gold. No flies on you."

The sarcasm stung. But Behan kept a tight grip on himself. Johnny Ringo was seemingly educated, but abrasive
by nature and given to outbursts of violence. On the run
from a double murder charge in Texas, he had joined the
Brocius gang only last year. Since then, he had killed one
man and shot another who refused to drink with him.
Though his whereabouts was known, no lawman in Arizona had attempted to arrest him. He and Doc Holliday
were considered the most dangerous men in Tombstone.

Thinking about it now, Behan reminded himself that
Ringo had a short fuse. He shook his head, spoke in an
agreeable tone. "Tell Bill he's got no cause to worry. Tomorrow the *Nugget* will announce that I've investigated
and found you boys to be in the clear."

Ringo chuffed a mirthless laugh. "That's the other question Bill wanted answered. He wasn't sure Harry Woods could swallow that hard."

"Harry knows which side his bread's buttered on. He always does the right thing by you boys."

"So I can relay that you've got things in hand? No trouble over a bunch of wise-ass Mexicanos?"

"No trouble," Behan assured him. "I've attended to it."

"Glad to hear it, Sheriff. Keep up the good work."

Ringo vanished into the shadows. Some moments later Behan heard hoofbeats from the rear of the house. As the sound faded, he had the strong sense that if he'd answered wrong, Ringo would have killed him on the spot. A breeze suddenly felt cold and damp on his face.

He realized he was sweating.

# Chapter Six

THE BIRDCAGE THEATER WAS A MONUMENT TO civic pride. Other mining camps were routinely visited by traveling variety shows. But the performances were held on makeshift stages, sometimes in gambling dives, more often in dingy saloons. The town fathers of Tombstone thought on a grander scale.

Their model was Denver, which had recently completed construction of an opera house. The Birdcage was a large edifice, with arches over the entrance and a carpeted foyer. On the ground floor the interior was appointed with candlelit tables, draped with fine linen. The upper floor was row upon row of seats, with several private boxes toward the front.

A proscenium stage, with foot lamps and velvet curtains, dominated the theater. Suspended high overhead were great chandeliers which bathed the interior in light. Waiters in crisp white jackets served champagne and brandy and choice whiskies, all at premium rates. The setting created an air of refinement more suited to a cosmopolitan city than a desert mining camp. Over the past year the theater had been able to attract such renowned stage entertainers as Lottie Crabtree and Eddie Foy.

Earp arrived a few minutes before the first show of the evening. He was accompanied by Lou Rudabaugh, owner of the Toughnut Mine, and George Parsons, president of the Lucky Cuss, a mining property controlled by eastern financiers. The men were attired in vested suits, starchy white shirts, and ties sporting diamond stickpins. A waiter ushered them to a reserved table in the front row, directly before the stage. Musicians began warming up in a sunken orchestra pit.

Rudabaugh ordered champagne. Within moments the waiter returned with a silver ice bucket, deftly popped the cork and poured for the men. Earp, who was more accustomed to whiskey, had only recently developed a taste for champagne. He lifted his glass as Rudabaugh proposed a toast.

"Good times, gentlemen," Rudabaugh said, smiling. "And good fortune."

"Indeed," Parsons added. "Good company as well."

After a sip, Rudabaugh nodded to Earp. "Excellent idea, coming here tonight, Wyatt. From what I hear, this Sarah Marcus puts on a fine show."

"Well, if nothing else," Earp said, "we'll get to judge Behan's taste in women. Word's around that she's quite a looker."

"Whatever the case," Parsons said in a wry tone, "she doesn't have much taste in men. Or maybe Behan neglected to tell her he's a Democrat."

Rudabaugh and Parsons were the acknowledged leaders of the local Republican party. While neither of them held political office, their immense wealth effectively provided control of party activities. Apart from other mine owners, and the town's bankers, few people were aware of the bonanza in riches being taken out of Tombstone. Even those who knew the actual figures found it somewhat staggering.

Ore from the mines assayed out to $2200 a ton. Ed Schieffelin, who originally discovered the silver field, had sold Parsons's group part of his claim for $90,000, and Rudabaugh shortly afterward bought another parcel for $130,000. Their companies invested heavily in stamp mill equipment, and within the first two weeks of operation produced $600,000 in pure silver. The amount was of such magnitude that the Sixth Cavalry, stationed at Fort Huachuca, agreed to escort the shipment to Tucson. From there it was transferred to the federal mint in San Francisco.

In the second year of the strike, Schieffelin had sold the remainder of his interests for $1,425,000. He then moved to San Francisco, married into society, and bought a mansion on Nob Hill. The mines, now controlled by financiers and interlocked corporations, continued to churn the earth and produce tons of silver. The remote district, once barren desert and cactus, had in two years yielded more than $40 million in bullion. The bonanza, cast into bars weighing two hundred pounds, was transported by Wells Fargo to Tucson. All of this took place in a time when the average working man earned less than forty dollars a month.

The mine owners, in a burst of civic benevolence, gave generously to the community. Funded by contributions, Tombstone now had four churches: Methodist, Presbyterian, Catholic, and Episcopal. Schools were established for the influx of children, and the educational system became a matter of great pride for the town's substantial citizens. Stores were stocked with silks and satins, and there were three elegant hotels, the Grand, the Occidental, and the Cosmopolitan. Stylish cafes, such as Delmonico's and Maison Doree, served cuisine previously unknown in the Southwest. And the Birdcage Theater, luxurious and ornate, stood as testament to Tombstone's continuing prosperity.

Earp sometimes thought himself in strange company. For a mule skinner and buffalo hunter turned lawman, he had come a long way in two brief years. Loans arranged by Rudabaugh and Parsons had permitted him to invest in mining properties and real estate. Though far from wealthy, the return on his investments had made him a man of considerable means. He had bought two homes in Tombstone, one for Virgil and one for Morgan, and another in California, for his mother and father. He wore tailored suits, handmade boots, and fancy silk ties. These days, when the occasion demanded, he even drank champagne.

Yet he was still more comfortable in the company of his brothers and Doc Holliday. He considered Rudabaugh and Parsons to be business associates and political allies rather than close friends. He was all too aware that their investment advice and financial assistance was directly linked to politics. Their goal was to bring Cochise County under Republican control, and they saw him as the man who could provide a public image of leadership. He often wondered what they would ask in return once he was elected. In his experience, there was no free lunch.

"Speak of the devil," Rudabaugh said now, nodding toward the entrance. "Look who's here."

Earp and Parsons turned in their chairs, watching as John Behan made his way to a table at the center of the theater. He was alone, and as he took a chair, he casually scanned the crowd. His gaze suddenly stopped, returning their stares, then shifted away. He busied himself with the waiter, ordering a drink.

"Damnable scalawag," Parsons said gruffly. "Those five Mexicans killed, and he's made no pretense of taking official action. How can the man call himself a peace officer?"

"Time will tell," Earp observed. "Abe Lincoln got it right when he said you can fool some of the people all of the time, and vice versa. Behan's time has about run out."

Rudabaugh chuckled. "That was a nifty piece Clum published in the *Epitaph*. I understand you gave him the idea."

"Nothing special." Earp feigned modesty. "What we need are more editorials on stagecoach holdups. Just stop and think about it for a minute." He paused for effect, looking back and forth at them. "The whole time he's been sheriff, Behan hasn't caught one robber. Lots of talk, but no action."

"Please, Wyatt," Parsons said, clearly disgruntled. "On average, there's one holdup attempt every week. And I'm reminded of it all too often by my partners in New York. Let's try to enjoy ourselves tonight."

The orchestra suddenly thumped to life. The curtains were drawn, and from the wings a bevy of chorus girls pranced on stage. Skirts flashing, their voices raised in song, they cavorted across the stage in a swirl of tossing legs and jiggling breasts. Then the tempo of the music quickened and they went into a high-stepping dance routine.

After several minutes the orchestra segued into a slower tempo and the chorus girls formed into a swaying semicircle upstage. A solitary figure emerged from the wings and crossed to stage center. Her dress was short, with a low neckline, but her entrance was curiously sedate. She stopped, bathed in the footlights, gazing out on an audience mesmerized by her appearance. Her clear alto voice softly emotional, she sang a sultry ballad, the theater gone quiet as a church.

Earp was no less taken with the girl then the rest of the crowd. She was scarcely twenty, her features exquisite, with creamy skin and a lush coral mouth that accentuated her high cheekbones. She was small but her jutting breasts tapered to a slim waist and were offset by perfectly rounded hips. She swayed gently to the music, her hands delicate and expressive, the lyrics of the song seemingly directed to every man in the audience. Earp thought she was the loveliest woman he'd ever seen.

Abruptly, with a blare of trumpets, the orchestra swung into a rousing tune. The chorus line surged forward and the girl led them in a frolicking, sometimes bawdy, dance number. She smiled and laughed, kicking high, transformed in an instant into a tantalizing nymph. The crowd roared with delight and gave her a thunderous ovation. Surrounded by the chorus line, she disappeared into the wings with one last flash of her magnificent legs. The next act, a team of acrobats, romped out to mild indifference.

The clientele of the Birdcage clearly wasn't much on gymnastic feats.

"By God!" Rudabaugh said with a nutcracker grin. "Behan finally did something for this town. That's one fine-looking woman."

"An understatement," Parsons said. "She's a beauty, and she can sing, too. What a voice!"

Earp was about to add his agreement when a door opened at the side of the stage. The girl stepped out, her costume covered by a loose silk gown, and began making her way through the tables. At the center of the room Behan rose from his chair, waiting expectantly. She moved in his direction.

On sudden impulse, Earp stood as she neared his table. He blocked her path and she stopped, looking up at him with a bemused smile. He nodded his head in a bow, trying for a courtly manner.

"Pardon the intrusion, Miss Marcus. I just wanted to tell you how much we enjoyed your performance. I'm Wyatt Earp, and these are my friends, George Parsons and Lou Rudabaugh."

"Thank you, Mr. Earp." She glanced around the table. "How very nice to meet you."

"Could we offer you a glass of champagne, Miss Marcus? We'd be honored if you would accept."

"I—"

Behan appeared at her side. He took her elbow, glaring at Earp. "You're out of line, Earp. Step aside and let the lady by."

"Oh, Johnny," the girl scolded softly, "Mr. Earp was a perfect gentleman. Don't make a scene."

Earp spread his hands. "Look, Johnny, we just offered Miss Marcus a drink. Why not join us?"

Behan's features flushed. "The lady doesn't want your drink. Is that plain enough?"

"You never know." Earp smiled at the girl. "Why not let Miss Marcus decide for herself?"

Behan took her arm and moved around Earp. She glanced back with an apologetic shrug. "I'm sorry," she said in a whispered voice. "He's terribly jealous."

Earp gave her a conspiratorial look. "Maybe we'll meet again."

Her laugh was throaty. "Maybe we will."

When Earp sat down, Rudabaugh slapped him on the shoulder. "You're a corker, Wyatt! You sure put Behan's nose out of joint."

"And with good reason," Parsons said. "She's the best thing I've yet seen in Tombstone."

Earp was in full agreement. He watched as Behan led the girl across the room. Something told him that their relationship was less than it appeared. So much so that Sarah Marcus would definitely see him again.

Sooner than she expected.

# Chapter Seven

MARSHALL WILLIAMS, WELLS FARGO AGENT FOR Tombstone, supervised the loading of the bullion on the evening stage. There were two strongboxes, each loaded with bars of silver. Several men muscled the boxes aboard, stowing them beneath the driver's seat. Williams then satisfied himself that the boxes had been lashed securely in place.

The driver, Bud Philpot, made one last check of the six-horse hitch. With the silver aboard, and a full complement of passengers, he carefully inspected the traces and rigging to ensure that all was in order. On the run to Tucson there were many steep grades, and even distribution of weight became a factor. He was concerned with the strain the load would place on his horses.

Bob Paul, the shotgun guard, stood just outside the stage office. A ten-gauge scattergun, loaded with buckshot, was cradled over his arm. His wide gun belt was stuffed with shotgun shells, and a Colt .45 rode on his hip. The strongboxes were his responsibility, from the beginning of the run until they were off-loaded in Tucson. His eyes constantly scanned the street, pausing now and then to inspect the passengers. He was highly paid to guard the shipment, and he trusted no one.

Finally, with the bullion loaded the passengers were allowed to board. There were seven passengers, three drummers and two businessmen traveling with their wives. The businessmen, their wives, and two of the drummers squeezed into the coach. The third drummer, a dry goods salesman, was forced to take the dicky seat at the top of the luggage boot. Shortly after eight o'clock Bud Philpot cracked the reins and the horses strained to get the load under way. He turned the coach north out of Tombstone.

Outside town the road was brightly lit by a full moon. Philpot worked his cud, studying the sky, and spat tobacco juice over the side. Beside him Bob Paul rode with the shotgun resting across his knees. They often worked the same run, and over time they had become friends. After the team had settled into a steady pace, Philpot jerked his head at the sky.

"Good night for it," he said. "Easy to see the road with that moon. Nothin' worse than a dark night and a heavy load."

"Yeah, there is," Paul noted. "Full moon makes it easier for highway robbers. Bright as day out here."

"Hell's bells, Bob, we ain't got nothin' to worry about. That cannon of yours would scare the devil hisself."

Paul rubbed the stock of the Greener. "Hope you're right, Bud. I'd sooner not meet up with trouble."

"Amen to that, pardner."

Philpot wasn't all that worried. Earlier in the year a pair of bandits had attempted to rob a stage under Paul's guard. The moment they appeared on the road, Paul had emptied both barrels, downing them with a hail of buckshot. One died on the spot, and the other, after a long recovery, had been sentenced to a term in prison. Paul, for his quick action, had been awarded a bonus by Wells Fargo.

Some ten miles up the road the stage pulled into the town of Contention. There, while a fresh team of horses was being hitched, the passengers were allowed to stretch their legs. Under such a heavy load, the teams would be changed five times on the seventy-mile run to Tucson. The next change would be made at Drew's Station, roughly twelve miles northwest of Contention.

Toward ten o'clock that night the moon was nearing its zenith. The countryside was awash with light, and the desert, always cool at night, became steadily colder as a crisp

October wind blew in from the north. Philpot and Paul now wore mackinaws and heavy gloves to ward off the cold. They hunched down, collars turned high and their eyes watering, as wind from the moving stage whipped their faces.

A mile or so out from Drew's Station the road went into the climb of a steep grade. Philpot hauled back on the reins, slowing the horses as they labored into the grade. Off to one side of the road a thick stand of chaparral was clearly visible against a landscape strewn with boulders. Three men, mounted on horseback, suddenly spurred their horses out of the chaparral. Waving pistols, they charged into the path of the stagecoach.

"Whoa back!" one of them shouted. "Nobody make a move!"

Slowed by the cold, taken by surprise, Bob Paul fumbled the heavy glove off his gun hand. As he eared back the hammers on his shotgun, the robbers opened fire. A slug whacked the seat beside his leg, another zipped past his ear, and a third struck Philpot in the chest. Thrown sideways, the driver slammed into Paul, spoiling his aim, and then tumbled from the seat onto the hindquarters of the rear horses in the team. The terrified horses bolted up the grade, scattering the robbers off the road. Wheeling their mounts around, the robbers loosed a volley of shots in an effort to down one of the team horses. The drummer on the dicky seat, hit by a stray bullet, toppled dead onto the road.

On the stage Paul fought to regain his balance as the coach jounced and swayed up the grade. He lowered the hammers on the shotgun, dropped it into the well, and began searching for the reins. Only then did he discover that Philpot, when he'd tumbled from the seat, had taken the reins with him. Paul gingerly lowered himself onto the coach tongue, gripping the seat panel with one hand, and retrieved the dragging reins from the ground. Bracing himself, he found a foothold and swung back into the seat well. As the coach crested the hill, he finally regained control of the horses. He whipped them into a run toward Drew's Station.

Behind, at the bottom of the grade, the three robbers milled around in confusion. The temptation to chase the stagecoach was weighed against the certainty of armed resistance they would encounter at Drew's Station. Worse, with the plan gone bad, it was no longer a matter of highway robbery. The driver and a passenger, both dead, lay stretched out before them in the moonlit road. One of the robbers reined his horse to face the others.

"Goddamn, boys!" he yelled. "We're up shit creek now. They catch us and we'll get strung up sure as hell."

There was a moment of deliberation. Then, as if in silent accord, they reined off the road and put their horses into a gallop. They rode south toward the San Pedro.

The Clanton Ranch lay in the foothills of the Whetstone Mountains. Across the vast emptiness there was a sense of desolation, the stark terrain brilliant under a moon on high. The land sloped sharply down as it stretched onward to the San Pedro River, broken occasionally by buttes and treacherous arroyos.

Some twenty miles outside of Tombstone, there was no road as such leading to the ranch. Instead, a rutted trail bordered the river, winding southwestward from the remote settlement of Charleston. A ramshackle collection of buildings, the ranch compound consisted of a main house, a cook shack and bunkhouse, and a log corral. No working ranch, it was a way station for Mexican cattle rustled by the Brocius gang.

The three riders splashed through the San Pedro at a gallop. Their horses were lathered and spent, and they slid to a dust-smothered halt before the house. Vaulting from their saddles, they left the horses wheezing and near collapse. Their leader, hurrying forward, pounded on the door.

"Hello the house!" he shouted. "Somebody open up in there!"

A lamp trimmed low suddenly flared from inside. The door edged open and Bill Brocius, pistol in hand, peered through the crack. "Who's out there?"

"Jim Crane," the man said. "Got Leonard and Head with me. Open up, Bill."

Brocius swung the door open. He was barefoot, dressed in longjohns, his hair tousled. "What the hell you doing here in the middle of the night?"

"We got trouble, Bill. Big trouble."

Crane, followed by Sam Leonard and Joe Head, stepped through the doorway. Ike and Billy Clanton appeared from a bedroom off the parlor. A moment later, guns in hand, Ringo and the McLaury brothers trooped in from the bunkhouse. Brocius looked at the three men, his eyes narrowed.

"What d'you mean, big trouble?"

"We hit the stage tonight," Crane blurted. "Just outside Drew's Station. Goddamn Bob Paul tried to make a fight of it."

"And?" Brocius demanded. "Don't appear he winged any of you."

"Well, no," Crane said, averting his eyes. "But there was some shootin' and—" He threw up his hands. "We kilt the driver and some jaybird on the back of the stage. Wasn't even aimin' at 'em, neither."

"You always were a peckerhead. Damned wonder you didn't get killed yourself."

"Don't be that way, Bill. Sometimes things just go haywire, that's all."

Brocius stared at him. "So why'd you come here?"

"Figgered you'd help," Crane said. "We never expected to see Bob Paul ridin' shotgun. Hell, he knows all three of us on sight. And the goddamn moon's bright as a diamond in a goat's ass."

"What kind of help are you lookin' for?"

"Fresh mounts. Our horses are plumb give out. We gotta make a run for it."

Brocius and Ringo exchanged a quick look. Then, almost imperceptibly, Ringo shook his head. Brocius turned back to the three robbers.

"No can do," he said. "What with the killin', the law's certain to get on your trail. They'll likely track you here, and that's bad enough. But if we—"

"C'mon, Bill!" Crane interrupted. "For chrissake, you gotta give us a hand."

Brocius's eyes hardened. "We give you horses and it'll look like we were part of it. You'll just have to fend for yourself."

The room went silent. The other gang members waited to take their cue from Brocius. He was a brutal man, with a hair-trigger temper, and given to sudden outbursts of violence. For a year now he had ruled the gang through fear, the certain knowledge that he would kill any man who stood in his way. Among the gang members, only Ringo could reason with him, sometimes divert his explosive temper. They watched, still waiting for a sign, as he stared at the robbers.

Crane and his men appeared desperate. They stared back at Brocius, seemingly on the verge of some foolish act. The standoff was broken when Ringo moved off to their side, began poking embers in the fireplace. The three robbers suddenly realized that the situation had turned dangerous. One false move and they knew Ringo would start shooting.

"Christ, Bill," Crane moaned. "You and me, we go back a long ways. I deserve better'n this."

"What you deserve," Brocius told him, "is to have your ass whipped. You shouldn't have brought your troubles to my door."

"On your way, boys," Ringo said in a cold voice. "We're through talking about it. Get on your horses and make dust."

Crane started to reply, then changed his mind. He brushed past Brocius and walked to the door. Leonard and Head followed him out in a cone of silence. Ringo moved to the door and watched as they mounted their horses. He turned back into the house when they rode out of the yard.

"What do you think?" he asked Brocius. "Will Behan track them here?"

Brocius laughed. "Behan couldn't track himself to the outhouse."

"So what are you worried about?"

"The Earps. Nothin' I can put my finger on."

Brocius and Ringo were of a similar mind about the Earps. Unlike John Behan, they knew the Earps could not be bought off or scared off. Should Wyatt Earp be elected sheriff, there was no question as to the outcome. Cattle rustling would suddenly become a hazardous occupation. The best they could hope for was a long stretch in prison.

Brocius was particularly obsessed by the thought. He'd worked too long, too hard building the rustling operation. The idea that it might be jeopardized by the Earps was like a thorn in his side. He had never allowed any man to crowd him, to block his way. He saw no reason to start with Wyatt Earp.

"So?" Ringo asked now. "What about the Earps?"

"Dunno," Brocius said. "Just a hunch."

"Yeah, like what?"

"I think they're gonna turn up on our doorstep."

# Chapter Eight

VIRGIL AWOKE TO SOMEONE KNOCKING ON THE door. By the light spilling through the window shade, he realized it was early morning. Allie stirred beside him, but buried her head in the pillow and went back to sleep. He eased out of bed, clad only in longjohns.

Quickly, he pulled on his pants and buttoned the fly. He reached toward his boots then changed his mind. Everyone knew that his workday as town marshal generally started at noon and ended long past midnight. For someone to be hammering on the door this early could only mean trouble. His suspenders hanging loose, he hurried into the parlor.

When he opened the door, he found Marshall Williams on the porch. The Wells Fargo agent was slowly stamping his feet against the early morning cold. Virgil waved him inside.

"You got me out of bed, Marsh. What's the problem?"

"Holdup," Williams said in a rush. "Or at least a botched attempt. Killed the driver and one of the passengers."

Virgil scrubbed his face with his hands, rubbing sleep out of his eyes. "Does Behan know about it?"

"I had the telegraph station take him a copy of the wire. Not that it means blue billy hell. He hasn't caught a stage robber yet."

"Yeah, but murder's a different kettle of fish. He'll have to get off his duff this time."

Williams appeared skeptical. "Tell you the truth, I don't

think he'd know where to start. He's a political hack, not a lawman."

Virgil walked to the stove. He opened the door, poked the banked coals to life, then tossed in chunks of firewood. When the flames caught, he closed the door and stood with his back to the stove.

"You'd think it was Alaska," he said. "Never get used to this kind of cold in the desert."

Williams nodded. "We're pretty near a mile high. Probably snow before long."

"Well, anyway, why come to me, Marsh? Behan's got the jurisdiction on stage holdups. And murder, too."

Williams removed his hat, swatted it against his leg. His eyes were rimmed with anger. "Virg, they killed Bud Philpot, one of the best drivers I ever had and a damn good man. Been with me ever since I opened the station here in '79."

"Everybody liked Bud," Virgil said. "Who was the passenger?"

"Roerig. Peter Roerig. A drummer out of St. Louis. He'd been here calling on the mercantile stores."

"Damn shame," Virgil said, his features tight. "Who was riding shotgun?"

"Bob Paul," Williams said. "The robbers started shooting and the horses bolted. We're lucky the stage didn't go off the road."

"So Paul didn't return fire?"

Williams briefly described the holdup, ending with Bob Paul's heroic effort to halt the runaway team. "Bob deserves a medal," he concluded. "Wasn't for him, we would've had a wreck on our hands. Probably lost the bullion and some more passengers killed."

Virgil looked troubled. "Marsh, what is it you want me to do? All this happened outside the town limits. I've got no legal authority."

"Well hell, Virg, you're a deputy U.S. Marshal! You ought to be able to do something."

"Don't you see, no federal crime was committed. If I had the authority, I would've taken after stage robbers long before now."

Williams shook his head like a mad bull hooking at cobwebs. "Then go jump on that good-for-nothin' Behan. Get him to organize a posse, or something!" His voice dropped, a catch in his throat. "I want Bud Philpot's killer caught and hung."

"Marsh, let me think on it awhile. You've got my word I'll do whatever I can. That includes a talk with Behan."

Virgil walked him to the door. When he turned back into the parlor, Allie emerged from the bedroom. She was a buxom woman, not yet thirty, with dark hair and lively eyes. She wore a housecoat over her nightdress.

"Guess you heard that," Virgil said. "Helluva mess to start off the mornin'."

Allie came to warm her hands by the stove. She studied his downcast features a moment. "What do people want?" she said at length. "You can't do anything unless Johnny Behan deputizes you. And that's far from likely."

"Never happen," Virgil said. "Hell'd freeze over before Behan deputized an Earp. But I keep thinking about Morg . . ."

"Morg?" She sounded confused. "What about him?"

"What if it'd been him on that stage instead of Bob Paul? Way it happened, anybody could've caught a bullet. We might be standin' here planning Morg's funeral."

"Morg just wants to be like his big brothers. He thinks the sun rises and sets on you and Wyatt."

Virgil smiled. "What about you?"

"Well . . ." She pulled him close, put her arms around his neck. "Let's just say I'm partial to one of the Earps."

She nuzzled against him, and he was still for a moment. Then she felt the tension return, the corded muscle in his shoulders gone tight, and he stepped out of her embrace. He started toward the bedroom.

"I have to get dressed."

"Why?" Allie said, suddenly alarmed. "Where are you going?"

"Gotta see Wyatt."

Some minutes later Virgil came out the door. He wore a heavy corduroy jacket, unbuttoned at the bottom for quicker access to the holstered pistol on his hip. On the porch he paused, staring across the street at Morgan's house.

Their scale of living had certainly improved. Upon arriving in Tombstone, they had lived in adobes for almost six months. Then Wyatt, who still preferred a hotel, had bought them homes. The houses were framed and shingled, painted white, with a shady porch for the summertime. Virgil reflected that things were looking up in their world.

After a moment he decided not to bother Morgan. There was nothing the youngster could do, and his wife, Jane, was sometimes a handful. She often badgered Morgan about working as a shotgun guard, and she was none too pleased about his duties as a deputy town marshal. Virgil thought it was fear, her fear that Morgan might get hurt or killed serving as a lawman. He knew that Allie had those same fears, which she kept to herself. Not that it would change anything if she were more outspoken. He was too set in his ways.

From the house, which was located on a corner, he turned down Fremont Street. A short while later he entered the Occidental Hotel, nodding to the desk clerk, and took the stairs to the second floor. He laughed to himself at the thought of waking Wyatt at such an ungodly hour. What with his partnership in the Oriental, and chumming around with Holliday, Wyatt seldom got to bed before three or four in the morning. Sometimes it seemed that his mining interests and business activities were at odds with the sporting life. Yet he had ambition to spare, and he somehow made it all work.

There was a long wait after Virgil rapped on the door.
When Earp finally opened it, he squinted as though half
blind. "What the hell time is it?"

"Little after nine."

"In the morning?"

"Rise and shine." Virgil waved him back into the room
and closed the door. "We're got to have ourselves a pow-
wow."

"Judas Priest," Earp groaned. "It's barely daylight.
What's so important?"

Virgil seated himself in an easy chair. The room was one
of the largest in the hotel, with a sitting area opposite the
bed and a tall wardrobe. He waited while Earp wrapped
himself in a woolen bathrobe and took the other over-
stuffed chair.

"Last night," he said, "three men tried to hold up the
stage outside of Contention. They killed the driver, Bud
Philpot, and one of the passengers."

Earp sat straighter, suddenly alert. "Any idea who the
robbers were?"

"Sorry to say it wasn't Brocius or the Clantons. But they
were identified."

"Who by?"

"Bob Paul," Virgil said. "He was riding shotgun, and as
you'll recall, there was a full moon last night. Bright
enough that he recognized all three of them. Jim Crane,
Sam Leonard, and Joe Head."

"How does he know them?"

"Marsh Williams got a long telegraph message from him
this morning. His hangout is the Alhambra, and he's seen
them in there lots of times. Says they work off and on as
cowhands."

"Which means they probably know Brocius and the
Clantons."

Earp sat lost in thought a moment. "Might work to our
advantage. If we could run down the killers and tie them
to the Brocius gang, we'd make Johnny Behan look like a

complete fool." He gave Virgil a slow smile. "That would be powerful stuff come election time. I'd likely win in a landslide."

"Yeah, likely so," Virgil agreed. "Only trouble is, killing people isn't a federal offense. Wasn't that what you said when those Mexicans got killed?"

Earp grinned. "Wells Fargo carries the U.S. mail. And any attempt to rob the mail service is a federal offense. As a deputy marshal, that puts it square in your bailiwick."

"So we use it as an excuse to go after the killers?"

"One reason's as good as another. The point is, it gives you the authority to take official action."

Virgil cocked his head. "Lots of stages get robbed. How come you never thought of this before?"

"Hell, Virg," Earp said, now wide-awake, "you never caught me at the crack of dawn before. I'm at my best with no sleep."

"How do we play it with Behan? By now he already knows about the killings."

"Put him on the hot seat. He can ride with you as deputy U.S. Marshal, or he can sit it out. His choice."

Virgil laughed. "That ought to get his bowels in an uproar. He'll squeal like a stuck pig."

"Let him," Earp said. "Just make sure he understands it's federal business—and he's along for the ride."

"You know, I've got the power to deputize my own posse."

"Even better!" Earp said, clearly delighted. "Deputize me and Morg and Doc—"

"Hold on," Virgil stopped him. "Much as I like Doc, that'd be a mistake. Folks just wouldn't approve, and that could hurt you in the election."

"Doc's liable to be offended, leaving him out."

"Not if you explain it, he won't. He'd jump through hoops if it'd keep you happy."

Earp hesitated, finally conceded the point. "I suppose you're right. Hold it to me and Morg."

Virgil stood. "We ought to leave by noon. Better to be on their trail while the tracks are still fresh."

"Get Morg, and round up enough supplies for three or four days. I'll arrange for horses down at the livery stable."

When the door closed, Earp sat there a moment longer. His expression congealed into a thoughtful frown. He wondered how he could explain it to Doc.

# Chapter Nine

EARP STRIPPED AND GAVE HIMSELF A BIRDBATH. The water was cold, but he still subjected himself to a good scrubbing. He figured it might be a while before he again saw a washcloth and soap. Outlaws on the run, and the men tracking them, seldom paused for a bath.

Toweling himself dry, he dressed in whipcord trousers and a wool shirt. Then he turned his attention to the weapons of a lawman's trade. He first unloaded his Colt .45, inspected it thoroughly, and tested the action. The pistol was blued steel, with a 5½″ barrel, and carried in a holster that had been soaked and allowed to shrink to the contours of the Colt. He oiled it lightly, loaded five shells, and lowered the hammer on an empty chamber.

Leaning in a corner was a Model 1873 Winchester. The rifle was chambered for .44-40 cartridges and had adjustable leaf sights. With the sights raised, and adjusted for range, he was confident of a hit out to five hundred yards. He worked the action, then dabbed oil on an old shaving brush and gave the rifle a light coat. Finished, he took a box of cartridges and stuffed forty shells into the loops of a wide cartridge belt.

From the wardrobe he selected an old hat with a raised crown and a wide brim, and a heavy mackinaw. The final item was a pair of roweled spurs, with the jingle bobs removed to eliminate any telltale sound. He strapped the spurs to his boots and left the room with the rifle in hand and the pistol cinched high on his waist. His years as a lawman had taught him that only a greenhorn carried his pistol low on the thigh. Quickest to hand in any practical situation was a gun carried at belt level.

In the hallway he rapped on Holliday's door. There was no answer, which surprised him, for it was now almost ten o'clock. He waited a moment, then turned back along the hall and went downstairs. Seated in chairs by the lobby window, two men paused in their conversation to stare. Ned Thomas, the desk clerk, gave him a curious once-over.

"Looks like you're loaded for bear, Mr. Earp."

"Here you go, Ned." Earp ignored the comment, passing the rifle and the cartridge belt across the counter. "Hang on to these for me. I'll be back directly."

"Sure thing, Mr. Earp."

Thomas and the men continued to stare as he crossed the lobby into the dining room. He treated himself to steak and eggs, with a stack of doughy pancakes, and strong black coffee. Experience had ingrained the lesson that a manhunt should always begin on a full stomach. Once on the trail, anything resembling a normal meal was little more than a memory. He finished breakfast to the last bite.

Outside the hotel he crossed the street to a tonsorial parlor. There, while the barber stropped a straight razor, he was again subjected to open curiosity. But he side-stepped the questions, interested only in a close shave. Hot water and shaving soap were in short supply on a manhunt, and he made it a rule to take the trail freshly shaved. When he emerged from the shop, he smelled strongly of bay rum lotion.

Downstreet, at the corner of Eighth and Allen, he entered Harrel's Livery Stable. Neither he nor his brothers owned horses. Their lives revolved around the town and seldom called for the need to travel on horseback. The livery stable catered to townspeople who found it more practical to rent rather than own. The proprietor was Bob Harrel, a grizzled old cavalryman, long since retired from the army. He prided himself on providing reliable top-notch stock.

The stable had a pleasant, musty odor of grain, loose hay, and horse droppings. Harrel turned from a stall where he'd been working. "Mornin', Mr. Earp," he said, smiling. "Help you with something?"

"Morning, Bob," Earp replied. "I need three horses. Give me geldings that can stay the course."

"How long you want'em for?"

"Three days, maybe longer."

Harrel eyed his clothing. "You figger to run'em hard?"

The question was less curiosity than a request for information. Harrel was an old campaigner, and he quickly calculated that the mounts were for the three Earp brothers, two of whom were lawmen. He wanted to know if the horses would be used hard in a long chase.

"Ought to plan on it," Earp said without elaboration. "Let's have a look at your stock."

Harrel led him along the stalls, inspecting horses. At the back of the stable they went through a rear door, where a dozen animals were quartered in an outside corral. Earp selected several horses for closer inspection of conformation and general condition. Finally, nodding to Harrel, he pointed to a gelding in the corral.

"I'll take that bay, and the two sorrels you've got in the stalls."

"Good pick," Harrel said with a note of approval. "You got an eye for horseflesh."

Earp chuckled. "From an old horse soldier, that's high praise. Not going to charge me extra, are you?"

"Not if you bring'em back in good shape."

"Have them ready at noon, Bob. Give me your best saddles, and I'll need rifle boot and saddlebags."

Harrel gave him a serious look. "Wherever you're headed—good luck."

"Appreciate the thought, Bob. I'll take all the luck I can get."

On the street again, Earp turned uptown. He thought to himself that the livery owner, as a seasoned campaigner, knew all of the signs. A man headed into a dangerous situation wanted a mount with staying power, in good condition. Often his life depended on the endurance, as well as the speed, of his horse. He was pleased by Harrel's offhand approval.

At Fourth and Allen he crossed the street as Sarah Marcus stepped out the door of the Grand Hotel. She caught sight of him and paused on the corner, her mouth curved in a bright smile. He stopped, reminded again of their first meeting at the Birdcage Theater and her revealing stage costume. Today she wore a short brocaded jacket and a fashionable high-necked dress. But the outfit did nothing to conceal her lush figure. He tipped his hat.

"Good morning, Miss Marcus."

"And good morning to you, Mr. Earp."

Earp smiled. "I'm surprised to see you out so bright and early. I thought theatrical people were night owls."

"Oh, we are!" she said merrily. "But I have some shopping to do and then a dress fitting. Time seems to fly."

She looked him up and down, from the battered old hat to the roweled spurs. Her eyes sparkled with curious amusement. "Are you in the cattle business, Mr. Earp? I somehow gathered you had other interests."

"For the most part, that's true," Earp said. " 'Course, as you may have heard, one of my brothers is a deputy U.S. Marshal. He's asked me to lend a hand with some official business."

"The stage holdup?" she asked. "I overheard people talking about it in the lobby. How terrible, those men being killed."

Earp thought it confirmed the adage that bad news travels fast. "These are hard times," he said. "Lots of men prefer robbery to an honest day's wage."

"And you're off to catch them? You and your brother?"

"We'll give it our best try. Never any guarantees when it comes to tracking down outlaws."

"How wonderful!" she bubbled, her eyes wide. "I so admire a man who goes in harm's way to uphold the law. And all the more so in your case, Mr. Earp."

"How's that, ma'am?"

"Well, after all, you aren't a sworn office holder. You're doing it out of a sense of civic duty, I'm sure. I find that very commendable."

Earp felt oddly taller under her praise. "Seems like the thing to do," he said with a stab at modesty. "Anyway, I couldn't let Virgil—that's my brother—tackle the job alone."

"Oh?" she said in a quizzical voice. "Won't Johnny—Sheriff Behan—ride with you, too?"

"I couldn't rightly say. Virgil's probably talking to him now."

Her eyes darted away. "I want you to know how very much I regret the other night. Mr. Behan presumes far more than he should. I was terribly embarrassed."

"Do I take it," Earp said, searching for the right word, "that you're not attached?"

"Heavens no," she said, blushing slightly. "Mr. Behan would like everyone to think so. But we're really just friends. Nothing more, I assure you."

Earp wanted to believe her. Yet the rumor around town implied that there was a personal liaison involved. Then, after an instant's thought, he decided it didn't matter either way.

"I wonder," he said, holding her gaze. "Would you like to have supper with me some night? Maybe an early supper, before your show?"

"Well . . ." She hesitated, suddenly flustered. "Yes, I would, Mr. Earp. I'd like that very much."

"Good," Earp said, grinning broadly. "I don't know how long I'll be gone. But when I get back, maybe we could make it official."

"I'll mark it on my calendar, Mr. Earp."

"And between now and then, maybe you could think about calling me Wyatt."

She laughed. "All my friends call me Sadie, short for Sarah."

They parted on that note. She proceeded uptown, and Earp cut across the street to the Oriental. A gambling establishment and saloon, the Oriental was one of Tombstone's finer gaming parlors. Just inside the door a mahogany bar ran the length of the wall. Behind it was a gaudy clutch of bottles with a gleaming mirror flanked by ubiquitous nude paintings. Along the opposite wall were keno and faro layouts, a roulette table, and a chuck-a-luck game. At the far end of the room were the poker tables, their baize covers muted by the cider glow of low-hanging lamps. The atmosphere was cordial and restrained, devoted solely to the pursuit of chance.

At one of the poker tables Doc Holliday and four other men were staring at their cards. Clearly, from the appearance of the players, it had been an all-night game that had yet to run its course. Save for a lone drinker at the bar, the rest of the room was empty. Earp took a seat at a nearby table.

After a moment Holliday tossed in his hand and got to his feet. He walked over to Earp's table, stretching his back, and sat down. His eyes were bloodshot and he looked near exhaustion. He idly waved a hand toward the men at the other table.

"Got'em gaffed," he said sardonically. "Damn fools don't know when to quit."

"You ought to get some sleep," Earp said. "You look like death warmed over."

"Never quit a winner, that's my motto. What got you out of bed so early?"

Earp briefly related the events of the morning. "I'm headed out with Virg and Morg," he concluded. "We figure to cut the robbers' tracks outside of Contention."

Holliday stared at him. "In a roundabout way, you're saying I wasn't invited to the party."

"We've got the election to think of, Doc. Deputizing you wouldn't sit too well with all those upstanding voters."

"Helluva note," Holliday grumped. "Was it Virgil's idea, or yours?"

"Nothing personal," Earp said, avoiding a direct reply. "It's just politics."

"Suit yourself." Holliday stood. "I've got lambs waiting to be fleeced. See you when you get back."

Earp rose and walked toward the door. He knew Holliday too well to be put off by the glib response. He'd offended a friend who deserved better. All for the sake of politics.

On his way out the door he was reminded of a saying he'd once heard. Ambition was a cruel master.

# Chapter Ten

By LATE AFTERNOON THE TRACKING PARTY AR-
rived at the site of the holdup. The bodies of the dead men
had been removed by stage employees at Drew's Station,
and the location was well marked. Dark stains on the
hard-packed ground indicated where Bud Philpot, the
driver, had been trampled by the horses and run over by
the stage. A short distance farther on, a patch of blood-
soaked earth revealed where the mortally wounded passenger had fallen onto the road.

There were five men in the tracking party. John Behan,
along with his deputy, Bill Breakenridge, had reluctantly
decided to accompany Virgil, Wyatt, and Morgan on the
manhunt. To refuse would have cast him in a bad light as
the chief law enforcement officer of Cochise County. Yet
he was clearly riddled with indignation and outrage,
openly hostile. He'd hardly spoken on the ride north from
Tombstone.

Behan dismounted, waiting with Breakenridge while the
Earps fanned out along the roadside. Neither he nor his
deputy had any skill as trackers, and they thought it wiser
to hang back rather than show their ignorance. Wyatt and
Virgil, who were experienced trackers from their time as
lawmen in Kansas, were drawn to the stand of chaparral
near the road. They quickly discovered where the robbers
had waited the night before, concealed by the chaparral
until the stagecoach slowed for the steep uphill grade.
From there they began a search of the rolling desert plain
to the southwest.

Morgan observed for a while, then walked back to the

road after a short conversation with Wyatt. At first he ignored Behan and Breakenridge, taking a long pull from his canteen. After replacing the canteen on his saddle, he took out the makings from his mackinaw pocket. He curled the paper with one hand, sprinkling tobacco from the cloth bag into the crease. Deftly, he rolled the paper between his fingers, licked the open edge and sealed the cigarette. He struck a match on his thumbnail and lit up in a haze of smoke.

Snuffing the match, he took a drag and slowly exhaled. Finally, as though stating the obvious, he glanced at Behan. "Looks like our boys skedaddled off in a southerly direction."

"Does it?" Behan said testily. "You want my opinion, this is a waste of time."

"How so?"

Behan consulted his pocket watch. "We're now eighteen hours or so behind them. I'd venture to say they've already crossed the border into Old Mexico."

"Maybe." Morgan studied the fiery tip on his cigarette. "Wyatt thinks they might've headed toward the Clanton spread."

Behan looked disturbed. "What have the Clantons got to do with this? They don't rob stages."

"Not much of a jump from rustling cows to stage hold-ups. A thief's a thief."

"No one's ever proved that they rustle cattle."

Behan regretted the words even as he spoke. He'd always thought Morgan Earp to be a young buffoon, a pale image of his brothers. But now, realizing that he'd been trapped into a reckless statement, his opinion was altered somewhat. He sensed that Morgan had been instructed to provoke him into some sort of damaging admission.

"Yeah, you're right," Morgan said easily. "Everybody in the county knows Brocius and his boys are night riders. Funny no one's ever got the goods on them."

Behan stiffened. "Is that remark directed at me?"

Morgan exhaled a wad of smoke. "Well, you're the sheriff," he said. " 'Course, what I was really wondering was whether you know these stage bandits. Crane, Leonard, and Head."

"Why would I know them?"

"Aren't they pals with Brocius and his bunch?"

The question was too casual, almost offhand. Behan saw where the conversation was headed. "I wouldn't have the least notion. Until this morning, I'd never heard their names."

"No kiddin'?" Morgan said, tapping an ash off his cigarette. "I thought you knew all the cowboys hereabouts."

"You thought wrong."

Morgan glanced at the deputy. "What about you, Billy? You ever crossed paths with these desperadoes?"

Breakenridge was a bluff man, not noted as a mental giant. His features creased in an abrasive scowl. "What makes you think I'd know'em?"

"Well, I've heard you spend a lot of time down around Charleston. Isn't that the hangout for men on the owlhoot?"

"Watch your mouth!" Breakenridge bristled. "You get smart with me and I'll tie a knot in your tail."

"Why hell, Billy." Morgan blew smoke in his face. "Anytime you get the itch, go ahead and give'er a try."

"That's enough!" Behan said sharply, stepping between them. "Let it drop, both of you. We've got other business to tend to."

"Now that you mention it," Morgan said, staring past him. "Looks like Virgil and Wyatt are ready to move on. We'd better get mounted up."

Some moments later the five men rode off to the southwest. Morgan exchanged an amused look with Earp and nodded. The byplay wasn't lost on Behan, and he understood it was for his benefit. There was an obvious effort to goad him, perhaps trick him in some unrevealed way where Brocius and the Clantons were concerned. He warned himself to play it close to the vest. The less said, the better.

Virgil took the point. Off to the west the sun slowly dropped toward the horizon. Long ago he'd learned that a wilderness manhunt required patience. A seasoned tracker always utilized the angle of the sun to cut sign. On hard ground the correct sun angle often made the difference between seeing a print or missing it entirely. The tracker stationed himself so that the trail would appear directly between his position and the sun. In late afternoon, with the sun at a low angle, he worked eastward of the trail. The westerly sunlight would then cast shadows across the faint imprints of man or horse.

A tracker seldom saw an entire footprint or hoofprint unless the ground was quite soft. On rocky terrain there was even less likelihood that complete prints would be spotted. What the tracker looked for instead were flat spots, scuff marks, and disturbed vegetation. Of all sign, flat spots were the most revealing. Only hooves or footprints, something related to man, would leave flat spots. Small creatures might leave faint scuff marks or disturb pebbles. But a flat spot, unnatural to nature, was always made by a hooved animal or a man.

The trail he followed now was roughly nineteen hours old but still faintly visible. He kept the sun between himself and the hoofprints of the three riders. From the length between prints, he knew the robbers had held their horses to a steady gallop. With a full moon last night, they'd had little problem negotiating an occasional arroyo, or clumps of cactus and chaparral. The tracks gradually veered off from a southwesterly direction to a course almost due south. Charleston and the Clanton Ranch, as well as the border with Old Mexico, were on a line with the tracks. Wherever the outlaws were running was still anyone's guess.

The tracking was slow and tedious. A good part of the time Virgil was forced to dismount and conduct the search on foot. At several points, particularly on hard ground, the hoofprints simply disappeared. He then had to rely on pebbles and twigs embedded in the earth's surface during past periods of rain. The number of pebbles and twigs dislodged indicated a hooved animal had passed that way. The direction in which they moved, invisible except to a skilled tracker, indicated the line of travel. Slowly, sometimes step by step, he clung to the trail.

At sundown Virgil called a halt along the banks of a shallow stream. He preferred the cautious approach, even though there would be a full moon again that night. However bright the moon, the tracks could easily be lost, or a misread sign could take them in the wrong direction. He would await sunrise to resume the trail.

There was a general air of frustration as they pitched camp beside the stream. The robbers gained ground with every hour that passed, and the slow tracking, though necessary, merely increased their lead. Yet a manhunt, by its very nature, was a roll of the dice. Sometimes the outlaws were caught, and at other times they simply vanished. A lawman learned to hope for the breaks, a lucky roll.

Supper that night consisted of coffee, beef jerky, and hardtack. While the other men were spreading their bedrolls, Earp walked off a distance from the small campfire. He stopped at the edge of the stream, his shadow cast across the water by moonlight. Shortly, he was joined by Virgil, who stood staring off to the south. After a moment Earp broke the silence.

"How do you figure it? Are they headed for the Clanton place?"

"One thing's for certain," Virgil said. "Hard as they were runnin' those horses, they had to stop somewhere. Otherwise they would've wound up on foot."

Earp grunted. "So we might get lucky, after all."

"I reckon we'll find out tomorrow."

Virgil walked back to the camp. Earp stared down at the

water, watching ripples run through his moonlit shadow. Tomorrow seemed too far away.

Late the next morning they forded the San Pedro. Their approach to the ranch compound had been observed while they were still far off in the distance. Brocius and Ringo, flanked by the Clantons and the McLaurys, waited for them outside the main house.

The Earps reined to a halt in the yard, their horses on a line. Behan and Breakenridge stopped off to one side, as though separating themselves from the three brothers. A tense silence settled over the compound, broken only by the horses stamping their hooves in the cool morning air. At length, Virgil nodded to Brocius.

"I'm here as a deputy U.S. Marshal. We're looking for Jim Crane, Sam Leonard, and Joe Head."

"That a fact?" Brocius said with a stony expression. "Guess you'll have to look somewheres else. Nobody here by them names."

"They were," Virgil said stiffly. "Their tracks lead right to your front door. We'll have to search the place."

"The hell you will!"

Brocius started to move, his face contorted with rage. Then, abruptly, he stopped as a gun appeared in Earp's hand, the hammer cocked. He stared across the sights at Brocius.

"You're talking to the law," Earp said coldly. "Pay attention and keep your lip buttoned."

Behan nudged his horse forward. "Everybody just simmer down!" He pointed a finger at Brocius. "Keep your head and don't do anything stupid. You hear me?"

Brocius stared at him hard. "You thrown in with the Earps, Sheriff? Christ, that'd be a laugh."

"Are the men they're looking for here?"

"Already said they wasn't."

"Then just hold still and let them search. Don't borrow trouble."

Earp kept his gun trained on the gang leader. Behan and his deputy traded an uneasy glance, kept their hands in plain sight. Virgil and Morgan dismounted, drawing their pistols, and quickly searched the house. Then, outside again, they cautiously approached the bunkhouse. After a fruitless search, Morgan returned to the main house, shaking his head at Earp. He stepped aboard his horse, gun still in his hand.

Virgil walked toward the corral. His eyes scanned the ground, sweeping outward in a broad arc. Suddenly he stopped, staring down at his feet, where the shallow angle of the sun created a shadow. He dropped to one knee and studied faint imprints in the hard-packed earth. As he inspected the track leading from the compound, he looked for the change of color caused by the dry surface of the earth having been disturbed to expose a moister, lower surface. Heat increased the rate at which tracks age, and the sun had been out now for more than five hours. The under surface of the hoofprints was almost restored to the normal color of the ground. All the sign indicated that they were some twenty hours behind the outlaws.

Satisfied, Virgil walked back to the house and mounted his horse. "They were here," he said to Earp. "Tracks run off to the west, straight as a string."

Earp's features revealed nothing. Yet he was surprised, for he'd thought the killers would make a run for the border. He looked at Brocius. "Too bad you didn't give them fresh horses. I'd have liked to take you in as an accomplice to murder."

Brocius glowered at him. "Mister, you'd be smart not to come around here again. Things wouldn't work out the same way next time."

"Yeah, they would," Earp told him. "You don't believe me, try it when you're feeling lucky."

Virgil backed his horse halfway to the corral. He pulled his rifle from the saddle scabbard and waited while the others reined their mounts out of the yard. Then, still looking over his shoulder, he fell in at the rear of the column. They rode west along the river.

The gang watched in shamed silence. Finally, as the riders faded into the distance, Brocius seemed to recover himself. His voice was tight, oddly gritty.

"Them bastards are gonna get theirs."

Ringo laughed. "You'd be smart to follow your own advice, Bill."

"What d'ya mean by that?"

"Steer clear of Tombstone."

"Yeah?" Brocius growled. "Why so?"

Ringo stared at the dust cloud growing smaller far upriver. He wagged his head as though he'd somehow seen into the future.

"Those gents play for keeps."

# Chapter Eleven

DUSK SETTLED OVER THE COUNTRYSIDE AS THEY rode into Tombstone. Streetlamps were already lighted and the business district was deserted. The gaming parlors along Allen Street, and the vice district farther downtown, were brightly lighted. Entertainment, in all its diverse forms, was open for the evening trade.

The lawmen had been on the trail for four days. Their pursuit had taken them west into the Santa Rita Mountains, where they had finally lost the tracks. They were covered with dust and grime, their faces peppered raw by the cold and blowing sand. Their attitude was one of weary disgust, for they returned empty-handed.

The posse separated near the town marshal's office. Behan and his deputy, Bill Breakenridge, turned onto Fourth Street. There was no parting as such, for the antagonism between the two groups had intensified over the last several days. The Earps went one way and the sheriff went another, without a word being spoken.

Outside his office, Virgil dismounted and handed the reins to Morgan. The sallow light from a streetlamp made his features appear worn and haggard. He stood for a moment, flexing his knees and swatting dust from his clothes. Then he looked up at Earp.

"Tomorrow, I'll see about getting some wanted dodgers printed. Not that it'll do a helluva lot of good. They're long gone."

"Never know," Earp said. "I'm still not convinced they headed for Nogales."

Virgil ducked his head. "Last tracks I saw was headed south. Only thing in that direction is Old Mexico."

"Like I said before, maybe that's what they wanted us to think. There at the end, they got real cute about covering their trail."

"C'mon, for chrissakes," Morgan said, interrupting Virgil's reply. "You two have been hashin' that around all day. Let's get a hot meal and some sleep."

The older brothers traded a look. "What do you think?" Virgil said, grinning at Earp. "Morg look like he's interested in a good night's sleep?"

"Not exactly," Earp said, amused. "Looks more like a tomcat to me."

"Yeah, five days on the trail does that to a man. His wife's liable to be sorry he's back."

"Lay off!" Morgan protested. "That wasn't what I meant."

"Says you," Virgil teased. "Young bucks always got one thing on their mind. And I never heard it called sleep."

"Whatever it's called," Earp interjected, "let's pack it in for the night. Virg, I'll see you tomorrow."

Earp and Morgan turned downstreet, leading Virgil's horse. At Fremont and Fourth they spotted light spilling through the front window of the *Epitaph*. Earp halted his horse in front of the newspaper and stepped down from the saddle. He handed the reins to Morgan.

"I've got to see Clum," he said. "Drop my gear off at the hotel and go on to the livery stable."

"Whatever you say." Morgan hesitated, then went on. "Wish we would have caught'em, Wyatt. I know how bad you wanted it."

"The game's still on. We might find them yet."

"Yeah, who knows, maybe we will. G'night, Wyatt."

Morg rode off, leading the two horses. Earp crossed the boardwalk and entered the newspaper. Clum was seated at his desk, pen in hand, working over a ledger. He glanced up with surprise, then his mouth split in a warm smile. He dropped the pen.

"Wyatt!" he said, half rising from his chair and extending his hand. "You're back."

Earp accepted his handshake. "Just rode in a couple of minutes ago."

"Good, good." Clum eyed him eagerly. "Got the killers, didn't you? I knew you would."

"No," Earp said flatly. "We never even got close. Complete washout."

Clum's mouth sagged. "What happened?"

"Nothing worth bragging about. We rode our butts off and finally lost their trail over in the Santa Ritas."

"How? How could you lose their trail?"

Clum's tone of voice was almost accusatory. Earp gave him a hard look. "Virgil's a damn good tracker, and I'm no slouch myself. We lost them on a long stretch of rocky ground, and no excuses needed. Anybody would've lost them."

"Wyatt, please," Clum said, suddenly flustered. "I wasn't criticizing you, or Virgil either. I was just . . . disappointed."

"How the hell do you think I feel? Five days in a saddle and nothing to show for it."

"What a waste," Clum muttered. "And how do I explain it in the paper? Anything I say will sound like an alibi."

"That's why I stopped off here," Earp said. "I want you to print a story about how we would've caught them, but they skipped across the border. Then say our investigation has turned up a new lead."

"What new lead? You just said they crossed into Old Mexico."

"A new lead I'll tell you about when we find it. Just leave your readers with the idea that we've only started. We won't quit till we get them."

Clum squinted at him. "And if you don't?"

"We will," Earp said tightly. "One way or another, we'll find them."

"What does Behan have to say about all this?"

"Whatever he says, you can bet Harry Woods will print it in the *Nugget*. So you need to hit the street first with our version."

Clum bobbed his head. "I'll play on the angle of this new lead, and hope to God you come up with one. For the time being, that should offset anything Behan has to say."

"Add something else," Earp said. "Work in that it's Virgil's investigation, as a federal marshal. That Behan was going to sit on his thumb until Virgil took over."

"I hit hard on that in my editorials while you were gone. But it's worth driving the point home again."

"Don't forget to mention that Behan was serving under Virgil. Play up the fact that the authority here is federal, and his name is Earp."

Clum looked thoughtful. "Are you aware that you've created a two-edged sword? Virgil as the authority, and now this new lead that might or might not exist." He paused, peering over his glasses. "Succeed and you get the credit. Fail and you'll get crucified by Behan and the *Nugget*."

"I don't intend to fail," Earp said forcefully. "Whatever it takes, I intend to put those men on the gallows. Or kill them, if they resist arrest."

"Yes, I understand. But first you have to find them."

"You just write your stories, John. Let me worry about bringing in the killers."

"I pray you do," Clum said. "You've put the Earp name on the line, and the election could easily be decided on this one issue. It's starting to look like an all or nothing proposition."

"When you're dealt a hand," Earp informed him, "you have to play it out. One fashion or another, I've been a gambler all my life. Why stop now?"

"Have you ever bet your entire bankroll on one turn of the cards?"

"After a manner of speaking, I've bet my life on one turn of the cards. I'm willing to risk an election."

"Speaking of your life," Clum said gravely, "the word's out that Brocius and the Clantons are making threats against you and your brothers. Apparently, they've been doing some loud talking in the saloon over in Charleston."

"Talk's cheap," Earp said. "Brocius backed down quick enough when I put a gun on him out at the Clanton place."

"Don't underestimate them, Wyatt. They've killed many people over the years."

"First thing I learned as a lawman was never to underestimate the other man. That goes especially for back-shooters like Brocius and the Clantons."

"Good," Clum said. "I'd wager money that this last episode was one insult too many. Sooner or later, they'll try something."

"I'm available," Earp said, with a faint smile. "They know where to find me."

With that, he left Clum to write a new editorial. He crossed over to Allen Street and walked toward the hotel. The boardwalks were crowded, and the gambling dens and dance halls were gearing up for a lively night. The thought occurred that he'd forgotten to ask Virgil who would police the town tonight. He had a feeling it wouldn't be Morg.

Approaching the hotel, he saw Holliday step off the veranda. As Holliday started toward the street, he called out. "Doc, wait up."

Holliday turned, inspecting his weathered appearance. "Well, now, home is the weary warrior."

"High time, too," Earp said. "Lots of water under the bridge since I spent five days in a saddle."

"Little tender here and there, are you?"

"Not tender, but I'm wore-out. I could use a long, hot bath."

Holliday wrinkled his nose. "Now that you mention it, you are a tad odiferous, Mr. Earp."

Earp waved him off. "Defending law and order, Mr. Holliday, carries a high price."

"So I heard on the grapevine. Appears you about gave Curly Bill conniption fits. Actually pulled a gun on him, did you?"

"Dumb bastard gave me no choice. He made a move and I moved a shade faster."

"That's your problem," Holliday said jokingly. "You lawmen always give the other fellow the first move. Get him before he gets you, that's my motto."

"Tell me about it," Earp said. "I've seen you in action before."

"Well, no question about it, I do good work. Fact is, you ought to keep that in mind."

"How so?"

"Take me along next time."

Earp studied him a moment. "You're not talking about stage robbers, are you?"

"No," Holliday said. "I'm talking about people who get pushed when they get in your way."

"Like Brocius and his bunch."

"Wyatt, you've been crosswise of that crowd damn near from the day we pulled into town. With Virgil a marshal, and you after Behan's job . . . it'll just get worse."

"No argument there," Earp agreed. "And you're saying you want to be included when push comes to shove, right?"

Holliday chuckled. "I'd be goddamn insulted if I wasn't. Stage robbers are one thing, but a personal matter—that's different."

"Doc, I think you just like a good fight."

"Spoil my day if I missed this one, that's for sure."

"You talk like it's just around the corner."

"I'd need a crystal ball to tell you that. But I'll lay odds it's sooner rather than later."

Earp stared off into the middle distance. "When we came here, I thought my fighting days were over. Figured I'd make my fortune and live like a rajah. Funny the way things work out."

Holliday laughed. "I'll let you ponder the ironies while you're steamin' in a bathtub. I've got a poker game that needs my attention."

Still laughing, he crossed the street to the Oriental. Earp watched him a moment, struck by a sudden thought. One he'd never had before.

Doc Holliday, who was waiting to die, found no mystery in life.

# Chapter Twelve

EARLY THE NEXT EVENING EARP EMERGED FROM the hotel. He was attired in a vested suit, white shirt and tie, and a flat-crowned hat. His pistol rode in a holster at waist level, just inside the skirt of his suit jacket. He took a seat in one of the rockers on the veranda.

Since arising late that morning, he'd spent the day attending to business affairs. Dividends on his mining properties were paid the middle of each month, and the statement for September had arrived while he was out of town. His share of the Oriental, which was accounted on a weekly basis, had also fallen due while he was away. Though he had a good head for figures, squaring the accounts had taken most of the afternoon.

Earp took out a cigar. He seldom indulged himself with tobacco, but tonight was something of an occasion. After clipping the ends, he moistened the cigar and lit it with a match. He idly puffed smoke, watching as crowds began gathering throughout the gaming district. The day had improved his mood measurably, particularly after he'd tallied his current bank balance. He was, to his way of thinking, in the chips.

The investment portfolio suggested by George Parsons and Lou Rudabaugh had performed beyond all expectations. By next month the original loans would be repaid, and in less than two years he would have effectively tripled his money. Today, in a cordial meeting, Rudabaugh had recommended reinvestment of three-quarters of his earnings. The road to wealth, according to Rudabaugh, lay in putting money to work rather than let it sit idle. In short, money made money.

Nothing was certain, but Earp was inclined to accept the advice. The mines around Tombstone continued to boom, and the risk seemed to him almost nonexistent. His experience in operating gaming parlors told him as well that money working at house odds was virtually assured of a substantial return. Mining investments, and business in general, appeared to him to be quite similar. Rudabaugh and Parsons, men with a nose for profit, allowed reinvestment to multiply their capital again and again. He thought he would be wise to follow their lead.

A year from now, perhaps two at the most, he saw himself as a man of independent wealth. Based on his accumulated return to date, he could expect his current investments to again double, or triple, in value. To a gambler's way of thinking, it was like playing with the house's money. Once you got ahead, you got further ahead by steadily increasing the size of your bets. As Doc Holliday was prone to say, "Never get off a winner." The mining investments were the largest stakes he'd ever wagered in his life. But he had no great qualms about laying it all on the line. He intended to walk away a rich man.

Puffing the cigar, he felt generally satisfied with the scheme of things. All the more so since he'd made further headway with Tombstone's newest stage sensation, Sarah Marcus. Early that afternoon he had sent a note to her hotel, inviting her to supper the following evening. She had replied in the affirmative, and with a promptness that indicated she found the prospect very appealing. At first, a good part of his attraction to her was the fact that she was John Behan's girl. But now, having spoken with her and seen her spirited manner, Behan was only a minor consideration. He was attracted to her in the way that bees sought out ripe, sweet-scented flowers. She was too tempting to resist.

For all his contentment, there was one matter that still

gave him pause. He had gambled on catching the three stage robbers, and he'd come up short. Their whereabouts was unknown, and there was small likelihood that wanted dodgers would result in a lead. Even though he had persuaded Marshall Williams, the Wells Fargo agent, to post a reward of $2,000 apiece, he had no great hope that they would be apprehended. The chances of a lawman in some out of the way spot happening across them was remote, at best. The chances were nil if they had crossed the border into Old Mexico.

The problem was one of some consequence. Having bragged that he and Virgil would track down the robbers, he was now in an awkward position. He had to deliver on the brag, or else risk a serious blow at the polls come election time. And unless he was elected sheriff, there was little question that his value to the mine owners would be greatly diminished. Lou Rudabaugh, in their meeting that afternoon, had alluded to the problem in roundabout terms. The questions had been tactfully phrased, but there was no doubt as to the meaning. Politics was the linchpin to future investments, and wealth.

The hotel door opened and Holliday stepped outside. He saw Earp seated in a rocker, smoking a cigar, and crossed the veranda. "You look like a man of leisure," he said. "Where've you been all day?"

"Business matters," Earp replied. "Had a meeting with Rudabaugh, and then I got accounts settled at the Oriental."

"The proverbial cat with a mouthful of feathers. Sitting out here counting your money, are you?"

"No need to count till I cash out. The last tally's the only one that counts."

Holliday lowered himself into a rocker. A sudden spasm racked him and he pulled a handkerchief from inside his coat. When the coughing subsided, he wiped his mouth and returned the handkerchief to his pocket. His face was pale.

"Cool this evening," he said without inflection. "Too much fresh air doesn't agree with my constitution."

There was unwritten agreement that the subject of his health was to be treated with some degree of levity. Earp played along. "You'll perk up once you get a game started. Nothing like a smoky saloon to improve a man's breathing."

"Exactly right," Holliday quipped. "How do you think I've lived this long?"

Earp's attention was suddenly diverted. Across the street he saw Ike Clanton rein his horse to a halt before the Alhambra Saloon. Holliday followed the direction of his gaze, and they watched as Clanton dismounted and entered the saloon. Holliday uttered a low chuckle.

"Ike always was the simpleton of the bunch. You'd think he would avoid town after you had that run-in with them."

"Maybe," Earp said, puffing the cigar. "Or maybe he's here for a reason."

"What would that be?"

"Well, like you said, he's not too bright. Brocius might've sent him in here as a scout, to test the water."

"Possible," Holliday allowed. "Brocius might want to find out whether or not he's welcome in Tombstone."

Earp sat with the cigar wedged in the corner of his mouth. His eyes narrowed in thought, as though he was weighing a matter of some import. After a moment his gaze shifted to Holliday.

"Doc, how would you like to do me a favor?"

"Fire away."

"Go over to the Alhambra," Earp said. "You and Ike are on speaking terms. Leastways, he doesn't see you as part of the problem with Virgil and me. Offer to buy him a drink."

Holliday's brow furrowed. "Why would I do that?"

"Give him some song and dance about how I'd like to make peace with Brocius. Tell him I want to talk to him, in private."

"Because it wouldn't do for you to be seen with him, right? Not after what happened between you and Brocius."

"That's the ticket," Earp said, nodding. "Let him think I want him to be the peacemaker."

"Small chance," Holiday observed dryly. "Mind telling me what you have up your sleeve?"

Earp told him. Holliday wagged his head in appreciation, then rose from the rocker. "See you out behind the Oriental."

Holliday crossed the street to the Alhambra. Earp waited a moment, then walked over to the Oriental. The bar was crowded, and the gaming tables were starting to fill with players. He wandered casually through the room, pausing at the roulette table and the faro layout, as though to inspect the action. He stopped at the dice table and spoke for a few minutes with Jack Slater, the partner who was responsible for daily operation of the Oriental. Then, after making his way to a storeroom at the rear, he went out the back door.

Holliday and Clanton were waiting behind the building. Clanton was short and wiry, in his late twenties, pugnacious by nature. In the dim starlight his features appeared set in a dubious scowl. He squinted at Earp.

"Doc says you wanna make peace with Curly Bill."

"Leave me out of it," Holliday said, walking toward the back door. "You gents make your own deal."

Earp waited until he was inside. When the door closed, he looked at Clanton. "Let's forget Brocius. The deal I want to make is with you."

Clanton looked skittish. "What're you talkin' about?"

"Ike, when's the last time you had six thousand cash to call your own?"

"What's that got to do with anything?"

"Wanted posters are being printed on those boys who hit the stage. Wells Fargo put a price of six thousand on their heads. Hard cash and no questions asked."

"Turn'em in?" Clanton said in an insulted voice. "What d'ya think I am?"

Earp smiled. "I know what you are, Ike. The question is, would you like to make an easy six thousand? And no one the wiser."

"Not on your tintype! I ain't no Judas."

"Stop and think a minute, Ike. Are you sidekicks with Crane, Leonard, and Head? You ever run with them?"

"Well, no," Clanton said, his eyes darting about. "I met'em through Curly Bill. Him and Crane were pards a while back."

"Where's the rub, then?" Earp asked. "Hell, they brought trouble to your doorstep by coming to your place. You can return the favor."

"Just ain't right, that's all. Besides, Curly Bill would blow my head off if he ever found out."

Earp saw an opening. "Suppose he never found out? We'll keep it to ourselves, and who's to know?"

"This reward?" Clanton said, still wary. "How'd it be paid?"

"From me to you, all on the hush-hush. I can arrange it with Wells Fargo."

"And nobody'd ever know? Not a solitary livin' soul?"

Earp sensed that greed had won out. "You deliver those boys and I'll deliver the six thousand. Who's to know?"

Clanton scuffed his toe in the dirt. He struggled with himself a moment, then surrendered. "What would I have to do?"

"Find out where they are and let me know. You get the money when I get them."

"Is this one of them 'dead or alive' rewards?"

"Don't worry," Earp said. "Either way, you still get paid."

"Awright," Clanton said stoutly. "We got ourselves a deal."

"How soon can you get word to me?"

"I dunno, and that's a fact. I'll nose around, but I'll have to be real careful. Curly Bill ain't nobody's dummy."

Earp decided to sink the barb deep. "For your sake, the sooner the better, Ike. Someone's liable to beat you to that reward."

"When'd you say them wanted dodgers go out?"

"First thing tomorrow."

"Kee-rist!" Clanton sputtered. "You're right, I got no time to waste. I'll get on it muy pronto."

There was no handshake. They agreed to pass messages back and forth between Doc Holliday. Then, with a furtive look over his shoulder, Clanton walked off into the dark. He vanished around a corner of the building.

Earp watched after him with a satisfied smile. His assessment of Ike Clanton had proved to be dead on the mark. Which merely confirmed the truth of an age-old axiom.

There was no honor among thieves.

# Chapter Thirteen

THE LOBBY OF THE GRAND HOTEL WAS CROWDED. As a wall clock struck five, Earp walked through the door. Apart from business travelers to Tombstone, most of those in the lobby were entertainers at the Birdcage Theater. The first show of the evening was at seven, and the performers usually had an early supper. They were a mixed lot of chorus girls, one comic, and three acrobats.

Earp moved toward the desk clerk. He was aware that the entertainers congregated in the lobby subjected him to a close once-over. Attired in his best suit, freshly pressed only that afternoon, he stopped in front of the desk. The clerk examined him with a thinly disguised smirk.

"Yes, sir. May I help you?"

"I'm here to see Miss Sarah Marcus. What's her room number?"

"Are you Mr. Earp?"

"I am."

"Miss Marcus will be down directly. She asked that you wait here."

All conversation in the lobby abruptly ceased. The desk clerk looked toward the stairs and Earp followed his gaze. Sarah Marcus descended the staircase as though making her entrance at an emperor's ball.

She wore an exquisite gown of teal-blue and a pearl choker with a sapphire in the center. The bodice of the gown was cut low and cinched at the waist, displaying her sumptuous figure to full advantage. Her hair was upswept and drawn back, with a soft cluster of curls fluffed high on her forehead. A velvet evening cape was thrown over her shoulders.

She looked at once regal and sensual.

Earp was momentarily transfixed. She was a vision of loveliness, and her entrance had clearly had the desired effect. He recovered himself, crossing the lobby as she reached the bottom of the staircase. Her mouth dimpled in an engaging smile.

"Good evening, Wyatt."

"Evening, Sadie."

Earp was distinctly uncomfortable. Her clothing was opulent compared to his serge suit, and he felt a cutaway coat would have been more fitting to the occasion. Adding to his discomfort, he was all too aware that they were the object of attention of everyone in the lobby.

Yet he was equally aware that this lovely young woman had staged her entrance for his benefit. She obviously meant to make an impression, one he would not soon forget. His discomfort was suddenly replaced by a sense of good fortune, as though he were the luckiest man in Tombstone tonight. He doffed his hat with a wide grin.

"You look mighty pretty," he said. "I'll be the envy of every man in town."

"Why, thank you, sir. I'm flattered you think so."

She tucked her hand inside his arm. Earp led her across the lobby, expecting the crowd to break out in applause at any moment. He held the door open for her, then clapped his hat on his head and stepped outside. On the street she again took his arm and they turned uptown. The air was brisk, and as they strolled along the boardwalk, she wrapped herself in the cape and hugged his arm tighter. He was acutely aware of the firmness of her breast against his arm.

Earp had planned the evening with care. He, too, meant to impress, and he'd made special arrangements for their early supper. He took her to the Maison Doree, considered to be the most exclusive restaurant in Tombstone. The menu was European, and the town's influential business leaders were regular patrons. The restaurant was owned by Henri Doree, an ingratiating man with a French accent and a pencil-line mustache. Earp thought the owner's name, as well as his accent, was a bogus front to attract a higher class clientele. But the service was impeccable and the food was referred to as cuisine. Everyone who was anyone ate there.

Monsieur Doree personally escorted them to their table. Diners at other tables paused, their conversation suspended, watching Sadie with appreciative stares as she preceded Earp across the room. The table was set with crystal, a full silver service, and fine linen. Doree held the chair for Sadie, waiting until Earp had seated himself. Then he snapped his fingers and a waiter materialized with menus. Doree bowed, glancing at Earp with a conspiratorial wink, and moved away from the table.

"How wonderful," Sadie said, slightly breathless. "It's so elegant . . . so continental."

"Food's good, too," Earp said, opening the menu. "Would you like me to order?"

"Oh, would you!" she said, closing her menu. "I'm afraid my French is limited to *Merci.*"

Earp studied the menu, most of which was printed in French. As the waiter hovered over him, he selected *bouef consommé* to start, followed by *oysters Doree,* and *pinions à poulett aux champignons* as a main course. If his pronunciation of the French dishes suffered, neither Sadie nor the waiter seemed to notice. He chose a fine white wine to accompany the meal.

"I know it's terrible," she said as the waiter whisked away with the menus. "But I really couldn't help myself. I asked around about you—and it's all true!"

"What's all true?"

"Well, you're a famous law officer from Kansas. Your brother's a marshal, and you invest heavily in mining stocks, and you're running for sheriff, and . . . just everything. It's all true, isn't it?"

Earp seldom spoke of his record as a peace officer. Yet dime novelists and newspapers such as *The Policeman's Gazette* had made his name a household word across the country. In Wichita, one of the largest cowtowns in Kansas, he had served as a deputy town marshal during the trail season of 1875. There he'd established a reputation as a fair but uncompromising lawman. Texas cowhands who broke town ordinances were treated to swift, and sometimes rough, justice.

A year later, in the spring of 1876, he had been hired as chief deputy marshal of Dodge City. Universally known as Queen of the Cowtowns, Dodge City was the last great railhead for western trail drives. While serving there he had formed lifelong friendships with Doc Holliday and Bat Masterson, another celebrated law officer. That same year Wild Bill Hickok had been assassinated, and the press quickly dubbed Earp as the West's most renowned shootist, a gunfighter who operated on the side of the law. By the time he departed Dodge City for Tombstone, his name was legend across the frontier.

But now, with Sadie awaiting his answer, Earp merely shrugged. "I suppose it's true enough," he said. "Although I'd wager you didn't hear it from Johnny Behan."

"Oh, please," she said with a charming little smile. "Let's just forget his name, shall we? I'd much rather hear about you."

Earp considered himself to be a good judge of character. He believed her interest to be genuine, and he was also flattered. He was aware as well that women, in an effort to charm a man, were not above playing on his ego. Still, if that was her intent, he didn't mind. She was too vivacious to deny her anything.

Over soup, and then the oysters, Earp allowed her to draw him out. He told her about his brothers, and his parents, who now lived in California, and how they had all drifted westward. She then got him to talk about his aspirations and goals in Tombstone, and the timbre of his voice took on greater enthusiasm. He concluded with what seemed to him a simple statement of fact.

"I've knocked around in my life, done lots of things. I figure Tombstone is the last stop, where I'll plant roots. When they write the history books on Arizona, I want the Earp name to mean something."

"It will," she said with utter conviction. "I just know it will."

The waiter served their main course. Her eyes were sparkling from several glasses of wine, and Earp decided to change the subject. "How about you?" he asked. "Were you always set on having a stage career?"

"Yes, always," she said, unable to contain the excitement in her voice. "Unless you're a performer, I know it's hard to imagine. But just think of the crowds, and the applause, simply being on stage . . . it's addictive!"

Earp coaxed her to tell more. Her full name was Josephine Sarah Marcus. Her father was a doctor and lived with her mother and a brother in San Francisco. Though her father had forbidden her a stage career, she had a good voice and she was headstrong. Only last year she'd run away with a traveling variety troupe that played engagements throughout the West.

Gradually her voice had won her top billing in the show. But then, following an engagement in Tucson, the show's owner had absconded with the company funds and a blond chorus girl. Along with the rest of the troupe, she had been stranded, with no funds and no prospects. John Behan, who was in Tucson on law business, had introduced himself only two nights before the disaster. He'd offered to help her, though there was nothing he could do for the troupe.

Behan returned to Tombstone, and the next day she had received a wire. He had somehow arranged star billing at the Birdcage Theater, as well as stagecoach passage to

Tombstone. With nowhere else to turn, it had seemed to her something of a godsend. She was enthralled with the Birdcage, not to mention the audiences, who had received her so warmly. But she'd been less than pleased with her sponsor, John Behan. While she was appreciative, and greatly in his debt, she felt that he asked too much in return. His demands for her attention were insistent, to the point that it had become a burden.

"Doesn't surprise me," Earp said when she was finished. "Behan's the type who trades in favors. Lending a helping hand doesn't fit into his scheme of things."

"So I've found out," she said. "But anyway, that's my problem, not yours. I'll just have to find a way to end it."

Earp liked a woman with pluck. All the more so if she turned heads when she entered a room. Whether Sarah Marcus was telling him the whole story hardly seemed to matter. Whether she was trying to use him as a foil against Behan was of no great concern, either. What mattered was that he was attracted to her, and he thought it was mutual. He was willing to accept her at face value.

"Want a suggestion?" he asked her. "About how you can end it with Behan?"

"Yes, I do, very much."

"You'll think I'm fast, and maybe a little forward. But no one ever accused me of being a smooth talker."

She laughed. "No, please go on. I won't be offended."

"One thing you can bet on," Earp said with a touch of pride. "Johnny Behan hates me worse than the devil hates holy water. Let it be known that we're keeping company and that's the end of him. Guaranteed."

"You mean—" She hesitated, uncertain of the right phrase. "Are you asking me to be your . . . girl?"

"We wouldn't be here now if the feeling wasn't mutual. Let's take it a step at a time and see where it goes."

She toyed with her wineglass a moment. Then, looking him directly in the eye, she smiled. "Suppose I think about it until after the show tonight?"

"Take your time," Earp said. "I'm not trying to rush things."

She laughed her throaty laugh. "On the contrary, Mr. Earp. I'd say you're trying to sweep me off my feet."

Later that evening Earp sat alone at a front row table in the Birdcage Theater. Nearby, at another front row table, John Behan was also seated by himself. Neither of them so much as acknowledged the other's presence. When the opening number ended, they sat sipping their drinks, watching the acrobats bound onto the stage. Some moments later the door off to the side opened and Sadie stepped out.

She walked without hesitation to Earp's table and took the chair he offered. There was a buzz of conversation from the audience as everyone waited for the sheriff's reaction. Behan stood, pulling a wad of bills from his pocket, and tossed money on the table. Then, his eyes straight ahead, he marched out of the theater. Murmurs from the crowd followed him out.

"Well, now," Earp said, smiling at her. "What would you say to champagne?"

Her eyes danced. "I'd love some champagne!"

He signaled the waiter.

# Chapter Fourteen

THE ORIENTAL WAS PACKED. THE SATURDAY NIGHT crowd jammed the bar and men waited in line at the gaming tables. Miners were paid once a week, at the end of their shift on Saturday, and payday was a time to celebrate. By midnight at least half the town would be drunk.

Earp stood at the far end of the bar, watching the action. He'd always been intrigued by the fact that Westerners seemed to hurl themselves into any celebration. In some early boomtown the phrase "Out to see the elephant" had been coined. What it meant was a wild spree involving liquor, gambling, and a visit to the whorehouse of a man's choice. Having seen the elephant, most men went away dead broke and virtually embalmed on rotgut whiskey.

Tradesmen fostered the tradition to their immense profit. A working man, with a week's wages in his pocket, generally looked to the essentials first. Mercantile stores, boardinghouses, and cafes that extended credit were paid something on account. Whatever remained was then devoted to a night on the town, where any vice was available at a price. Saloons and gaming parlors, along with women of lost virtue, profited most from this weekly binge. A man with empty pockets invariably went away happy.

Tonight, observing it all, Earp was in a rare mood. For three days now, since Sarah Marcus had made her choice, he'd been in high spirits. Part of it could be attributed to the envy he saw in the eyes of Rudabaugh and Clum, and even Doc Holliday. There was a certain male pride in the fact that he'd captured the affections of the most stunning

woman in town. But a larger part stemmed from the fact
that her affections were now without limitation, the union
complete. Last night, for the first time, she had invited
him to her room at the hotel. He still felt somewhat intoxi-
cated by a night spent in her bed.

Later tonight he would catch her last show at the Birdcage. There was no question in his mind that she would
again invite him to her room. She had proved to be a
hungry lover, uninhibited yet curiously tender, and the
thought of it left him filled with anticipation for the night
ahead. Tombstone was in many ways a small town, and by
now their liaison was common knowledge. But he was
bothered neither by the gossips nor the hatred he had kindled in John Behan. A mortal enemy seemed a small price
to pay for what he'd found in her arms.

One thought sparked another. Over the past five days
he had grown increasingly confident that he would defeat
Behan in the election. His confidence was born out of an
absolute certainty of Ike Clanton's greed. Cattle rustling
was profitable, but the prospect of a quick six thousand
dollars would goad Clanton to action. The one uncertainty
was how soon Clanton would uncover the whereabouts of
the stage robbers. The *Epitaph* editorials had promised a
break in the case, and the public wanted results. To win at
the polls, the killers had to be captured, and soon. Delay
merely served to erode the gains already made.

A shout attracted Earp's attention. Across the room he
saw a miner at the faro layout laughing and waving his
arms. Ganged around him were several miners no less en-
thused by his good fortune. Apparently he had won a large
bet, and the crowd was drawn to any man with a run of
luck. The miner whooped at the top of his lungs.

"Look out now! I'm gonna buck the tiger."

Earp wandered over to observe the play. Faro was one
of the more popular games in western mining camps. Its
name derived from the image of an Egyptian pharaoh on

the back of the cards, and the game had originated a century earlier in France.

Cards were dealt from a specially adapted box, and the player bet against the house. Every card from ace to king was painted on the cloth layout that covered the table. A player placed his money on the card of his choice, and two cards were then drawn faceup from the box. The first card drawn lost and the second card won. The player could "copper" his play by betting a card to lose instead of win. There were twenty-five turns, since the first and last cards in the deck paid nothing. When the box was empty, the dealer shuffled and the game began anew.

Normally, the house hired an experienced gambler to operate the game. The dealer worked for a salary, plus a small share of the winnings. Sometimes, when a gambler had developed a reputation and a following, the house leased him the concession and he backed the faro bank with his own money. The house received a weekly payment for the concession, plus a percentage of the winnings. But the odds greatly favored the house, and Earp had rejected any number of offers to lease the concession. Instead, he and his partners had hired a dealer who knew how to work a crowd as well as the pasteboards.

Having just turned the last hand, the dealer deftly shuffled the cards and allowed the miner to cut. Then he placed the deck in the dealing box and burned the top card, commonly referred to as the "soda" card. Glancing up, he nodded, indicating the game was open to play. The miner juggled his handful of gold coins, placed one above the ace, another between the five-six, and still another between the jack-queen. By playing several cards at once, he immediately marked himself as an experienced player. The system was known as "coppering the heel," and increased the chances of winning. The dealer pulled two cards from the box, a king and a four.

"Close," he said in the slick cadence of a pitchman. "Give'er another go."

"Keep dealing!" The miner laughed, scattering coins across the layout. "I'm on a streak tonight."

The dealer was adroit and quick. His hands flashed between the box and the layout with practiced expertise. Cards popped out of the box in speedy pairs, and just as rapidly he paid the winners and collected the losers. The miner continued to "copper the heel," but for every bet he won, he lost double and sometimes more. He blithely tossed coins about the layout, alternately chuckling and cursing with the gusto of a man who was enjoying himself immensely. By the time the "hoc" card, the last card in the deck, was turned the last of his gold coins had disappeared. Within a matter of minutes, he'd been trimmed for something more than a hundred dollars.

"Stick with it," the dealer cajoled, shuffling the cards. "The worm's bound to turn."

"No more for me." The miner laughed, turned to the crowd of onlookers. "Boys, I done been et by the tiger!"

Earp walked back to the bar. Over the course of the years, he had seen many men get "et by the tiger." He knew the miner would end the night drunk, bragging loudly that he'd won and lost a month's pay. Gambling, for the miner and his friends, was a high form of entertainment, a diversion from their grueling labor in the underground shafts. For the Oriental, it was a veritable money tree. The odds inevitably took any man's toll.

At the rear of the room Earp saw Holliday deep in a poker game. There were seven men in all at the table, and Holliday, as usual, appeared to be winning. His skill at poker was uncanny, so much so that some men thought he now and then gave luck an assist. Yet he prided himself on honest play, and anyone brash enough to accuse him of cheating was given an option. They could recant, offering an abject apology, or test him at another game of skill. Those who opted for a pistol over an apology went to an untimely reward. Holliday was rarely bested at cards, and never at guns.

Turning back to the bar, Earp saw Virgil step through the front door. Virgil hurriedly scanned the room, then spotted him, and motioned. Earp circled the bar and walked toward the door. Virgil was waiting for him outside.

"Got some bad news, Wyatt."

"What's wrong?"

"The postal system operates pretty speedy these days. You recollect those wanted posters I sent out the first of the week?"

Earp looked surprised. "You've already heard something?"

"Not ten minutes ago," Virgil said. "Word came in over the telegraph from a town marshal in New Mexico. Crane, Leonard, and Head were killed earlier today."

"Killed?" Earp said, astounded. "Who killed them?"

"The marshal and his deputy. He's claiming the Wells Fargo reward."

"How'd it happen?"

"Way it appears, they switched from stages to robbin' banks. They pulled a holdup and got killed for their efforts. Those boys just weren't cut out to be bandits."

"Dammit!" Earp smacked his fist into his palm. "Why'd they have to get themselves killed? That leaves us a day late and a dollar short where the election's concerned."

"Yeah, I know," Virgil said solemnly. "Hated to bring you the news. Seems like we just weren't meant to catch that bunch."

"We played into bad luck. From the very start, nothing went our way."

"Behan's sure to rake us over the coals. By tomorrow, he'll spread the word that some New Mexico lawman got the job done while we were standing around scratchin' our butts."

Earp nodded agreement. He stared off down the street, silent for a long moment. There was little doubt that Behan would use the turn of events to political advantage.

Finally, still frowning, he shook his head. "We're not through yet," he said. "Hell, we're the ones that organized the posse, not Behan. Except for us, nobody would even know the robbers' names."

"You got a point there."

"On top of that, we sent out those wanted posters. If we hadn't, nobody would ever know they were dead. So you might say we had a fairly big part in justice being served."

Virgil gave him a sly look. "You sound like you're writing an editorial for the *Epitaph*. Clum ought to put you on the payroll."

"First thing tomorrow," Earp said, "I'll get Clum hot on it. Whatever credit's due, it falls to us. That's more than Behan can say."

"Might just work, too. Behan sure as hell can't claim any credit."

Earp looked past him. Virgil turned and saw Marshall Williams approaching along the boardwalk. The Wells Fargo agent was listing, his stride unsteady. He was known to have a fondness for liquor, sometimes to excess. Tonight appeared to be one of those times.

"Wyatt! Virgil!" he said in high good humor. "You look sober as a couple of deacons."

Earp smiled. "We've got some news that's liable to sober you up, Marsh."

"Not if I can help it. But you're welcome to try."

Sticking to the salient points, Earp brought him up to date on the robbers' unexpected demise.

"Hooray and hallelujah!" Williams bellowed when he finished. "Somebody got Bud Philpot's killers. Maybe there's a God in heaven, after all."

"More like the devil's own, Marsh. Those boys won't get anywhere near heaven."

Williams suddenly broke out laughing. "Speaking of the devil's own! Your Judas Iscariot won't get the reward money now. With them dead, Clanton's left out in the cold."

Earp had sworn the Wells Fargo agent to secrecy about his arrangement with Ike Clanton. He gave Williams a scolding look. "Watch what you say, Marsh. That's still private information. No need to let it out."

"Gotcha." Williams winked and tapped a finger to his lips. "No slips out of me."

"Well, anyway, it's over now. You can advise Wells Fargo on Monday."

"Only wish't I'd shot those bastards myself. Double damned deserved what they got."

Williams wobbled off into the Oriental. Virgil watched after him a moment, then wagged his head. "I wish we'd shot 'em. Trouble is, we never got the chance."

"Luck of the draw, Virg."

"How do you mean?"

"Simple," Earp said. "We got dealt the joker."

They went inside and drank to lost opportunity.

# Chapter Fifteen

IKE CLANTON ENTERED TOMBSTONE FROM THE south. Nightfall had settled over the town and streetlamps flickered brightly in the dark. At the intersection of Fourth and Allen he turned west and halfway down the block reined into the O.K. Corral. A stablehand, working the night shift, came to take his horse. •

Some three years ago, when Tombstone sprang almost overnight from the desert, the O.K. Corral was the first stable to be built in town. Frequented largely by ranchers and cowhands, it was also a stopover for teamsters who hauled goods overland to resupply the town's stores. Cattlemen preferred the outside corral, where their horses could run loose in the fenced enclosure.

Ike walked back to the corner of Fourth. He entered the Can Can Cafe and took a seat at a table by the front window. One of the regular waitresses took his order, beefsteak with beans and potatoes. He was hungry, having ridden the twenty miles from the San Pedro that afternoon. Yet his stomach rumbled and felt a little queasy, for he was suffering from a bout of mixed emotions. He felt both worried and relieved that the three stage robbers had been killed.

News of their deaths had reached the Clanton Ranch late yesterday. According to the story in the *Nugget*, they had been killed in New Mexico after a bank holdup. Brocius and Ringo took morbid amusement from the story, noting that the three men were poor cowhands and rank amateurs as robbers. They took even greater amusement from the lambasting Virgil and Wyatt Earp had received in a scathing editorial. Ringo, in his caustic way, had remarked that the Earps were a bunch of carpetbaggers with overblown ideas.

Ike was not asked to comment. Nor would Brocius or Ringo have paid any attention if he'd voiced an opinion. For almost a year now, since his father had been killed during a raid into Sonora, he'd been forced to play third fiddle in the gang's affairs. Brocius had appointed himself leader of the outfit, and Ringo had assumed the post of lieutenant and chief enforcer. Brocius was the brains and Ringo was the muscle, in the sense that a fast gun tended to forestall argument. No one had dared challenge their takeover of the gang.

For his part, Ike went along to get along. He was no mental giant, and the first to admit it. All his life he'd taken orders from the Old Man, his father, who was the planner and schemer of the family. His brother Billy was no better, just another rustler whose grand ambition was to be a notorious gunslinger. Yet Ike was resentful of Brocius, and in time he had become disgruntled. Taking over the gang was one thing, for Ike understood that someone with brains had to run the operation. But Brocius had also appointed himself lord of the ranch, claiming the Old Man's bedroom and favorite chair as though he was the family heir. That was a bitter pill to swallow.

The waitress brought Ike's supper along with a steaming mug of coffee. He attacked the steak as though he was cutting out Curly Bill's gizzard. Only that morning, Brocius had ordered him to ride into Tombstone. He was to hit the saloons, keep his ears open, and determine whether or not Wyatt Earp's campaign for sheriff had been damaged by his failure to capture the stage robbers. Brocius trusted no one, including Johnny Behan, and he wanted a reliable report on the state of affairs. Cattle rustling would become a hazardous occupation if Earp were somehow elected sheriff. He intended to see that it didn't happen.

Finished with his meal, Ike rolled himself a smoke. He lit the cigarette and sat staring out at the street. Tomorrow his brother and the McLaurys were coming into town for food and various supplies needed at the ranch. He'd been sent ahead on a lone scouting mission, the thought being that one man would draw less attention and thereby tend to hear more by way of the grapevine. That gave him one night to gather information, and at the same time, attend to some business of his own. One way or another, he had to make contact with Wyatt Earp.

The three stage robbers getting killed had instantly set Ike to worrying. His deal with Earp made him valuable only so long as he was able to deliver the robbers. With them dead, his value to Earp had also died, and that made the situation dangerous. Should Earp forget that their deal was based on secrecy, and become talkative, then the fat was in the fire. Word would spread, and Brocius would soon hear that he'd agreed to sell out Crane, Leonard, and Head. The outcome was simple to predict, and too scary to contemplate. At a nod from Brocius, Ringo would fill him full of holes.

The immediate problem was how to contact Earp. Ike sat smoking his cigarette, trying to concoct a plan. Were he to be seen with Earp, that would raise suspicions in itself. So it had to be accomplished in secret, again using Doc Holliday as the go-between. Yet he was leery of walking into the Oriental, where Earp spent his evenings, and trying to get a word with Holliday. Someone might put it together and he'd be worse off than before. The best idea was to drop by the Alhambra and hope that Holliday would again show up there. Only as a last resort would he go near the Oriental.

Ike doused his cigarette in the coffee mug and dropped a silver dollar on the table. Outside the cafe, he rounded the corner and turned down Allen Street. What he'd worked out wasn't the greatest plan in the world, but it was a place to start. He just had to hope that Holliday was on the prowl tonight.

Some minutes later Ike came through the door of the Alhambra. Any Tuesday night in Tombstone was slow, and tonight was no exception. There was only one poker game in progress, and Ike noted that Holliday was not among the players. Several men lined the bar, and the one nearest the end was Marshall Williams. Ike was barely on civil terms with the Wells Fargo agent, but a thought popped into his mind. He could use Williams to gather information for Brocius.

Halting at the end of the bar, he ordered whiskey. Williams was slouched against the bar, his eyes bloodshot and his features flushed with drink. One glance confirmed that he was staggering drunk, and Ike thought the situation was made to order. A drunk could be steered to talk about anything.

"Howdy," he said, nodding to Williams. "How's things?"

"Peachy keen," Williams said with a lopsided smile. "Matter of fact, I'm celebrating. Been celebrating for three days."

"Yeah?" Ike said amiably. "What's the occasion?"

"Glad you asked." Williams's speech was slurred. "The occasion is in honor of Bud Philpot, and the glorious demise of the rotten bastards who killed him. All of them your pals, I might add."

"Nosiree, you're wrong there. Those boys weren't pals of mine."

"A point well taken." Williams drew himself erect, clutched the bar for support. "Hell, they couldn't've been much of anything to you, could they?"

Ike was taken aback by the turn of the conversation. He tried to wave it off. "Tell you the truth, I hardly knew them boys."

"Hardly knew 'em?" Williams thundered drunkenly. "Why, you little shitheel, you sold 'em out! Or you would've, if they hadn't got killed."

"No such thing!" Ike said in a shaky voice. "Why would I do a thing like that?"

"For thirty pieces of silver, you goddamn Judas. Sold 'em to Wyatt Earp for the reward money. And I reckon I oughta know. Wells Fargo would've paid it."

"Earp told you that?"

Williams looked at him with a gloating smile. " 'Course he told me, and it's true, too. Written all over your face."

All the color drained from Ike's features. His head reeling, he spun away from the bar and hurried toward the door. Everyone in the saloon had heard the exchange, heard Williams brand him a Judas. Before the night was out, the word would spread to every dive in town. By tomorrow, or the next day at the latest, Brocius would hear it, and then Ringo would . . .

Ike slammed to a halt on the boardwalk outside. He pulled a great draught of cold air into his lungs, trying to clear his head. His mind thumped with questions. Should he get his horse and ride for the border? Or should he lie to Brocius, try to bluff it out? But standing there, even as he posed the question, he knew he would never fool Brocius. In the end he'd be caught out and killed. So what the hell was he to do?

Frozen in place, all but paralyzed, his gaze wandered across the street. He suddenly tensed, staring a few doors downstreet at the Eagle Lunch Counter. Through the plate-glass window he saw Doc Holliday seated at the counter beside Morgan Earp. All thoughts of Brocius and Ringo were abruptly set aside. His mind focused instead on Holliday and a way around what had now become a life and death predicament. He told himself there had to be some way, a way out. He rushed across the street.

Ike burst through the door of the cafe. Holliday turned on his stool at the counter, his senses immediately alerted. Ike Clanton looked like a crazed man, wild-eyed and strangely out of control. Holliday had no idea what was wrong, but he'd stayed alive by following his instincts. He motioned for Morgan to remain seated, then got to his feet and took a step away from the counter. His elbow, in a casual movement, brushed his coat away from the pistol he carried at belt level.

"Doc!" Ike said, halting in front of him, "I gotta talk to you."

"What about?"

"You got me into this mess and you gotta get me out."

Holliday stared at him. "What mess?"

"With Earp," Ike said loudly. "Marsh Williams is over at the Alhambra tellin' the world that we made a deal. You gotta set him straight."

"Why would I do that?"

"Goddammit, Doc! What we done was private. You know that."

"No," Holliday said quietly. "I don't know anything of the kind. I wasn't there."

"Well Earp was!" Ike grated out. "And now the sorry sonovabitch done went and told—"

Holliday backhanded him in the mouth. "You're heeled," he said in a low, cold voice. "Use it."

Blood trickled down Ike's split lip. His tongue darted out, tasting the blood, and he shook his head. "I haven't got no fight with you."

"You do now," Holliday told him. "Defend yourself."

"You're tryin' to make me draw, aren't you? 'Cause I called Earp a name. Well, thanks all the same, Doc. I ain't gonna let you kill me."

Holliday slapped him again. "Come on, yellowbelly, show a little guts. What do you carry a gun for?"

"I won't do it. I'm walkin' out of here."

Ike backed away a step, then turned and headed toward the door. His movements were jerky, his pace curiously slow, almost as though he expected to be shot in the back. Everyone in the cafe, their food forgotten, watched as he opened the door.

Morgan pushed away from the counter and stood. He looked at Holliday. "Let me try him. He might fight."

"Stay out of it, Morg. It's between him and me now."

"So what are you gonna do?"

"Kill him."

# Chapter Sixteen

DELMONICO'S BOASTED THAT IT WAS THE FINEST restaurant in Tombstone. Unlike its chief competition, the Maison Doree, the fare on the menu was prepared without fancy sauces or continental airs. The dishes were proudly American, the specialties of the house featuring prime beef, elk, venison, and other native game. Nothing delicate, the food was for hearty eaters.

Earp was working on a thick slab of steak that required a platter. The outside was charred and the inside was rare, oozing succulent juices. Across from him, Sadie picked at a fillet that would have fed three women her size. The food was excellent, the beef cooked to perfection. But the size of the portions left her somewhat overawed.

"Wyatt."

"Hmmm?" Earp paused, with a hunk of beef speared on his fork. "How's your fillet?"

"Oh, wonderful." She trimmed a dainty bite with her steak knife. "But I was just thinking. Do you realize I could feed the entire chorus line with the food on this table?"

Earp surveyed the table a moment. In addition to the generous cuts of beef, there were a variety of vegetables and thick slices of fresh baked bread. "You're right," he said, deadpan. " 'Course, with all this food, the girls might lose their figures."

"Well!" she said with mock indignation. "What about me?"

"No worries there. Not the way you keep me chained to the bed. You need all the strength you can get."

She stifled a laugh. His dry humor was one of the things she liked about him most. She glanced around, alarmed that someone at a nearby table might have overheard his remark. But then, all things considered, it wouldn't have mattered. By now everyone in town knew of their affair.

Sadie had long ago grown accustomed to the stares and whispers. Women who worked in variety theaters were admired and often lavishly courted by men. Yet those men's wives, as well as preachers and an assortment of do-gooders, were quick to label stage performers as women of easy virtue. She was more amused than miffed by their hypocrisy.

In mining camps across the West many of the most respected women in a town had begun as stage performers. For that matter, some of the grand dames of society had started out in parlor houses, any man's woman for a price. Even the so-called respectable women, beneath their veneer of virtue, were bawdier than their church pastors suspected. Women talked among themselves, and secrets were shared by the ladies in any sewing circle. Fewer than imagined took their wedding vows with their virginity intact.

So the opinions of other people were only of passing concern to Sadie. All the more so when she felt positively aglow with happiness. She was unable to look at Wyatt without a tingle of warmth spreading over her. Contrary to what she'd expected, she had found him to be gentle and thoughtful, considerate of her every wish. His reputation as a tough lawman was no doubt deserved, and she admired the strength of character that underlay his dedication to the law. But the man she'd taken to her bed was gentle rather than tough, the lover she had always hoped to find, and hold. Quickly, almost delirious with joy, she felt herself falling in love.

Some wellspring of intuition told her it was the same for him. He was reserved, not given to open displays of affection, but she sensed it nonetheless. Looking at him now, she knew deep inside that she had found her man. She thought he'd found his woman, too.

"You ought to stop looking at me that way."

Earp's voice broke her reverie. She blushed, suddenly aware that she'd been mooning over him. "I can't help it. I like to look at you."

"Keep it up and I'll have to drag you back to the room. That kind of look gives a man ideas."

"Well, first of all," she said gaily, "you wouldn't have to drag me. I'd go quite willingly, thank you. But I regret to say it's almost show time."

Earp checked his pocket watch. "Going on six-thirty, all right. Guess we'd better get you to the theater."

"You'll come by later . . . won't you?"

"With bells on."

Outside the restaurant they bumped into Virgil. Earp had formally introduced them several days ago, and Virgil approved of his choice in lady friends. He tipped his hat to Sadie.

"Evening," he said pleasantly. "All ready for another big show?"

"No thanks to him," she said, cutting her eyes at Earp. "The way your brother stuffs me with food, it's a wonder I can dance. I've never eaten so much in my life."

"Don't believe her," Earp said. "A bird couldn't live on what she eats."

She laughed and took Earp's arm. Virgil fell in beside them and they continued along the boardwalk. In the next block, they dropped Sadie off at the Birdcage Theater. Earp promised he would return in time for the last show.

"Tell you," Virgil said as they walked away. "Like her better every time I see her. She's got lots of spunk."

"And then some," Earp added lightly. "She's a regular ball of fire."

"Well, you always were partial to spirited women. Maybe you've met your match."

"Virg, you might be more right than you know."

Virgil scrutinized him closely. "Does that mean what it sounds like?"

"Yeah"—Earp wagged a hand back and forth—"maybe."

"Maybe, my dusty butt! You're thinking about gettin' hitched, aren't you?"

"You think it's too fast? I've only known her a couple of weeks."

"Why, hell no," Virgil said firmly. "The minute I laid eyes on Allie, I knew we'd get married. Sometimes it just happens that way."

"Guess it does," Earp agreed. "Tell you the truth, I feel a little bit like a schoolboy. Looking at her makes my ears buzz."

"High time, if you want my opinion. A good woman can be a comfort to a man."

"That the voice of experience speaking?"

"Hell, ask Allie, not me. She's been tellin' me that since the day we got hitched."

As they crossed the intersection, they saw Ike Clanton lurch out the door of the Eagle Lunch Counter. Even from a distance he looked peculiar, his stride ungainly and his manner somehow harried. Then, hard on his heels, Holliday emerged from the cafe, followed closely by Morgan. Holliday had a hand on his holstered pistol.

*"Clanton!"*

Holliday's shout brought Ike to a stop. He turned with the look of a cornered rat, his eyes wild. He shook his fist at Holliday.

"Leave me alone, goddammit! I got no quarrel with you."

"You stinkin' pisswillie," Holliday said, advancing on him. "What's it take to make you fight?"

"Hold it, Doc!" Virgil yelled out. "Let's not have any trouble."

Ike turned as Virgil and Earp approached from upstreet. On opposite sides of the street passersby had taken cover in doorways at the first sign of trouble. Virgil stopped in front of Ike, blocking him from Holliday. He looked from one to the other.

"What's going on here?"

"Ask him," Holliday said. "He's the one with a big mouth. Called Wyatt a son of a bitch."

Earp moved forward. In the lamplight he saw blood on Ike's mouth, and he could imagine that Holliday had tried to provoke a fight. He gave Ike a hard stare. "What's your problem?"

"You're my problem," Ike said angrily. "You went and told Marsh Williams about our deal."

"So?"

"You gave me your word you wouldn't tell nobody."

"You're wrong, Ike," Earp said. "To get the reward money, I had to tell Williams. Figure it out for yourself."

"Horseshit!" Ike exploded. "You just flat out lied to me. No other word for it."

"Ike, I don't allow any man to call me a liar. Maybe we ought to settle this between ourselves."

"Yeah, you'd like that, wouldn't you? Holliday and your brothers backin' your play. Well, it don't change a goddamned thing. You still broke your word."

Earp hit him a hard clubbing blow. He went down in the street, an angry welt forming along his jawline. He rolled over, slowly levering himself to his knees. Virgil stepped between them.

"That's enough," he commanded. "Ike, get on your feet and get out of here. Otherwise I'll arrest you."

"Arrest me!" Ike scrambled to his feet. "I'm the one that's been assaulted. Whyn't you arrest Holliday and your brother?"

"Because you're the one that went huntin' trouble. So far as the law's concerned, you got what you deserved. Let it go at that."

Ike glowered around at them, his eyes smoky with rage. He looked first at Virgil, then Holliday and Morgan, and finally at Earp. His features contorted, he backed off a step.

"You just think you've seen trouble. Tomorrow, Billy and the McLaurys are gonna be here. You'll get your fight then! Wait and see if you don't."

Before anyone could reply, he whirled around and strode off along Allen Street. The crowd on the boardwalks slowly dispersed, satisfied that the problem had been settled for now. Within moments the four men were standing alone in the street. Morgan broke the silence with a soft whistle.

"That's boy's mad," he said. "You think he meant that, about tomorrow?"

"Ike's a blowhard," Virgil remarked. "He'll get over it by morning."

Holliday and Earp exchanged a look. Holliday shook his head. "You're wrong about him, Virg. He won't cool off."

"What makes you say that?"

"Because he's more afraid of Brocius than he is us. Only one way he'll convince Brocius he didn't turn Judas for the reward. He'll have to brand Wyatt a liar—and fight."

Virgil appeared doubtful. "You agree, Wyatt?"

"Hard to say," Earp replied. "Ike's a coward at heart. But cowards do dumb things when they're cornered. Doc might just have a point."

"Maybe so." Virgil still sounded unconvinced. "I don't think he'll cause any more trouble tonight. Let's wait and see what happens tomorrow."

Virgil and Morgan separated for their nightly patrol of the town. One headed for the vice district and the other went off to check saloons. As they walked away in opposite directions, Holliday grunted. His sallow features were set in an expression of mild disgust.

"Virg should've let me kill him. Tonight didn't solve anything."

"Wish I'd never brought him in for the reward. But you

remember something, Doc. If he needs killing, I'm the one to do it."

"Figure he's your responsibility, do you?"

"Yeah, that's how I figure it."

"Whatever you say, Wyatt." Holliday chuckled. "Just get yourself a good night's sleep."

"Why so?"

"I think you're gonna get your chance tomorrow."

# Chapter Seventeen

ALLIE WAS CONCERNED. VIRGIL WAS NORMALLY A heavy sleeper. But last night he'd been unusually restless, tossing and turning in the bed. She had been asleep when he arrived home long after midnight, and they hadn't spoken. Yet his fitful manner had awakened her several times.

Virgil arose shortly after ten o'clock. Allie had already stoked the fire and the house was warm. She had changed into a gingham dress by then, and she began preparing breakfast. After putting on his clothes, he entered the kitchen, nodding to her without his usual morning greeting. He walked directly to the washstand.

Allie took biscuits from the oven and placed them in a warmer. She began frying bacon as he went about his morning scrub. Afterward he stropped his razor, lathered his face, and began shaving. She set the bacon to one side and put eggs to frying in the hot grease. Virgil muttered a curse and she looked around, saw that he'd nicked himself with the razor. Her concern deepened, for she suddenly realized that his nerves were on edge, his hand unsteady. He never cut himself shaving.

Finally, at the table, she could contain herself no longer. She poured coffee from a galvanized pot, watching as he spread jam over a biscuit. "Honey, what's wrong?" she asked. "You're not yourself today."

Virgil broke the yellow on his eggs and began eating. He shrugged. "Had some trouble last night. Nothing to worry about."

"Was that why you practically wrecked the bed? I've never seen you pitch around like that."

"Guess I must've had a bad dream."

Allie's reply was cut short. A knock sounded at the door and Virgil jumped. He collected his pistol from the bedroom and went to the door. When he opened it, Morgan stepped inside with a blast of cold air. Morgan glanced at the pistol in Virgil's hand, waiting until the door closed, then moved to the center of the parlor. He saw Allie framed in the kitchen entrance.

" 'Mornin', Allie."

"Good morning, Morg. Would you like to join us for breakfast?"

"Thanks anyway," Morgan said. "Janie already fed me."

"Well, come sit with us. I'll pour you some coffee."

Allie knew something was dreadfully wrong. Morgan followed them into the kitchen, tossing his hat onto a chair. He accepted the coffee, but he appeared agitated, unable to sit still. Virgil resumed eating, stuffing the pistol into his waistband. After a moment, Morgan stood and walked to the window, scanning the street in both directions. Allie finally lost her patience.

"All right, Virgil," she demanded. "You two act like you have ants in your pants. What's going on?"

Virgil munched a mouthful of biscuit and egg. He washed it down with a swallow of coffee, his expression grim. "I'm trying to keep Doc from killin' Ike Clanton."

"The rustler?" Allie looked confused. "Why would Doc kill him?"

Virgil briefly explained. He covered Earp's deal with Ike Clanton, and the various factors that had caused it to fall apart. He concluded with a chilling comment.

"Ike's threatened to make a fight. Doc thinks he'll do it."

"By himself?"

"Billy Clanton and the McLaurys are supposed to be here this morning. Ike will likely pull them into it."

"Omigod," Allie said. "All this to get Wyatt elected sheriff? It's gotten out of hand."

"Yeah, I know."

Morgan shoved away from the window. "Wyatt's coming up the street."

They moved into the parlor. Virgil opened the door as Earp crossed the porch. He was wearing a topcoat over a vested suit, his gun belt cinched just beneath the vest. He nodded to Allie and Morgan, then looked at Virgil.

"They're here," he said in a flat voice. "Billy Clanton and the McLaurys. I just saw 'em pull into the O.K. Corral."

"Did they spot you?"

"Don't think so. Clanton was driving a wagon and the others were on horseback. They'd just turned the corner onto Allen Street."

Virgil knuckled his mustache. "Any idea where Ike's at?"

"Grand Hotel," Earp said. "Leastways that's where he spent the night. I got out early and checked around."

"So what's your plan?"

Allie wasn't surprised by the question. Even though Virgil was five years older, he invariably deferred to Earp's judgment in moments of crisis. Over the years, she'd badgered Virgil to assert himself, but to no effect. Earp was the dominant force in the family.

"I don't want any killing," Earp said. "Let's try to find Ike and take him into custody. Without him, the others might listen to reason."

"What charge do we bring against Ike?"

"Knowing Ike, he'll give us an excuse."

Ten minutes later the brothers separated at Third and Fremont. Earp cut over to Allen Street, to begin a search of the saloons. Virgil and Morgan continued along Fremont, strolling past the rear entrance to the O.K. Corral stable. None of the gang members were visible, but they saw two saddle horses and a wagon team hitched outside the corral. At the end of the block, they rounded the corner onto Fourth. Some thirty paces ahead they saw Ike Clanton walking toward Allen Street. He was carrying a Winchester carbine and a pistol was strapped on his hip.

Virgil and Morgan increased their stride, rapidly closing

the distance. As they approached, Ike heard their drumming footsteps on the boardwalk and glanced over his shoulder. His features went rigid and he quickly turned, swinging the Winchester around. Virgil grabbed the barrel of the carbine, twisting it aside. He pulled his own pistol in the same motion and buffaloed Ike with a hard blow.

Ike's forehead spurted blood at the crack of steel on bone. He dropped to his knees, releasing his hold on the Winchester, and pitched forward onto the boardwalk. Morgan stood a step away, his pistol drawn, while Virgil stooped down and relieved the fallen man of his six-shooter. After a moment, Ike groaned and rolled to his hands and knees. He wobbled to his feet.

"You bastards," he said, blood dripping down over his face. "You're still gonna get yours."

"Let's go, Ike," Virgil said, motioning with the Winchester. "You're under arrest."

"The hell you say! What's the charge?"

"Violation of the city ordinance against carrying firearms in town."

"Jesus Christ!" Ike howled. "Nobody pays no mind to that asshole law. Everybody packs a gun!"

"Today's the day we start enforcing it."

Morgan took Ike by the collar and waltzed him along the boardwalk. Virgil stuffed the extra pistol in his waistband and followed, still carrying the Winchester. Storekeepers and people on the street stopped to watch as the three-man parade went past. During their crosstown walk, Virgil kept a sharp eye out for the other gang members. He was wary of encountering them with Ike in custody.

A few minutes later they entered the city court. Ike was placed in a chair while the court clerk went to summon the municipal judge. The only sound in the courtroom was the steady tick of a large clock mounted on the wall. From his hip pocket Ike pulled out a filthy bandanna and tied it around the bloody cut on his forehead. The front door opened, and they all turned as Earp walked into the courtroom.

"Good work," he said to Virgil. "I was over at the Alhambra looking for him. Somebody ran in and said you were bringing him here."

"Had to bust his head," Virgil observed, hefting the carbine. "He swung around on me with this."

Earp glanced at the prisoner. "You're bound to get yourself killed, aren't you, Ike?"

"You and your shitpoke brothers are the ones bound to get killed. You can mark it down as gospel, Earp."

Morgan drew back a hand to cuff him. He stopped, lowering his fist, as a door opened at the rear of the courtroom. Judge David Wallace, an attorney recently elected to the post, looked at them as he came through the door. He walked to the bench and took his seat. He nodded to Virgil.

"What's the problem, Marshal?"

"Violation of the city code, Your Honor."

Virgil held up the Winchester and pulled the six-gun from his waistband. "Apprehended this man—name's Ike Clanton—carrying these on the street. The pistol was concealed, covered up by his coat."

Other than disorderly drunks, Judge Wallace had never fined anyone for carrying firearms. He sensed that there was more here than met the eye. "Anything else, Marshal?"

"Yessir," Virgil said. "He turned on me with the Winchester. Deputy Morgan Earp was a witness."

"Did he actually point the rifle at you?"

"Never got the chance, Judge. I whacked him over the head while he was still turnin' around."

Wallace looked down at Ike. "What do you have to say for yourself, Mr. Clanton?"

"I say he's a liar!" Ike snapped, rising from his chair. "I turned 'cause he was comin' up on me so quick. And carryin' weapons ain't no reason to arrest me. This whole town's a walkin' arsenal."

"Not quite, Mr. Clanton. What's your recommendation, Marshal Earp?"

"Stiff fine on the firearms violation, Your Honor. And ten days in jail for threatening an officer of the law."

Wallace looked skeptical. "I'll fine him twenty-five dollars on the firearms violation. But to be quite frank, Marshal"—the judge nodded to the blood-soaked bandanna around Ike's head—"I think a cracked skull is punishment enough for the alleged threat."

"Judge, I'm tellin' you this man—"

Wallace banged his gavel. "You've heard my decision, Marshal. Prisoner will pay the court clerk twenty-five dollars fine. Are you prepared to do that now, Mr. Clanton?"

Ike shrugged. "I got the money."

"Case closed."

Judge Wallace walked from the courtroom. Ike moved forward to a table where the court clerk was seated. He paid the fine from a roll of greenbacks, then turned to Virgil. His eyes glittered.

"How about my guns?"

"Pick them up on your way out of town."

Earp's features were wreathed with disgust. As Ike waited for a receipt from the clerk, he spun around and moved toward the street door. The door was open and he saw Tom McLaury peering into the courtroom. McLaury abruptly jerked his head back and closed the door.

Outside, Earp found McLaury standing on the board-walk. He was facing the door with his hands jammed in his back pockets, hidden by the drape of his mackinaw. He gave Earp a cold look.

"What's all that about with Ike?"

"Broke the law," Earp said curtly. "Got caught carrying a gun."

"You're shittin' me," McLaury said. "Every sonovabitch and his dog carries a gun hereabouts."

"How about you?" Earp said, walking toward him. "What've you got behind your back?"

"Stay the hell away from me, Earp! I'm warning—"

Earp's pistol appeared as though by sleight-of-hand. He laid the barrel of the Colt upside McLaury's head with a mushy thunk. McLaury staggered backward, then folded at the knees. He rolled off the boardwalk into the gutter.

Stooping down, Earp reached inside his coat and pulled a pistol secreted in the waistband at the small of his back. Earp turned, the pistol in hand, as Virgil and Morgan came out of the courtroom.

"Godalmighty," Virgil said, staring at the man in the gutter. "What's happened here?"

"Virg, I think they're gonna force us to fight."

# Chapter Eighteen

IKE CLANTON STEPPED OUT THE DOOR OF THE courtroom. He stopped with the door still half open, startled by the sight of Tom McLaury lying in the gutter. For a moment he didn't move, vaguely aware of a small crowd gathered on the opposite side of the street. Then, recovering his wits, he rushed across the boardwalk.

McLaury groaned, struggling to sit upright. His hat was on the ground and his left temple was swollen by an ugly, bruised knot. Ike bent down, got him under the arms and assisted him to his feet. McLaury swayed, then caught himself and put a hand to his temple. He winced, his eyes squeezed tight with pain.

"Tom?" Ike said, still supporting him. "What the hell happened?"

McLaury gingerly explored the knot on his head. His eyes cleared and he steadied himself. "Got cold-cocked. Earp whapped me with his pistol."

"Which one?"

"Wyatt, the sonovabitch."

"Virgil got me the same way. Snuck up from behind and busted me over the head."

McLaury took a closer look. He noted the bloodstained bandanna covering Ike's forehead. "That's why I showed up here. Went to get some smokes and heard you'd been dragged off to court."

"Where's the rest of the boys?"

"Last time I seen 'em was at the dry goods store. Billy was ordering supplies."

"Let's go find'em. We got a score to settle with the Earps."

On Fremont Street, near the corner of Fourth, they ran into the other members of the gang. With them was Will Claiborne, a cowboy sometimes used in their rustling operation when an extra hand was needed. Having just ridden into town, he was leading his horse by the reins. Billy Clanton and Frank McLaury stared at the injured men with open amazement. Ike was recovered, the blood caked dark brown on his bandanna. But Tom was still dizzy, weaving slightly as he stopped. The five of them gathered in a tight knot outside the Capital Saloon.

"Holy Christ!" Billy marveled. "Who'd you boys tangle with?"

"The Earps," Ike said, somewhat abashed. "Virgil got me and Wyatt got Tom."

"What the hell for?"

"They're out to kill us, that's what for."

Ike knew that it was now or never. He had to plant the seed of anger and enlist their support. To that end, he had to convince them that the Earps intended to force a fight. At the same time, he had to walk a fine line where his secret deal with Earp was concerned.

"Last night," he went on, "Holliday would've killed me if I'd give him half a chance. Little later, the whole bunch jumped me and Wyatt knocked me down in the street. First thing today, it started all over again."

Ike quickly explained the events of the morning. At his prompting, Tom related how he'd been buffaloed by Wyatt outside the courtroom. When Tom finished, Ike once again drove home the message. "No doubt about it," he said. "Them bastards aim to plant us on Boot Hill."

Frank McLaury stared at him. "Why'd they pick a fight now?"

Overnight Ike had thought it through, and he was prepared for the question. "Wyatt Earp ruined his chances for sheriff when he didn't catch them stage robbers. Way I figger it, he means to use us as the next best thing." He paused, gave them a knowing nod. "Not any secret that Johnny Behan's on our side. Earp plans to get us and use it against Johnny in the election. It's all politics, boys."

"Maybe," Frank said skeptically. "Somebody over at the dry goods store told us an interesting story. Said the word's around that you sold out them robbers—Jim Crane and his bunch."

"Goddamn lie!" Ike fumed. "That's what started the trouble last night. When I heard the story, I braced the Earps and Holliday. They tried to kill me so's I wouldn't brand them liars."

Frank appeared confused. "Why'd they come up with a story like that, anyway? Don't see where it gains them nothin'."

"Hell it don't," Ike said. "They got my dander up, and that gave'em an excuse to pick a fight. Slick bastards suckered me real good."

"Sure did," Billy agreed. "And if they'd got you, that would've made the rest of us fight. All so's Earp can win his goddamn election."

"Listen here," Ike said, glancing around the street. "Let's walk over to the gunsmith shop. Tom and me are naked, and I'd hate to run across the Earps without a gun."

There was a general murmur of agreement. The men walked to the corner and turned onto Fourth. Will Claiborne, leading his horse, followed along in the street. Halfway down the block, they trooped into the gunsmith shop, with Claiborne's horse left ground-reined outside. Fred Hamer, the gunsmith, greeted them politely.

"What can I do for you gents, today?"

"Pistols," Ike said. "What've you got?"

"Just about anything you'd want."

Hamer opened the display case. One by one he took out a Colt Peacemaker, a Smith & Wesson breaktop, and a double-action Colt Lightning. He spread the weapons on the countertop for their inspection.

"Hey, looky here," Ike said, hefting the Colt Lightning. "Heard tell this here's what Billy the Kid used."

A mounted deer's head was hung on the rear wall. He raised the pistol, sighted on the deer head, and pulled the trigger. Unlike the Colt Peacemaker, which required that the hammer be cocked before the trigger would operate, the Lightning could be fired simply by pulling the trigger. He grinned as the hammer rose and fell each time he squeezed the trigger.

"Pretty nifty," he said. "Smooth as butter."

"A fine weapon," Hamer intoned. "And you are right about William Bonney. This was his pistol of choice."

"Maybe so," Tom McLaury said. "But Mr. Billy got his ass shot off last summer. Think I'll stick with the ol' tried-and-true."

He took the Colt Peacemaker off the counter. Thumbing the hammer, he drew a bead on the deer head and snapped the trigger. He smiled, blowing imaginary smoke from the end of the barrel.

"Dead between the eyes. Never fails."

"What the hell!" Frank McLaury suddenly barked. "There's that goddamn Earp again."

Will Claiborne's horse had stepped onto the boardwalk and stood looking in the doorway of the gun shop. Earp had hold of the reins and was backing the horse into the street. Frank McLaury, who was nearest the entrance, hurried outside. The others crowded into the doorway.

"Hold on!" Frank growled. "Where you going with that horse?"

Billy Clanton edged through the shop door. His hand gripped the Colt holstered beneath his heavy mackinaw. One foot on the boardwalk, the other still in the doorway, he suddenly stopped. He saw Virgil and Morgan some ten feet away, positioned to cover anyone coming out of the gun shop. Their coats were open, hands resting on the butts of their holstered pistols. Billy held his place, watching them intently.

Frank ignored them. He crossed the boardwalk and took hold of the horse's bridle. "You didn't answer me," he said roughly to Earp. "What right you got to mess with this horse?"

Earp dropped the reins at his feet. "Horses aren't allowed on the sidewalk. That's a violation of the city ordinance."

Tugging at the bridle, Frank backed the horse into the street. "That satisfy you?"

"Keep him there," Earp said. "Otherwise you'll have to appear in court."

"You fellers are big on takin' people to court. Understand you conked Ike and my brother for carrying guns."

"I see you're carrying one, too."

"That's right," Frank said. "Don't intend to take it off, neither. Not with all you Earps on the street."

"You have a choice," Earp told him. "Take it off or leave town. That's the law."

"Mister, you just keep pushin', don't you?"

Earp smiled. "Any objections?"

Frank glanced sideways at Virgil and Morgan. He calculated the odds, with the rest of the gang wedged in the doorway, and found them not to his favor. "When we're done here," he said, "we'll take the horse over to the corral. That suit you?"

The answer was evasive, but Earp decided to let it go. "I gave you a choice," he said. "Take the smart way out."

"Whatever I do, you'll know about it."

Earp studied him a moment. The thought occurred that Frank McLaury was sharper than the others, and might somehow convince them to leave town. Whatever the chances, he decided not to push it any further for now. He turned, nodding to Virgil and Morgan, and walked toward Allen Street. At the corner, they stopped outside Hafford's Saloon.

Frank waved the others back inside the gun shop. When he came through the door, he motioned to Ike and

Tom. "You boys better finish your business here. They're keepin' an eye on us from the corner."

Ike pulled out a wad of bills. He bought the Colt Lightning for himself and the Peacemaker for Tom McLaury. He purchased cartridges as well, and the loaded pistols were stuck in their waistbands. They stuffed extra cartridges into the pockets of their coats.

"What about you, Will?" Ike asked. "You ain't heeled."

Claiborne shrugged off the suggestion. "I've got a saddlegun on my horse."

"Suit yourself."

Frank led the way out the door. Outside they were all too aware that the Earps continued to watch them from the corner. Claiborne took the reins of his horse and trailed along as they walked in the opposite direction. No one spoke until they rounded the corner onto Fremont Street.

"Dirty bastards!" Ike raved. "You see what I was talkin' about, Frank? They're gonna kill us or drive us out of Tombstone for good. Either way, they win."

"Nobody drives me nowhere," Frank said stubbornly. "I'll leave town when I'm damn good and ready."

Tom McLaury was having second thoughts. "Why get ourselves in a shootin' scrape? We could just ride out and wait for things to blow over. Or leastways come back with Curly Bill and Ringo."

Ike inwardly flinched at the thought of Brocius and Ringo. He looked around. "What the shit's the matter with you, Tom? Earp like to cracked your head wide open. You gonna turn tail and run?"

"I'm with Tom," Claiborne chimed in. "We stick around and we're liable to get ourselves killed."

"Like hell!" Billy Clanton crowed. "Frank and me could plumb shoot their lights out. Anybody gets killed, it'll be them Earps. Ain't that so, Frank?"

"Mortal fact," Frank said with mild sarcasm. "You're a regular *pistolero*, Billy."

Ike realized that the others were looking to Frank for leadership. Without Brocius and Ringo around, the older McLaury brother was generally the man whose word carried the most weight. There was no question in Ike's mind that the others would follow his lead today. Yet, though he was smart, Frank was also bullheaded. That could work to advantage.

"Tell you one thing," Ike said. "No Earp's gonna make me show the white feather. How about you, Frank?"

"I'm thinkin' on it, Ike. I'm thinkin'."

They walked toward the O.K. Corral.

# Chapter Nineteen

"THINK THEY'LL RIDE OUT?"

Virgil's question was more of a statement. He and his brothers stood outside Hafford's Saloon, watching as the gang turned onto Fremont Street. The thought uppermost in his mind was the hope that the rustlers would leave town. He wanted to avoid bloodshed.

"Depends," Earp said. "Ike is spoiling for a fight. Frank McLaury might talk them out of it."

"What makes you say that?"

"Frank's stubborn as a mule. But he's got more common sense than the rest of them. I don't think he likes the odds."

"C'mon," Morgan said quickly. "Five to three? They've got the best of it."

"Maybe not," Earp observed. "Ike never shot anybody in his life, except from ambush. I doubt that Frank puts much faith in back-shooters."

Morgan looked at him. "Cornered rats have been known to turn and fight. Besides which, Ike is trying to cover himself with Brocius. You said that yourself."

"I'm just telling you how I sized up Frank."

Earp was none too certain himself. The situation had degenerated to such an extent that the gang would probably fight. From their reaction outside the gun shop, it was clear that Ike had worked them into a dangerous mood. Yet Frank McLaury had backed off, listening to some inner voice of reason. For the moment, at least, he'd chosen not to accept the challenge.

Long ago Earp had learned the cardinal rule in dealing

with lawbreakers. The most effective play was to seize the
initiative, force the other man on the defensive. He'd used
the horse outside the gun shop as a pretext, to intimidate
the gang and throw them off stride. Surprise was the best
of all tactics, and it had thrown them into a state of confusion. Frank McLaury, who'd kept his head, wisely elected
to avoid a showdown. Whether his reasonable attitude
would hold remained to be seen.

"So what'd we do now?" Virgil asked. "Hold off or keep
the pressure on?"

"Hold off," Earp said without hesitation. "Let them chew
on it awhile. Frank might just convince them to let it
drop."

"Or he might not," Morgan said. "Ike's got his tit in a
wringer. He'll argue long and loud to make a fight of it."

There was no question of Morgan's courage, his willingness to go in harm's way. Yet he was sometimes rash, eager
to take action at the expense of tactics. Earp wasn't given
to lectures, but he thought a word of caution was in order.

"Never rush to a fight, Morg. Show the other fellow his
options and give him a chance to cool off. Often as not,
he'll take the easy way out."

Morgan snorted. "You really think those boys are gonna
back down? Way it's worked out, they'd be tagged yellow
as cur dogs."

"No," Earp said pointedly. "After what's happened today, I tend to doubt they'd let it drop. But on the chance
that they will, we'll wait."

Morgan understood that the matter was no longer open
to debate. His brother could be blunt when his authority
was questioned. For now, he was not soliciting opinions or
asking advice. They would wait until he said otherwise.

On the opposite corner, they saw two men huddled in
conversation. One was Arnie Wilton, the night bartender
at the Alhambra. The other man, his face covered by a full
beard, wore rough work clothes, his pants' legs stuffed into
mule-eared boots. After a moment Wilton bobbed his head

and turned, pointing across the street. His finger was aimed at Virgil.

The bearded man moved toward them at a fast, shuffling pace. His features were twisted in a worried expression, as though he'd just read something disturbing in the paper. He was upwind, and a few steps away they caught the distinct odor of a man whose days, and nights, were spent working horses. He stopped in front of Virgil.

"That feller"—he jerked a thumb across the street—"told me you're the town marshal. That so?"

Virgil nodded. "I'm the marshal."

"And your name's Earp?"

"Virgil Earp."

"I'm Hobart Sills," the man said. "Teamster from over Tucson way. Pulled in with a load of mercantile goods yesterday 'bout sundown."

"What can I do for you, Mr. Sills?"

"I just suspect it's the other way 'round, Marshal."

"How so?"

"Well, sir," Sills said, "I got the goods unloaded late this mornin'. Figgered I'd give my animals a day's rest before I headed back to Tucson. Don't pay to work animals too hard, you know?"

"I'm sure you're right."

"Anyways, like I said, figgered to let'em loaf the rest of the day. So's I took'em over to the O.K. Corral."

The teamster suddenly had their attention. Earp and Morgan moved to stand beside Virgil. Sills cocked one eye, squinting at the three of them in turn. He wagged his head, as though agreeing with himself.

"Three peas in a pod," he said. "All you gents named Earp?"

"These are my brothers," Virgil acknowledged. "What was it you wanted to see me about?"

"Well, don't you see, I figgered to get some shut-eye myself. So I bunked down in the back of my wagon. Then these boys commenced talkin' and I forgot about shut-eye. They was talkin' about killin' some people name of Earp."

"Describe them," Virgil said. "What'd they look like?"

"Don't generally butt in," Sills said. "But what with such talk, I peeked through the sides of the wagon. There was five altogether, but three of'em done most of the talkin'. One with the biggest mouth had a blood-dirty bandanna 'round his head."

"Ike," Virgil said, glancing at Earp. "How about the other two?"

"Second one was a young pup, clean-shaved. Kept sayin' he was for killin' the whole bunch. Meanin' you gents, of course."

"Billy Clanton," Virgil said.

"Last one was older, pushin' thirty. Recollect he had a mustache."

"Frank McLaury," Virgil remarked. "You remember anything particular he said?"

"Yessir, I do," Sills affirmed. " 'Cause the others seemed to listen when he spoke up. Just before they walked off, he says plain as day, 'I reckon there's no way around it. We'll have to fight.' "

"Just before they walked off where?"

"That vacant lot down a ways behind the corral. Don't know why, but two of'em was leadin' horses. Others was on foot."

Virgil grilled him for several minutes. Finally, he thanked Sills and they shook hands all around. The teamster went past them and toward Hafford's Saloon. He had the look of a man who needed a drink.

"No doubts now," Virgil said as the teamster entered the saloon. "Ike's got them primed for a fight."

"Let's oblige the bastards," Morgan said. "They want it so bad, we'll give it to them."

Virgil knuckled his mustache. "What do you say, Wyatt? Are we through waitin'?"

"Yeah, I guess so," Earp said. "Way it appears, they've made their choice."

"I'll be back in a minute."

Virgil walked into Hafford's Saloon. Some moments later he emerged carrying a ten-gauge double-barrel shotgun. The barrels had been sawed off to within three inches of the forestock. He opened the breech, inserted two massive shells loaded with buckshot, and snapped it shut. He caught Earp's look.

"Borrowed the house scattergun. A double dose of buckshot ought to even out the odds."

From downstreet Doc Holliday approached along the boardwalk. Attired in a suit and tie, he wore a gray, full-length overcoat against the brisk afternoon wind. He stopped, glancing at the shotgun crooked over Virgil's arm.

"I take it the game's afoot."

Virgil nodded. "The Clantons, the McLaurys, and Will Claiborne. They're determined to make a fight."

Earp took out his pocket watch. "Two o'clock," he said, closing the lid. "You almost missed the party, Doc."

Holliday hawked and spat. His phlegm was tinged with red where it kicked up dust in the street. He smiled. "I'm always there when the music starts."

"Sure you want to lend a hand?"

"Wouldn't miss it for all the tea in China."

"Just to make it legal," Virgil interrupted, "you're all deputized. You included, Doc."

Holliday grinned. "A man of the law at last. Do I get a badge?"

Before Virgil could reply, a shout brought them around. John Behan motioned wildly as he emerged from a barbershop across the street. He hurried toward them, mounting the boardwalk, his features flushed. He smelled of rose water and pomade.

"Marshal," he said, addressing Virgil formally. "Somebody just came in the barbershop and said there's to be a fight. Between your men and the cowboys."

Virgil gave him a look. "As usual, Johnny, you're late getting the word."

"Is it true?"

"I intend to disarm them, if that's what you mean. They're in violation of the city ordinance."

"Good God!" Behan muttered. "You can't be serious."

"Never more serious in my life."

"But they won't surrender their arms—not to you!"

"That's their call," Virgil said stolidly. "I have a duty to perform."

Behan turned to Earp. "Wyatt, you've got to stop this. You know what will happen."

Earp studied him with contempt. "You have an uncommon concern for rustlers, Sheriff."

"Where are they?"

"Last we heard," Virgil said, "they're in that vacant lot beside the photograph gallery."

"Let me disarm them," Behan said. "I'm sure they'll listen to reason."

"Tell them to lay off their arms while they're in town and the quarrel's ended."

"I'll attend to it." Behan started away. "Just give me time to talk to them."

"Johnny."

Behan turned back. "What?"

"Those boys threatened to kill us on sight. We have witnesses."

"Don't do anything hasty, Virgil. Let me handle it."

Behan rushed off toward Fremont Street. A moment of silence ensued as they watched him turn the corner. Then, with a laugh that ended in a harsh cough, Holliday shook his head.

"God save us," he said. "Johnny Behan's on our side."

Virgil handed him the scattergun. "Stick that under your coat. Keep it out of sight."

"I'm not a shotgun man, Virg."

"They see a shotgun and they're liable to get spooked. Maybe we can still pull this off without bloodshed."

Holliday took the shotgun in his left hand and wrapped it into the long skirt of his overcoat. He looked at Earp with a wry smile.

"I'm laying seven to three that Virgil's wrong."

"You always bet the sure thing, Doc."

"Hell, why not? I've got the shotgun."

# Chapter Twenty

JOHN BEHAN STRODE SWIFTLY ALONG FREMONT Street. He passed the *Epitaph* on his right and the *Nugget* on his left. For an instant he was tempted to turn into the *Epitaph* and solicit the aid of John Clum. But then, in the next instant, he set the thought aside. Clum would never be able to stop the Earps.

Only one thing, Behan told himself, would stop the Earps. He must somehow convince the Clantons and the McLaurys to surrender their arms. They were willful men, Billy Clanton a braggart and self-styled gunman, and they were certain to resist his arguments. Yet reason must prevail over temper, for that was their only chance. The Earps would never shoot down unarmed men.

An overriding concern for Behan was his pact with Bill Brocius. He turned a blind eye to Brocius's rustling activities in exchange for political support from the county's ranchers. But he had no doubt as to Brocius's reaction if he allowed the Earps to kill trusted members of the gang. At the very least, Brocius would withdraw his support, and influence ranchers to do likewise in the upcoming election. At worst, because Brocius was a vengeful man, he would extract a final form of payment. His enforcer, Johnny Ringo, would be the messenger.

Behan himself felt somewhat like a messenger of death. As he passed Bauer's Butcher Shop, it occurred to him that he might well be carrying a death sentence. Unless he brought all his powers of persuasion into play, there would be blood on the street. For there was no question in his mind that the Earps would resort to force unless a

surrender were affected. He believed them when they said
their lives had been threatened. The bad blood was of long
standing, and the gang had proved themselves all too capable of murder. So the Earps, properly so, took the threat
seriously. Their nature was to act rather than await attack.

Yet there was an opposite side to the coin. As he strode
past the assay office, he was reminded that pride governed
men's lives in large degree. The Clantons and the
McLaurys wore their pride on their sleeves. They were
rough, violent by nature, and they set great store in their
reputation as hardcases. To back down and show the white
feather went against their code. They were more concerned with the opinion of other rough, violent men than
they were with the prospect of death. To be judged a coward was a low form of dishonor, a shame too onerous to
bear. They would not easily hand over their guns.

Ahead, Behan saw them gathered in the vacant lot. The
lot was bordered on one side by Fly's Lodging House and
on the other by the home of the Harwood family. To the
rear of the boardinghouse was Fly's Photograph Gallery,
and beyond that the outside enclosure of the O.K. Corral.
As Behan approached, he observed Mabel Fly in the doorway of the lodging house. Her mouth was pursed and her
gaze went to the men in the vacant lot, then shifted back
to him. Her expression was one of disapproval.

The men were ranged along the wall of the Harwood
home, on the far side of the lot. Billy Clanton was nearest the street, flanked by Ike. Tom and Frank McLaury
were next in line, with Will Claiborne on the end. Behind
the men, two horses stood ground-reined beside Tom
McLaury and Will Claiborne. Their conversation turned to
silence as they spotted Behan approaching from upstreet.
They watched with a mixture of confusion and apprehen-
sion, waiting motionless during the time it took him to
cross the lot. He stopped in front of the McLaurys.

"Listen to me, boys," Behan said sternly. "The Earps
agreed to hold off until I talked with you. This foolishness

has to end here and now. I want you to give me your arms."

"No soap," Frank said brusquely. "Not while the Earps have got theirs. We're not lookin' for trouble, but we'll defend ourselves."

"They say you've threatened their lives. They're determined you must give up your weapons."

"Horseshit!" Ike spread the flaps of his coat. "I ain't even packin' a gun. See for yourself."

"Me neither," Tom said, spreading his coat. "I'm clean as a whistle."

Behan was not fully convinced. He knew they might have pistols jammed in their pants, at the small of their backs. In towns with strict laws, men often carried in that manner, to better conceal a weapon. But he decided not to press the issue, nodding instead to Will Claiborne.

"What about you?"

"Not my fight," Claiborne said, suddenly deciding he wanted out. "I was just fixin' to leave town. Told these boys they oughta come along."

Behan turned to Billy Clanton. "No question you're armed, and so are you, Frank." His eyes went to the pistol on McLaury's hip. "Play it smart and let me have your guns."

Frank looked mulish. "Already told you no and that's final."

"All right," Behan said reasonably. "Come to my office and I'll put you under sheriff's protection. That'll give me time to get this mess straightened out."

"Save your breath," Frank said. "We don't need your protection."

"Too late, anyhow," Billy said, looking upstreet. "Here they come."

Behan spun about. He saw the Earps and Holliday round the corner onto Fremont Street. They walked forward at a steady pace, spread out on line. Earp was on the near side, with Virgil and Morgan in the center. Holliday, somehow ghostly in his gray overcoat, was at the opposite end. Behan thought they looked like death on the march.

"Stay here!" he ordered. "I'll stop them."

Hurrying upstreet, Behan went to meet them. He rapidly closed the distance, on a line to intercept Virgil. As the only sworn law officer, Virgil had the authority to make the others call it off. Searching for an argument as he rushed forward, none came to him that he hadn't already tried. Desperate now, he decided to resort to a bald-faced lie. He met them as they neared Bauer's Butcher Shop.

"For God's sake!" he shouted. "Don't go down there."

Virgil kept coming. "I mean to disarm those men."

Behan backpedaled to keep pace. "Marshal, that's what I'm trying to tell you—I've already disarmed them."

"Why don't I believe you, Johnny?"

Virgil brushed past him. The four men were now approaching the assay office. Ahead, they saw the gang standing stiff and watchful next to the Harwood house. Earp took his pistol from the holster and jammed it into the side pocket of his knee-length overcoat. He was vaguely aware of people crowded into doorways, and Behan trailing them a few steps behind. But his attention was focused on the gang, every nerve alert to the slightest movement. He kept his thumb hooked over the hammer of the Colt.

Mabel Fly ducked back inside as they passed the lodging house. Like a gate swinging around, they turned in unison into the vacant lot. Behan darted along the wall of the lodging house, moving into the breezeway that connected it to the photo gallery. The gang remained frozen in place, and Earp noted that Frank McLaury's eyes were fixed on Virgil. In a matter of moments, they crossed the lot, still spread out on line. Virgil halted, Earp on his left, Morgan and Doc Holliday on his right. Not more than four feet separated them from the gang.

A fragment of time slipped past in silence. Like skirmishers meeting on contested ground, the opposing sides stood staring at each other in the eerie quiet. Then, his face rigid, Virgil rapped out a command.

"Throw up your hands!"

Billy Clanton and Frank McLaury reached for their guns. In the same instant, Earp pulled the Colt from his overcoat pocket. Only a beat behind, Morgan and Doc Holliday drew their pistols.

Frank McLaury fired a quick snap-shot at Virgil, and missed. Earp brought his arm level, aimed, and touched the trigger. The slug drilled McLaury in the stomach and he slammed back into the building. At the first shot, Will Claiborne crossed the lot at a run and disappeared into the photo gallery. Ike Clanton scuttled forward, his face constricted in sudden terror.

"Don't kill me!" Ike cried out. "Don't kill me!"

He grabbed Earp's left arm, pleading for his life. Earp was on the verge of shooting him, then roughly pushed him aside. "Fight or get out."

Ike sprinted away, heading for the photo gallery. Holliday turned, firing two shots, and sent splinters flying on the doorjamb as Ike scrambled into the breezeway. Across the lot, Billy Clanton fired at Earp and glass shattered from the boardinghouse window. Morgan twice dropped the hammer, aiming at Billy, and missed. Edging out into the street, Billy returned fire and Morgan went down, his left shoulder shattered.

Tom McLaury jumped behind one of the horses and fired wildly over the saddle. Suddenly the horses spooked and bolted into the street. Holliday holstered his pistol, swung the shotgun from beneath his overcoat and triggered both barrels. His chest shredded by buckshot, McLaury hurtled backward and dropped to the ground. Holliday tossed the shotgun aside and pulled his pistol.

Virgil finally got his Colt unlimbered and winged a shot at Billy Clanton. On the heels of the report, Morgan fired, still sitting sprawled on the ground, and sent a slug ripping through Clanton's chest. Clanton clutched at the wound and staggered farther into the street. Behind him, firing at Earp and Morgan, Frank McLaury hobbled toward the front of the house. Morgan and Earp returned fire in the same instant that Holliday brought his pistol to bear on McLaury.

The three shots echoed as one. McLaury lurched sideways, slowly toppled over against the house, and fired one last shot. The bullet struck Holliday's holster, ripping a bloody furrow across his hip. Off to the side, Virgil was now trading lead with Billy Clanton. Virgil's leg suddenly buckled from the impact of a slug and he hit the ground on his rump, bracing himself upright with his left arm. Earp and Virgil fired simultaneously, one shot breaking Clanton's wrist and the other boring through his skull. He dropped dead in the street.

A tomblike lull fell over the lot as the firing abruptly ceased. For a moment a thick cloud of gun smoke hung in the air, then washed away on a breeze. Morgan slumped onto his side, and Virgil, in an effort to staunch the flow of blood, began knotting a handkerchief around his leg. Tom and Frank McLaury, several feet apart, lay dead along the side of the house. In the street, Billy Clanton was spreadeagled, blood and gore oozing from his head.

Earp and Holliday were the only ones still standing. In the frozen tableau, with the dead and wounded scattered around them, they seemed stunned to find themselves alive. Then, at last convinced that the fight was over, Earp knelt down at Virgil's side, and Holliday went to assist Morgan. After a quick look at Morgan's shoulder, Holliday turned back to the street.

"Somebody go fetch Doc Goodfellow!"

From around the street people began appearing in doorways. Slowly, edging closer to the battleground, they appeared dazed by the sight of the carnage. A man moved forward and stared down at Billy Clanton's grotesque death mask. No one went near the McLaury brothers, but others rushed to help with Virgil and Morgan. Earp climbed to his feet, trading a look with Holliday, and finally holstered his pistol.

The wind was thick with the scent of death.

# Chapter Twenty-One

JOHN CLUM AND HARRY WOODS WERE AMONG the first to arrive on the scene. The offices of the rival newspapers were only a short distance up the street. The newsmen felt somewhat like war correspondents approaching a battlefield littered with wounded and dead. The victors, as in any war, were those left standing.

The thing that most impressed Clum was the bearing of the victors. In the aftermath of the gunfight, Earp appeared calm and unshaken, coolly directing the care of his brothers. Doc Holliday, though wounded, was equally composed, his manner almost impassive. After a quick survey of the scene, Clum moved through the gathering crowd toward Earp. His veins pumped with printer's ink, and he wanted a quote from the one man to emerge unscathed from the shootout. The man he now felt confident would be elected the next sheriff of Cochise County.

Harry Woods immediately sought out the current sheriff, John Behan. Upon arriving, he saw Behan emerge from the photo gallery and circle the vacant lot, clearly avoiding any contact with Wyatt Earp. The three dead men lay where they had fallen, and Behan moved from one to the other, his expression dour. Woods noted that his features were pasty in color, and he moved like a man who had awakened to find that the nightmare was no dream. He was staring down at Billy Clanton when Woods approached him.

"Good God, John," Woods said. "What happened here?"

"Murder," Behan said dully. "These boys were murdered in cold blood."

"You saw it?"

"From start to finish. I was watching from the photo gallery."

Woods pulled out his notepad. "Who started the fight?"

Behan flicked a glance across the lot. He lowered his voice. "Wyatt Earp and Doc Holliday fired the first shots. Opened fire before those boys even had a chance to surrender."

"Wasn't there anything you could have done to stop it?"

"I tried to stop them, Harry. Tried everything within my power. The Earps just wouldn't listen to reason."

On the opposite side of the lot, Clum waited silently by Earp. Dr. George Goodfellow knelt on the ground, examining Morgan's shoulder. Morgan's clothing was soaked with blood, and though he was conscious, he appeared dazed, all the color leeched from his face. His overcoat, suit coat, and shirt had been pulled aside for a better look at the wound. He groaned as the surgeon gingerly explored the wound itself and then the back of his shoulder. Goodfellow looked up at Earp.

"I'll have to operate," he said. "The bullet's still in there."

"You," Earp ordered, pointing to a bystander. "Get the first wagon and team you see on the street. Bring it here right now."

"Yessir, Mr. Earp."

The man took off running up Fremont Street. Dr. Goodfellow got to his feet and walked to Virgil, who was being attended to by Holliday. Earp turned in that direction, and for the first time seemed to notice Clum. His eyes were cold, pale as blue ice on a frozen pond. He nodded absently.

"Where'd you come from?"

"I heard the shooting," Clum said. "Sounded like a war, Wyatt. But, my God . . ." He paused, motioning in disbelief at the dead and wounded. "It couldn't have lasted more than thirty seconds."

Earp seemed distracted. "Things happen fast when there's gunplay."

"What started it?"

"Ike Clanton got his brother and the McLaurys all wound up. They threatened our lives."

"Ike?" Clum searched the lot for another body. "I don't see him here."

"Yellow bastard ran," Earp said. "Got the others killed, but wouldn't fight himself. Ducked out when the first shot was fired."

"Why did they threaten your lives?"

"That's a long story, John. Let's save it for another time."

"I understand." Clum nodded to where Behan stood talking with Harry Woods. "I saw Behan come out of the photo gallery. What was he doing in there?"

"Hiding," Earp observed sourly. "Sorry son of a bitch told us he'd disarmed these boys. I ought to shoot him on general principle."

"I hope you're not serious."

"Doesn't matter either way. Behan wouldn't fight if you put a gun to his mother's head. He's yellow as they come."

Earp's gaze touched on Behan, then moved around the lot. Dr. Horace Matthews, the county coroner and a local physician, had just finished examining the dead men. He walked to Behan and they began conversing in hushed tones. Harry Woods listened intently, his pencil flying, taking copious notes.

"Trouble's brewing," Clum said, staring at them. "Look for Behan's version of this affair in tomorrow's edition of the *Nugget*."

"Yeah, you're right," Earp said. "Catch me later and I'll give you the whole story. I've got to look after Virgil and Morg."

A wagon and team pulled up to the lot. The man pressed into service by Earp walked forward with the driver. They offered their assistance, and with Dr. Goodfellow supervising, Virgil and Morgan were loaded into the back of the wagon. Holliday, who was limping noticeably, had to be assisted aboard. The physician rode with the wounded men, and Earp took a seat by the driver. Clum began interviewing witnesses as they drove off.

Earp directed the driver to Virgil's house. The wounded men were off-loaded and carried inside. Upon seeing Virgil, Allie's face drained of color, but she quickly collected herself. The driver went across the street and returned with Morgan's wife, Jane. Her hand went to her mouth when she saw Morgan, and then, like Allie, she fought back her fear. At the doctor's direction, the woman began boiling water and ripping clean sheets into bandages.

Virgil and Morgan were placed side by side in the bed. Virgil was in considerable pain, but his wound was not critical. Dr. Goodfellow dosed Morgan with laudanum, waiting until the opiate took effect. Then, with Allie and Jane assisting, he began probing for the bullet. Morgan groaned, struggling to evade the digging of steel in flesh, his face beaded with perspiration. With Jane at the foot of the bed, and Allie at the head, they were able to hold him down. Virgil lay staring at the ceiling, unable to watch the operation.

In the parlor, Earp and Holliday tried to ignore the cries from the bedroom. Holliday unbuckled his gun belt, lowered his trousers, and pulled down his longjohns. The slug from Frank McLaury's gun had gouged a bloody furrow through the meaty flesh above his hipbone. He sponged the wound clean with hot water and wadded sheet cloth, teeth gritted as he worked. After padding the wound with clean cloth, he got back into his clothes. His face flushed, Holliday pulled out his flask and took a long slug of whiskey.

Earp was seated in a chair, his hands knotted into fists. A muscle ticked in his jawline each time Morgan cried out. He had watched Holliday minister to himself without comment, his features void of expression. Holliday knew the look, recognized it as a mix of suppressed fury and a sense of helplessness. To sit there, listening to Morgan's agonized cries, was perhaps the most tortuous part of the day's ordeal. Far worse than facing men with guns.

Holliday tried to divert him from the noises in the bedroom. "I'm losing my touch," he said casually. "Took two shots at Ike when he was running for the photo gallery. Missed both times."

Earp looked around. "Wondered where he took cover. I lost sight of him when things got hot."

"Out of curiosity," Holliday asked, "why didn't you shoot him when you had the chance? He was right on top of you."

"Doc, I'll never know. Maybe because he hadn't pulled a gun. Maybe because he was begging for his life. Beats the hell out of me."

"You should've killed him and been done with it. One way or another, he'll come back to haunt you."

"Wish I had," Earp said quietly. "Almost did, but something stopped me. Still haven't figured it out."

"Spilt milk now," Holliday said. "Question is, will Brocius and Ringo try to settle the score? Whatever Ike tells them, it won't be the truth."

"After today, they won't come at us head-on again. I suspect next time it'll be from behind."

"So how do we keep from gettin' back-shot?"

The question went unanswered. Dr. Goodfellow walked from the bedroom into the parlor. His sleeves were rolled up and he was wiping his hands on a towel. Specks of blood dotted his shirtfront, and his expression was neutral. He nodded to Earp.

"They'll live," he said. "Morgan's shoulder wasn't as bad as it looked. He ought to be up and around in a week or so. Of course, he'll have to take it easy."

"What about Virg?"

"The bullet went clean through his calf. In and out, no bones broken. He's a lucky man."

Earp seemed to relax. "So they're in the clear?"

"Barring infection," Goodfellow noted. "That's always a concern with gunshot wounds. I'll come by to check on them at least once a day. Meanwhile, I've instructed the women on their care."

Goodfellow collected his black bag, then slipped into his coat. Earp walked him to the door and they shook hands. Holliday was feeding wood into the stove when he turned back into the parlor. A moment later there was a knock on the door.

Thinking the doctor had forgotten something, Earp retraced his steps. When he opened the door, Behan and his deputy, Bill Breakenridge, stood on the porch. Behan appeared nervous, a slight tremor touching the corner of one eye. His voice was strained.

"Wyatt, I don't want any trouble. I'm here to arrest you and Doc. The charge is murder."

Earp stared at him. "Do you have a warrant?"

"I don't need a warrant to arrest you for murder. I can hold you until there's a court hearing."

Holliday moved across the parlor. He took a position that gave him a clear shot at the men in the doorway. Behan flicked a nervous glance at him, then looked back at Earp. The tic in his eye jumped.

"Let's not have any trouble, Wyatt. I'm here in my official capacity as sheriff."

"The hell you are," Earp said tersely. "You're here to make a headline for tomorrow's *Nugget*. How Earp and Holliday refused to be arrested."

"Are you?" Behan said too quickly. "You're telling me you won't submit to arrest?"

"Show me a warrant and I will. Otherwise you're wasting your time."

"I could always come back with more men."

"Don't push it," Earp said in a cold voice. "I should have shot you when you lied about disarming those boys. Give me half an excuse, and I'll still do it."

Behan swallowed hard. He blinked, a pinpoint of fear in his eyes, then turned away. Breakenridge hastily followed him off the porch. Earp closed the door as they started across the yard.

"What do you think, Doc? Will he be back?"

"No, you're right," Holliday said. "He was hunting a newspaper headline."

"I halfway wish he would come back."

"Someone will, Wyatt. We haven't seen the end of it yet."

Earp studied him a moment. "Are you talking about Brocius and Ringo?"

"I'm saying today was the start, not the finish."

Earp walked to the chair and sat down. Holliday went back to warm himself by the stove. Neither of them spoke, for there was nothing left to say.

# Chapter Twenty-Two

IKE CLANTON CHOSE THE LESSER OF TWO EVILS. Had he stayed in Tombstone, he was convinced that Wyatt Earp or Doc Holliday would kill him. With Virgil and Morgan wounded, perhaps dying, his life could easily be forfeit. The risk was too great.

So he elected instead to take his chances with Brocius. He was prepared to lie, even get down on his knees and beg for mercy. Whatever happened, he knew the odds were better with Brocius than with Earp. There was virtual certainty that Holliday would shoot him on sight. Which left nowhere else to turn. He rode toward the San Pedro.

Earlier, when the gunfire had died away, he'd watched from a window in the photo gallery. He could hardly bear to look at his brother, who lay sprawled in the street. Nor was it any easier to look at the bodies of the McLaurys. Whatever excuses he made, however much he lied to himself, the truth was there in that vacant lot. He had gotten them killed.

To his own ends, he had goaded them into the fight. Then, at the last moment, he'd lost his nerve and left them to die in his place. The amazing part, something that defied belief, was that Earp hadn't killed him on the spot. But he'd escaped, running like a rabbit looking for a hole, and taken refuge in the photo gallery. Though he had survived, the shame of what he'd done had overtaken him instantly. He saw it in the eyes of John Behan, who had pulled him through the door.

He would be branded a coward for the rest of his life.

From the window, he had watched as Virgil and Morgan

were carted away in a wagon. Shortly afterward, the undertaker had arrived, and he couldn't bring himself to watch as Billy and the McLaurys were loaded into the hearse. At that point Will Claiborne had walked out, having never spoken a word, and disappeared in the direction of the corral. A short time later Behan had returned to the photo gallery. Their brief conversation was still brutally vivid in his memory.

"I want the truth," Behan said sharply. "Did you and those boys threaten the Earps?"

"God as my witness," Ike lied, "we never made no threats. You gotta believe me."

"Then what started the fight?"

"I dunno, and that's the truth. First thing this morning, they started bustin' our heads."

Behan scrutinized him. "Word's around you had some deal with Wyatt that went sour. Was that the cause of it?"

"Wasn't no deal," Ike said, lying faster. "Earp made that up just to start trouble. Him and Doc Holliday lied their heads off."

"Given a choice, I think I'd take their word over yours. Lucky for you, I don't have a choice."

"I don't follow you."

"Why, it's simple enough," Behan said. "I'd rather hang Earp out to dry. So I'm stuck with your story."

"Honest to God's truth, Johnny. I swear it."

Behan just looked at him. "What do you want done with Billy and the McLaury boys?"

"Well . . ." Ike suddenly appeared forlorn. "Have the undertaker fix 'em up with the best. Tell him not to spare anything. I'll pay for the whole works."

"Shouldn't you arrange that with the undertaker yourself?"

"Handle it for me, won't you, Johnny? Tell him I'll be there for the funeral."

"I take it you're headed back to the ranch?"

"Yeah, think so," Ike said. "Not too safe for me around town."

Behan started out, then turned back. "Just for the record," he said, "you're about as yellow as they come. Nobody should let his brother die like that."

Even now the words still echoed through Ike's mind. Dark had fallen by the time he forded the San Pedro. Ahead, lamplight spilled out the windows of the main house. As he neared the compound, he saw a strange horse tied to the corral fence. But he gave it no thought, for his head whirled at the prospect of facing Brocius. He dismounted and left his horse at the corral. Walking toward the house, he was overcome by a question that had nagged him all the way from Tombstone. How was he to explain that he'd survived the gunfight?

When he opened the door, Brocius and Ringo were seated in chairs before a blazing fireplace. At the far end of the room a man he recognized as Frank Stilwell turned from the cook stove with a cup of coffee. They looked around, staring at him without expression. Then Brocius uttered a short, barking laugh.

"Here's our hero! Figgered you'd show up."

Ike was confounded. "What d'you mean?"

"Why hell, Ike, where else would you go? We're the only family you've got left."

"I—" Ike faltered, disbelief etched across his face. "You've already heard?"

Brocius waved a hand. "Tell him, Frank."

Stilwell moved to the fireplace. "Word came in over the telegraph at Charleston, late this afternoon. When I got the news, I rode out to tell Bill."

"Yessir, he did," Brocius said. "Figgered I ought to know my boys got their asses shot off by the Earps. All except one with a yellow streak a yard wide."

"Now, hold on, Bill. I can explain—"

"What's to explain, you gutless little shitheel? You run

for your life and left them other boys to do the fightin'. The telegraph message had all the juicy details."

"Wasn't like it sounds, Bill."

Brocius rose from his chair. He advanced across the room with a disarming smile. Then, without warning, he backhanded Ike in the mouth. "Tell me all about it. And none of your goddamn lies! Why'd the Earps come after you boys?"

"I dunno." Ike pulled his hat off, pointed to the bloody bandanna. "Busted me over the head first thing this mornin'. Little later, they near about split Tom's skull. Just kept pushin' us into a fight."

"You're a sad and sorry liar, Ike."

"No, I ain't neither. Swear to Christ I ain't."

"Tell him what you told me, Frank."

Stilwell motioned with his coffee cup. "I rode over to Charleston this morning. Spent last night in Tombstone." He stared straight at Ike. "Heard all about your deal with Earp. How you turned Judas for the reward money."

Ike's mouth dropped open. He stood as though bolted to the floor, expecting to be shot at any moment. Brocius let go a guttural laugh.

"What d'you think, Johnny? Should we kill him now or later?"

Ringo stirred in his chair. "I wouldn't dirty my hands. You kill him."

Brocius had no intention of killing him. After hearing the story from Stilwell, he'd thought about it a long time. He concluded that Ike, for all his faults, was still valuable. The ranch was in the Clanton name, and it provided an established base for the rustling operation. Apart from that, he had another use in mind for Ike. One he hadn't yet revealed to anyone.

Still, for all his clemency, he was furious. Ike's ignorance and greed had cost him three good men, most of his gang. On top of that, it had made him look the fool where the Earps were concerned. He felt some form of punishment was in order.

"Tell you what, Ike," he said. "I'm not gonna kill you."

"You're not?"

Ike thought he'd heard wrong. He was on the verge of wetting his drawers, and he'd suddenly been granted a reprieve. The idea was still spinning around in his brain when Brocius hit him. The first punch stunned him, and the second buckled his knees. Brocius grabbed him by the collar, holding him upright, and clubbed him to the floor with a looping haymaker. Ike's mouth leaking blood, he rolled onto his side. He muttered something under his breath.

"What'd you say?" Brocius demanded.

Weary and beaten, shamed once again, Ike summoned a spark of defiance. "You're so tough, whyn't you take on the Earps yourself? How come you never go into Tombstone?"

Brocius kicked him in the ribs. "You little pissant! I got plans for the Earps. Don't you worry about that."

Ike rolled himself into a ball, protecting his head with his hands. When he made no response, Brocius grunted and turned away. He walked back to his chair and sat down, staring into the fireplace. At length he looked up at Stilwell.

"Now that we got that settled, go ahead with what you were sayin'!"

"After today, you're sort of shorthanded, Bill. I'd like to join up with you, and I can bring in two other men. That'd replace the three you lost."

Brocius rubbed a raw knuckle. "Who are the other two?"

"Pete Spence and Florentino Cruz. I can vouch for'em both. We've pulled some jobs together."

Stilwell was a former deputy sheriff. He had served briefly under John Behan before switching to the other side of the law. The grapevine had it that he and two other men had pulled at least one payroll robbery at the mines.

He was known as a man who would go the limit, not above killing when necessary.

"Out of curiosity," Brocius said, "why would you go from payroll holdups to rustlin' cows? Seems like harder work."

"Maybe," Stilwell conceded. "But it's safer and it's lots more steady. Nobody bats an eye when you boys raid the greasers."

"That's a fact," Brocius said. "One of them names you mentioned sounds like a Mex hisself."

"Half-breed," Stilwell remarked. "Good man with a gun, too. Pete Spence is no slouch, either."

Brocius appeared to drift off into thought. Ringo and Stilwell watched as Ike slowly got to his feet. He was shaky, clutching at the wall for support, but made his way into one of the bedrooms. The door closed and their attention returned to Brocius. He nodded, as though having decided a weighty matter.

"Awright, Frank," he said. "Bring those boys around and we'll have a look at 'em. If they pass muster, we'll go from there."

"I'll bring'em around tomorrow, Bill. You're gonna like what you see."

Stilwell shook their hands, smiling broadly, and walked to the door. They sat in silence, warmed by the fire, until they heard hoofbeats fade into the distance. At last, rousing himself, Brocius looked around.

"Well?" he said. "Think Stilwell will do?"

Ringo shrugged. "No worse than Billy and the McLaurys. Doesn't take Jesse James to steal cattle."

Brocius was quiet a moment. "I've been thinkin' about the Earps."

"What about them?"

"I want you to ride into Tombstone. Arrange a meeting for me with Behan. Somewheres private."

Ringo nodded. "Somewhere you won't be seen together."

"That's the ticket."

"Mind telling me what you've got in mind?"

Brocius told him, and Ringo liked it. He laughed. "That's sinister stuff, Bill. Downright sinister."

"Don't use them two dollar words. Spell it out in English."

"You're cruel and crafty, my friend. A spider spinning his web."

Brocius smiled. "This time we're gonna snare the Earps."

# Chapter Twenty-Three

EARLY THE NEXT AFTERNOON EARP WAS SUM-moned to Lou Rudabaugh's office. A message had been waiting for him when he and Holliday returned to their hotel late that morning. The message was subtly phrased, but nonetheless insistent. His appointment was for one o'clock.

Earp and Holliday had spent the night at Virgil's house. By that morning the medical situation had improved to the point that their presence was not required. They were still dressed in the clothes worn at the gunfight; their appearance was soiled and rumpled, with dark bloodstains on their coats. Neither of them felt particularly presentable as they entered the hotel.

Upstairs, Earp stripped and dropped his clothing in a heap. A houseman delivered the hot water he'd ordered, and his clothes were taken away to be cleaned. He scrubbed himself thoroughly with a strong yellow soap and a hot washcloth. Then he lathered his face, stropped his straight razor, and gave himself a close shave. Finished, he inspected the image in the mirror and thought he'd made a passable job of it.

At noontime, attired in a fresh suit and tie, Earp went downstairs. When he entered the hotel dining room, there was a momentary lull in the conversation. Some people looked at him, then quickly glanced away, and others rose to shake his hand. He ordered the blue plate special and asked the waitress to bring him both newspapers. As he ate, ignoring stares from around the room, he scanned the articles. The opposing views explained the mixed reception he'd received from the noontime crowd.

The *Nugget* branded him a murderer. There was a quote from John Behan to the effect that he had refused arrest. Behan further stated that the dead men had been in the act of surrendering when they were killed. An investigation was under way, and there was a promise of official action. The *Epitaph* told an entirely different story. Earp, his brothers, and Doc Holliday were lauded as stalwart lawmen performing their sworn duty. The Clantons and the McLaurys were roasted as outlaws operating in open defiance of the law. John Behan was severely scorned for his protective attitude toward the outlaws.

The tone of the stories was much as Earp had expected. He was faintly amused by the disparity in the reporting. Anyone reading the articles would be left with the impression that two separate and very different gunfights had taken place. Though he was infuriated by the lies in the *Nugget*, he was hardly surprised. Last night, when he'd met with John Clum at Virgil's house, he had predicted how their opposition would portray the incident. The facts had been twisted and distorted, with critical details purposely left out with the fabrication then presented as the truth. Some people would believe it.

Earp walked uptown after his meal. The reaction of passersby on the street was quite similar to what he'd received in the hotel dining room. Some people rushed forward to grab his hand, as though congratulating him on having survived the shootout. Others avoided looking at him, or crossed the street, as though skirting contact with a dangerous killer. By rough calculation, Earp scored the reaction at two to one in his favor. He entered the offices of the Toughnut Mining Company at the appointed hour.

A clerk ushered him into the inner office. Lou Rudabaugh, who believed in advertising the company's prosperity, was seated behind a massive walnut desk. The furnishings were upholstered in lush brown leather, with scenic paintings decorating the walls. He rose from behind the desk with a warm smile, his hand extended.

"Good to see you, Wyatt," he said as they clasped hands. "I must say, you look no worse for wear."

"Pure luck," Earp said. "Yesterday wasn't my day to get it."

"And your brothers, how are they faring?"

"Not too bad, all things considered. Morg will be out of action for a while. Virg ought to be hobbling around in a week or so."

"Excellent." Rudabaugh waved him to one of the leather chairs in front of the desk. "I thought we might have a talk about this unfortunate affair."

Earp crossed his legs, hooked his hat over his knee. "What's there to talk about?"

"Well, for one thing, the political implications." Rudabaugh leaned forward, pushing a copy of the *Nugget* to the front of his desk. "How do you think that will affect your campaign for sheriff?"

"People who read the *Nugget* won't vote for me anyway."

"Perhaps that was true in the past. But these headlines will attract unwanted attention, and a great many new readers. You'll have to admit, these are very serious allegations."

Earp shrugged. "These allegations, as you call them, are a pack of lies. Anybody who wants to know the truth reads the *Epitaph.*"

"Not necessarily," Rudabaugh amended. "The truth is what the majority of people choose to believe at any given moment. Elections are often won by men who concoct the greatest lies."

"Let's not beat around the bush, Lou. What's your point?"

"I spoke with George Parsons this morning at some length. We're both concerned about the notoriety you've gained from this . . . incident."

Earp gave him a level gaze. "We killed three men who

threatened our lives and were breaking the law. Does that make me notorious?"

"I'm afraid so," Rudabaugh said. "Overnight, it seems, the story has spread to the national press. George received a telegraph from his partners in New York. The newspapers there have already dubbed it the 'Gunfight at the O.K. Corral.'"

"Why not call it the 'Gunfight at Fly's Photo Gallery'? That'd be closer to the truth."

"The press deals in sensationalism. A gunfight at a corral fits the public's perception of the West. And unfortunately, the perception is too often accepted as the truth."

Earp saw where the conversation was headed. "You're saying folks might not want a 'notorious' man as their sheriff. Is that it?"

"Actually, Wyatt," Rudabaugh said blandly, "we see it as a liability rather than an asset. We thought you might have some idea as to how the situation could be turned to a more positive note."

"You're jumping at shadows, Lou. Allegations don't mean a hill of beans. Especially when they're founded on lies."

"So you don't anticipate formal charges being lodged?"

"Not a snowball's chance in hell. We were in the right, and the facts support our actions. Let the *Epitaph* keep pounding the drum and all this will blow over. Take my word for it."

"I see." Rudabaugh steepled his fingers. "And your friend, Doc Holliday? A truly notorious man deputized at virtually the last instant. Will that blow over as well?"

"Let's get something straight," Earp said. "Holliday saved our bacon yesterday. Except for him, somebody named Earp would be dead. Does that answer your question?"

"No, not entirely. To be more specific, has his involvement jeopardized your chances in the election?"

"No more so than before. You knew about Doc when you backed me for sheriff. Why get jumpy now?"

"Not jumpy," Rudabaugh corrected, "merely concerned. We have a lot invested in you, Wyatt."

"Don't worry about it," Earp said, rising from his chair. "One way or another, Johnny Behan will shoot himself in the foot. He'll win the election for us."

"I admire your confidence."

"Take it to the bank, Lou. You're betting on a sure thing."

Outside, Earp cursed under his breath as he headed downtown. He thought Rudabaugh had a point about perception and truth being one and the same. An old saying popped into his mind, with a slight twist on the words. A twist that left him suddenly uneasy.

Dead men sometimes tell too many tales.

Late that afternoon, Earp and Sadie emerged from the Grand Hotel. She held onto his arm tightly, as though she might never let go. Her face was radiant with happiness.

Last night, even though she knew he was alive, she'd been unable to sleep. When he appeared at her door that afternoon, she had thrown her arms around him and peppered his face with kisses. The next several hours had been spent in bed, her lovemaking curiously desperate. She acted as if she'd lost him and found him, and never would again.

She chattered on about nothing as they walked toward Delmonico's. She had read both of the newspapers, and everyone in town talked of little else except the shootout. Yet she'd made no mention of it, and evidenced not the slightest interest in what had happened, or why. She was instead bubbly and vivacious, and clearly thrilled that he was safe. Her sole interest in the entire affair was that he had walked away alive.

Upstreet from the hotel, they strolled past the funeral parlor. Earp suddenly stiffened, and for an instant he broke stride. His gaze was fixed on the large plate-glass window that fronted the funeral home. Her gaze was drawn there as well, and she lost her breath in a low gasp. Upright in the window, rigid in their coffins, were the three dead men. Their faces were waxen in appearance, their arms folded across their chests. A hand-painted sign rested at the foot of the coffins.

MURDERED ON THE STREETS OF TOMBSTONE

Earp took it all in at a glance. He held Sadie's arm tighter and moved on past the funeral parlor. She sensed a sudden tautness about him, like a coil spring wound too tight. His features were stern and his eyes seemed to bore through people they passed on the boardwalk. She was aware of the political battle being waged and the effort to tar Earp with the image of a murderer. But she cared nothing for politics, or the mudslinging that was all part of the process. She cared only for the man at her side.

"Sugar." Earp appeared not to have heard her. His eyes were fixed on some distant point, visible only to him. "Wyatt?"

"Sorry." Earp seemed to awaken from a funk. "Did you say something?"

"I started to say that you shouldn't let these things upset you. You're alive and you won and that is all that matters."

"I haven't won, not yet. Unless I'm elected sheriff, then what happened yesterday was for nothing."

The meeting that afternoon with Rudabaugh was uppermost in his mind. However tactfully phrased, the threat had been delivered. His business investments, even his acceptance by the town's business leaders, all hinged on his election to sheriff. His value to them was in the political arena, and unless he won there, then the conclusion was foregone. He would be cut loose.

Yet he'd shared none of this with Sadie. Whatever his emotional attachment to her, he couldn't bring himself to talk of the deal he had struck with Rudabaugh and Parsons. Nor could he reveal that his ambition, and the extent of his success, was governed largely by the dictates of other men. There was, in the mix, the sense of having mortgaged his independence to underwrite his ambition. He was too proud to tell her that he'd bartered a part of himself.

"Honestly!" she said, in a sudden fit of pique. "Johnny Behan is behind all this nonsense. The article in the *Nugget* and that sign on those poor dead men. He's just spiteful, that's all!"

"Spite might be part of it," Earp agreed. "But where politics are concerned, all the rules are thrown out the window. He's prepared to play dirty in order to win."

Her eyes narrowed in concentration. After a few steps farther, she looked up at him. "I don't know much about these things. But sometimes, especially in politics, aren't you forced to play by the other fellow's rules? I mean, do you really have a choice?"

Earp realized that, whether by design or by accident, she had revealed another side of herself. At bottom she was a pragmatist, and far shrewder than she let on. She was telling him that the end justified the means, particularly when your opponent was a liar and a scoundrel. He thought it was wise advice.

"Good point," he said. "What I need to do is rig a surprise of some sort for Behan. Something he doesn't expect."

"Oh, sugar!" She laughed. "Between us, it's absolutely sinful what we could dream up. Johnny Behan doesn't stand a chance!"

Entering Delmonico's, Earp ignored the stares from those in the room. As they were escorted to their table, his attention centered on Sadie and her willingness to join in his fight. She was eager and sharp, a very determined lady.

He thought they'd make a good team.

# Chapter Twenty-Four

THE MEETING PLACE SELECTED WAS HALFWAY BE-
tween Tombstone and Charleston. The site was a water
hole, fed by an underground spring, situated a short distance off the road. Midnight was the appointed time, and
the sky was ablaze with stars. The water hole, at that hour,
was deserted.

Brocius and Ringo were the first to arrive. They tied
their horses in a clump of stunted trees bordering the water hole. Never one to take anything for granted, Ringo
then ghosted off into the boulders ringing the site. Some
minutes later he returned, satisfied that they were alone.
He and Brocius sat down to wait.

John Behan arrived shortly after the hour. Last night
he'd been contacted outside his house by Ringo. No reason
was given for the meeting, and there was no thought of
refusing. The summons was an order rather than a request,
and Behan understood that he had no choice in the matter. Whatever Brocius wanted to discuss, it was clearly related to yesterday's shooting. If nothing else, Behan was
certain of that much.

"Step down," Brocius said as he rode into the clearing.
"Find yourself a soft patch of ground."

Behan dismounted, hitching his horse to a tree. "Evening, Bill," he said, seating himself near the two men.
"Long time no see."

"Yeah, I reckon so. Near as I recollect, the last time was
when we made our deal."

Behan thought of it as a pact struck with the Devil. His
share of the rustling operation amounted to a tidy sum.

But he often wondered if he'd sold his soul in the bargain. Tonight, he told himself now, could be the night he found out.

"What can I do for you, Bill?"

"Other way 'round," Brocius said. "I'm gonna get you reelected to sheriff. How's that sound?"

At what price? was the question that leaped to Behan's mind. But he resisted the temptation to ask it. In the pale starlight, he could make out the features of Brocius and Ringo. He had the eerie sense of sharing a water hole with two brutes from some ancient tribe. He almost expected to see the clearing littered with gnawed bones.

"I welcome your help," he said with feigned good humor. "Every vote counts."

"Gawddamn right," Brocius said. "And I aim to get'em all for you. Every last one."

"How do you plan to do that?"

"Simple as fallin' out of a tree. You're gonna be the man who got Wyatt Earp hung for murder."

Behan looked unimpressed. "I'm already working on that."

"No, you're not." Brocius took out the makings, began rolling a smoke. "All that stuff in the *Nugget* won't get Earp hung. Words don't hurt nobody."

"As a matter of fact, I plan to arrest Earp shortly."

"I heard you tried that last night. What happened?"

Behan thought he already knew the answer. "I didn't have a warrant last night. Next time, I will."

"That's pure horseshit." Brocius popped a match on his thumbnail, lit the cigarette. "You gotta have proof to get a warrant—and you don't have none."

"What makes you think so?"

"Ike told me the whole story. Billy and Frank pulled first, and that takes the Earps off the hook. They was just lawmen doing their job."

Behan shrugged. "I suppose it depends on your point of view."

"What it depends on," Brocius said, exhaling a stream of smoke, "is an eyewitness. I got two that'll swear it was cold-blooded murder."

"Two?"

"Ike was standin' right there when the guns was drawed. So was Will Claiborne."

Behan warned himself to take care. "They would have to perjure themselves . . . swear false."

"Naturally," Brocius said, grinning. "That's the whole idea here, Sheriff. We're gonna railroad the Earps."

"Ike I can understand. He'd do anything to get back at the Earps. What about Claiborne?"

"Don't worry your head about Will Claiborne. He'll do what I tell him, or else I sic Ringo on him. Ain't that right, Johnny?"

Ringo smiled. "Whatever it takes, he can be persuaded. He'll do his part."

" 'Course, he will," Brocius said. "We'll feed him the words and he'll spit'em out like a Polly parrot. Him and Ike will tell a helluva story."

"I don't know," Behan said doubtfully. "There were other witnesses around yesterday. That'll contradict whatever Ike and Claiborne say."

"Maybe so." Brocius took a drag, stared at him over the fiery coal. "But it won't make a good gawddamn one way or another. Not when the sheriff backs their story."

"Me?" Behan blurted. "You want me to lie under oath?"

"Why, perish the thought, Sheriff. You're gonna tell the God's honest truth. How the Earps pulled first and gunned them boys down in cold blood."

"That wasn't the way it happened."

"Yeah, it was," Brocius told him. "You and Ike and Claiborne are gonna swear to it. With you the chief law dog hereabouts, nobody'll believe otherwise."

"Sounds risky," Behan said. "Ike's got no more nerve than a grub worm. He's liable to break under cross-examination."

"I'll jam a board up his ass. Give the little bastard some backbone."

"Claiborne turned yellow and ran too. What about him?"

Brocius dusted off the objection. "Wasn't never Claiborne's fight, anyhow. But like I said, don't worry yourself none. They'll stick to their stories."

"I don't like it," Behan persisted. "You're asking me to row a boat that's full of leaks."

"Not askin'," Brocius said in a hard voice. "I'm tellin' you how it's gonna happen. You're smart enough to see that, aren't you, Sheriff?"

Behan's throat went dry. He felt Ringo's eyes drilling holes into him, and he knew the outcome if he refused. His body would be found at the water hole.

"Let me ask you," he said, clearing his throat. "Why not just bushwhack the Earps, if you want them dead? Why go to all this trouble to put them on the gallows?"

Brocius slapped his knee. "Why hell's bells, that's the whole point. I wanna see the look on their faces when the hangman's knot gets cinched up tight. I wanna see the sonsabitches swing."

"You're saying you want to see them suffer."

"Now you got it!" Brocius flipped his cigarette stub into the water. "Just killin' them ain't near enough. I wanna see 'em get the cold sweats when they're face-to-face with the short drop. Be worth the price of admission, won't it, Johnny?"

Ringo chuckled, a low raspy sound. "I'd pay top dollar for a front row seat. Especially to see Wyatt Earp step off into air. That'd be some sight."

Behan felt himself shiver. From the day he'd become involved with them, he had known that they were sadistic killers. But now, listening to them gloat over the spectacle of a hanging, he saw them in a new light. He was in the presence of evil men, sinister and vengeful.

"All right," he said, repulsed by his own fear. "How do we go about this?"

"Nothing simpler," Brocius said. "Tomorrow them three boys are gonna be buried. After they're planted, Ike will come by your office and bring murder charges against the Earps."

"And Holliday," Ringo interjected. "Don't forget him."

"Yeah, the whole gawddamn bunch. With Ike, you got all you need for a warrant, right?"

Behan nodded. "That should do it."

"So how long till they stand trial?"

"First, there has to be a preliminary hearing. But with testimony from Ike and Claiborne—and myself—they'll be bound over for trial. I'd think by the end of November."

"A month!" Brocius howled. "Jesus Christ, why's it take so long?"

"To kill a man legally," Behan said, "he has to have his day in court. That's how the law works."

"You hear that, Johnny?" Brocius said over his shoulder. "We're gonna kill the bastards legally. Don't that take the cake?"

"Well, it's different," Ringo allowed. "Ought to be a regular circus."

"Gawddamn if it won't! I think I'm gonna enjoy this."

Later, on the way back to town, Behan remembered those last remarks. He thought their response to legally killing a man perfectly summarized the code of Bill Brocius and Johnny Ringo. To them, it was different for the best of reasons.

They normally acted as judge, jury, and executioner.

Earp was cautious now. He moved slowly down Allen Street, scanning the faces of men on the boardwalk. He was alert to sudden movement and particularly watchful when he passed a darkened alleyway that opened onto the street. Over the years, he had seen many lawmen fall to an assassin's bullet. Vigilance, though an imperfect defense, was the only safeguard.

Earlier, after their supper at Delmonico's, he had dropped Sadie at the theater. Walking uptown, he'd then spent the rest of the evening at Virgil's house, sitting with Virgil and Morgan. At his direction, a blanket had been tacked over the bedroom window, obstructing the view from outside. Virgil kept a pistol on the nightstand beside the bed, and the women had pistols secreted in both the parlor and the kitchen. Their instructions were to open the door only to family, close friends, and Dr. Goodfellow.

Entering the Oriental, he was in a low mood. The constant state of vigilance, at Virgil's and on the street, kindled a simmering anger. Earp bitterly resented the need to govern his life around the possible threat of death. Later, when he joined Sadie for the night, his mood would improve and he would be able to relax. For now, he felt strung a turn too tight.

Holliday was seated alone at one of the poker tables. He looked up from dealing a hand of solitaire as Earp took a chair. "How's Virg and Morg?" he asked. "Any better?"

"Some," Earp replied. "They're keeping Morg dosed on laudanum. Virg bitches a lot about being stuck in bed. That's probably a good sign."

"How about infection?"

"Doc Goodfellow says everything's fine. Just take time for them to mend."

"How about you?" Holliday said, inspecting him. "You look a little peaked."

"I'll get by," Earp commented. "Suppose I just hate to see Virg and Morg forted up in that house. It's not much of a way to live."

"Same goes for walking down the street. I've begun wishing I had eyes in the back of my head."

"Sometimes it's tough operating within the law. Ties our hands, in a way."

"Told you before," Holliday said. "What we ought to do

is clean out Brocius and his crowd once and for all. Take the fight to them rather than wait."

"Doc, I'd like nothing more," Earp said. "Trouble is, that would make us no better than them. We have to have a reason to act."

"Well, the odds are they'll give us one. The question is, at what price?"

"Guess we won't know till they up the ante."

Holliday slowly shuffled the cards. "Got a funny feeling, Wyatt. Like when you smell rain in the air before it gets here."

Earp looked at him. "One of your hunches?"

"Never failed me yet."

"So what does it tell you?"

"Sleep light, and keep a gun close at hand."

Holliday dealt another game of solitaire. Earp watched the cards fall, troubled by a new sense of unease. One that had to do with a gambler's faith in hunches.

He'd never known Holliday to be wrong.

# Chapter Twenty-Five

BURIAL SERVICES WERE HELD THE FOLLOWING AF-ternoon. Fresh graves had been dug on Boot Hill, the cem-etery outside town. The mourners included Ike Clanton, Will Claiborne, and a few townspeople who had known the deceased. Conspicuous by their absence were Curly Bill Brocius and Johnny Ringo.

A local preacher had been persuaded to say a few words at graveside. There was no eulogy for the dead, and no one to sing hymns. Ike and Will Claiborne, uncomfortable in their store-bought suits, stood solemnly while the last words were spoken. Then the coffins, one at a time, were lowered into the ground. The gravediggers waited with shovels to fill in the holes.

Ike looked on with a mixture of grief and guilt. He mourned the loss of his brother, and to a lesser extent the passing of the McLaurys. But his overriding emotion was guilt at having been the instrument of their deaths. He was angry as well that Brocius and Ringo had considered dis-cretion the better part of valor. Neither of them thought it prudent to make an appearance in Tombstone, even at a public funeral. They opted instead for the relative safety of the San Pedro.

To Ike, their absence was a sign of cowardice. They talked big, and among their own kind they were feared in the way schoolyard bullies frighten other children. Yet it was all too apparent by their actions that they wanted nothing to do with the Earps and Doc Holliday. Had a chance encounter occurred, they would probably have ac-quitted themselves with reasonable courage. Still, they rarely took chances, and killing was something better done from ambush. In Ike's view, that made them cowards.

For all that, he nonetheless feared them. At night, when he lay awake with his own thoughts, he reluctantly admitted that he was the bigger coward. Their way was the smarter way, taking action only when the odds were stacked in their favor. His way, when he looked back, was dumb as dirt. He'd forced a fight, then turned tail like some witless dimdot. So they stuck to the San Pedro, and fostered the notion that they were a couple of tough-nuts. He was meanwhile pegged a coward by anyone who could read a newspaper. Somehow, it didn't seem fair.

Nor was he eager to undertake their latest scheme. He would follow orders and bring charges against the Earps as well as Holliday. But he felt like a cat caught between two large, surly dogs. Unless he obeyed, there was a strong likelihood that Brocius would let Ringo off the leash. On the other hand, by bringing charges, there was every likelihood that the Earps would have no need to restrain their dog. Doc Holliday would gladly kill him, and never ask permission.

Will Claiborne, who stood beside him at the graveyard, was no less apprehensive. He was fidgety, shifting from foot to foot, and appeared scared out of his wits. Overnight, after a visit from Johnny Ringo, he had agreed to swear false witness against the Earps and Holliday. He was caught as well between those large, surly dogs. His life was forfeit if he refused Ringo, and equally forfeit if he antagonized Holliday. His one hope was that Holliday and the Earps would be hanged, thereby freeing him from threat. He longed for the peaceful life of a simple cow thief.

The preacher shook their hands and walked toward his buggy. The gravediggers, who were not much on ceremony, began shoveling dirt onto the coffins. As though the last to be notified, Ike and Claiborne realized that the services were concluded. They turned from the gravesite as the handful of mourners trudged down the hill. Off to the side, more observer than mourner, John Behan waited in his capacity as sheriff. Harry Woods, there to report on the funeral, stepped forward.

"Mr. Clanton," he said, "I'd like to extend my condolences."

Ike bobbed his head. "Much obliged."

"I know it's a bad time, but I go to press in a couple of hours. Would you mind a few questions?"

"About what?"

"Just a quote or two," Woods said. "Something to add to my story on the services here today."

"Sure," Ike agreed. "Ask away."

"Have you anything to say about your brother, or the McLaurys? A message for our readers?"

"Well, you can say for me that they was good men shot down in the prime of life. All their friends are sorry they're gone."

"On that subject," Woods said, "their being shot down, I mean. Could you explain why you chose to leave the field of battle?"

"How's that again?"

"C'mon, Ike," Claiborne said impatiently. "He's askin' why you quit the fight."

"Oh," Ike said, reddening slightly above his stiff shirt collar. "Well, don't you see, I didn't have no gun. I had to quit or get shot."

Woods was astounded. "Do I understand you correctly? You were unarmed?"

"Me and Will both." Ike tried for an earnest tone. "Ain't that right, Will?"

Claiborne averted his gaze. "Yeah, that's right. Neither one of us had guns."

John Behan clapped a hand on Woods's shoulder. "Harry, I need to talk to you."

Startled, Woods looked around. "Won't it wait a minute? I'm interviewing these men."

"Sorry." Behan kept hold of his shoulder and walked

him off a short distance. "Harry, I want you to do me a favor."

"I'll certainly try, John."

"Hold off on interviewing those boys. Trust me, you won't be the worse for it. Drop by my office later and I'll give you a front page story."

Woods eyed him closely. "Something to do with the Earps?"

"I'll tell you later," Behan said. "Just go along for now and you won't regret it. All right?"

"This had better be good, John."

"Harry, it's the icing on the cake."

Woods went reluctantly. When he was out of earshot, Behan walked back to the men. His expression was cloudy as he looked from one to the other. His tone left no room for argument.

"Here's the way we'll work this. You probably noticed that I brought a buggy. I want you boys to climb in back and keep out of sight."

Ike and Claiborne glanced past him to a four-passenger surrey with the top raised. "Why so careful?" Ike asked nervously. "You think the Earps are layin' for us?"

"Not too likely," Behan said. "Even the Earps wouldn't try anything on the day your brother was buried. But there's no harm in playing it safe."

"Amen," Ike said quickly. "The safer the better, so far's I'm concerned."

"Christ," Claiborne muttered. "Wish to hell I'd never gotten myself in this fix."

Behan still had great reservations about the scheme. He was none too certain that either Ike or Claiborne would deliver on a witness stand. In his view, they would be easy prey for a clever defense attorney. Yet he had given his word to Brocius and he would have to see it through. He nodded to Claiborne.

"Don't get any ideas about backing out. You know where that would lead."

A quick image flashed through Claiborne's mind. Last night at the saloon in Charleston the message delivered by Ringo had been brief and to the point. Either he went along with the plan, or somebody would put a leak in his ticker. The threat seemed no less ominous to him now.

"Nobody's backing out," he said. "I know what's got to be done."

"Let's get about it, then."

A short while later the carriage rolled to a stop behind the county courthouse. Behan led them through the rear door and along a hallway to his office. His chief deputy, Bill Breakenridge, and a clerk were waiting for them. Behan locked the door.

Ike and Claiborne were motioned to chairs before the clerk's desk. At Behan's direction, they each dictated statements charging the three Earps and Doc Holliday with the murders of Billy Clanton, Tom McLaury, and Frank McLaury. The language was precise, relating to the circumstances surrounding the killings, with sufficient details to provide substance to the charges. After the statements were signed, the clerk locked them in the desk drawer. Behan looked at the two men.

"Here's the way things work. I first have to get the judge to sign an arrest warrant. With that, I can then take the Earps and Holliday into custody."

Claiborne appeared uneasy. "When's all this come out in the open?"

"I'll try to keep it quiet until I've made the arrests. But I want you boys to stay out of town between now and the day we go to court. I'd strongly advise you to lay low."

"Be honest," Ike said. "You think the Earps will come lookin' for us?"

Behan considered a moment. "I'll try to get them held without bail. But with Virgil Earp a lawman, that's not too likely. They'll probably make bail and be released till the court hearing."

"So?" Claiborne said anxiously. "You still haven't answered Ike's question."

"Offhand, I'd say the Earps will take their chances in court. Doc Holliday is another matter entirely. I think he'd kill you on sight."

"Jesus," Ike mumbled. "How long till this court hearing?"

"I'll have to talk to the judge. Unless the docket's full, I'd think no more than a couple of days."

"And meantime," Ike said, "we've got to be on the lookout for Holliday."

"Stick close to the ranch," Behan said. "I seriously doubt he'd come there. I'll get word to you about the court date."

Their faces were blank. But their eyes were bright with fear. Behan motioned to Breakenridge. "I want you to walk these boys over to the stable. Stay with them until they're on their horses and headed out of town. Get the picture?"

"Sure," Breakenridge said with a shrug. "Keep 'em away from Allen Street—and Holliday."

Ike and Claiborne rose from their chairs. Escorted by Breakenridge, they trooped out of the office. Behan walked to the window and stood watching as they emerged onto the street. Numb with fright, they trudged along behind the deputy. Their appearance was that of men being led to face a firing squad.

Behan thought they were dead men. Their one hope was that Doc Holliday would be held without bail, brought to trial, and quickly hanged. But their fate was of no great concern to him either way. His attention turned now to the matter of politics. Though Brocius would settle for revenge, his priorities were of a different nature. He meant to ensure his reelection as sheriff.

A good deal of thought had gone into the next step. In his opinion, there was a fifty-fifty chance at best that the Earps would ever go to trial. Yet the scheme hatched by Brocius opened the door to an opportunity almost as great. Behan considered himself a worthy tactician, and the plan he'd concocted was nothing short of a political coup. Trial or no trial, it would result in the downfall of Virgil Earp. And with him the Earp name.

Behan turned from the window. He waited until the clerk unlocked the desk drawer, then took the written statements and crossed the office. His mouth was set in a faint smile as he stepped into the hallway.

He walked toward the chambers of Judge Wells Spicer.

# Chapter Twenty-Six

An EMERGENCY SESSION OF THE TOWN COUNCIL was convened at seven-thirty that evening. The meeting had been called by the deputy mayor, Joseph Walsh. Stores in the business district were dark as the council members filed into the town hall. Walsh greeted them at the door to the mayor's office.

There were seven members on the council. Four were merchants and storekeepers, one was president of the Exchange Bank, and the deputy mayor was the owner of the town's largest mercantile emporium. The seventh member, Mayor John Clum, arrived just as the others were taking chairs around the room. He appeared to be out of breath.

"What's going on here? Who called this meeting?"

"I did," Joe Walsh said. "We have an important matter that has to be discussed tonight."

"Why wasn't I informed?" Clum demanded. "Why didn't you contact me to call the meeting? I was only advised of it ten minutes ago."

"To be frank, Mr. Mayor, I consulted with some of the other council members. In light of the matter to be discussed, we weren't sure you would agree to an emergency session."

"What are you talking about? Why wouldn't I agree?"

Walsh offered a shrug. "We felt you would be influenced by a conflict of interest."

Clum glared at him. "What conflict of interest?"

"Your association with Wyatt Earp and his brothers."

The tone of the statement made it sound like an allegation. Yet Clum had an immediate sense of why the meeting had been organized in secret. Joe Walsh was a leader in the Democratic party, and a strong supporter of Sheriff Behan. In large part, he had been elected to the town council as counterpoint to a Republican mayor. On any issue, he stood in opposition to John Clum.

"Speak plain," Clum said indignantly. "What does this meeting have to do with the Earps?"

"Since we're here," Walsh said, "why not call the meeting to order? Then we can get down to business."

Clum saw that he'd been outmaneuvered. He took his chair behind the desk and formally called the meeting to order. "Get to it," he said, glowering at Walsh. "What's on your mind?"

Walsh rose from his chair. "Late this afternoon, I had a visit from Sheriff Behan. He informed me that he has a warrant for the arrest of the Earp brothers and Doc Holliday."

"On what charge?" Clum said stiffly.

"The murder of William Clanton, and Franklin and Thomas McLaury. I might add that the charge is with premeditation. First degree murder."

"That's tommyrot!" Clum sputtered. "Some trumped-up nonsense courtesy of Johnny Behan."

"On the contrary," Walsh said with a smug look. "The charges were brought by Ike Clanton and Will Claiborne. The warrant for arrest was issued by Judge Spicer."

There was a murmur of conversation among the council members. Three were Democrats and three were Republicans, but their political differences were momentarily forgotten. The news brought into issue the most hotly debated subject in town. Not everyone was convinced that the Earps had acted in the interests of the law.

Walsh raised his hands for silence. "I bring before the council tonight a matter of grave consequence. As you all know, Virgil Earp is our town marshal. Yet he now stands charged with first degree murder."

"For God's sake," Clum fumed, "you're talking dirty politics here, Walsh. The law says a man's innocent until he's been proved guilty."

"So it does," Walsh admitted. "But we're not discussing some petty misdemeanor. Our chief law enforcement officer has been charged with a hanging offense."

Clum appealed to the other council members. "Gentlemen, you belittle yourselves by listening to this tripe. Any damn fool can bring charges on anything. But that doesn't make it a fact! Especially when the charges are brought by a common cow thief."

The councilmen merely stared at him. No one nodded agreement or raised a voice in support. At length Arnold Lockhart, the banker, shifted in his chair. An avowed Republican, he was nonetheless respected by everyone for his moderate views. He looked at Walsh.

"What is it you're proposing here, Joe?"

"Nothing pleasant," Walsh said with a grim expression. "For the good of the community, I propose that we suspend Virgil Earp from the office of town marshal. On such a divisive issue, I believe we have no other choice."

"Suspend him," Lockhart queried, "rather than fire him? Why is that?"

"For the reason Mayor Clum pointed out. Let the courts decide his guilt or innocence. In the meantime, we need someone to restore law and order to the community. Someone with no taint of suspicion."

Clum had to admire the gambit. By suggesting a mere suspension, Walsh removed the onus from the councilmen. Their action would be seen as prudent and wise, awaiting confirmation of Virgil's innocence or guilt. Any politician, given a choice, took the middle ground on questionable issues.

"Wake up!" Clum exhorted them. "He's asking you to compromise principle for expedience. Have you forgotten that Virgil Earp is also a deputy U.S. Marshal? Would you sacrifice his character and good name simply because it is expedient?"

From their expressions, he saw that he had lost. Walsh put the proposal in the form of a motion and it was quickly seconded. The vote was six to one, with Clum the only dissenter. As the three Republican councilmen voted in the affirmative, he knew that the party line had been solidly broken. They were afraid to be censured for supporting an accused murderer.

The vote placed Virgil on indefinite suspension, without pay. When the subject of a replacement was raised, one of the Democrats immediately nominated a local gadfly, James Flynn. The fact that he was Joe Walsh's brother-in-law, and had no experience in law enforcement, was never brought to discussion. The vote was four to three, but nonetheless a majority. Jim Flynn was the new town marshal.

Clum advised the council members to read tomorrow's *Epitaph.* They could expect a full report on the quid pro quo of their politics. He then stormed out of the town hall.

Ten minutes later Clum burst through the door of the Oriental. His face was flushed and he was puffing as though he'd sprinted across town. He found Earp observing the action at the roulette table.

"Wyatt," he said, breathing hard. "I need to speak with you—now."

Earp caught the anger in his voice. "You've practically got steam coming out of your ears. What's wrong?"

"Where can we talk in private?"

"Let's try the office."

A door at the rear of the Oriental led to the storage room. An area to the right of the door had been partitioned off into an enclosed office. There was no one about, and Earp led the way inside. He motioned the editor to a chair. Clum declined. He was too agitated to sit still.

"I just came from a council meeting," he said, pacing back and forth as Earp seated himself behind the desk. "Virgil has been suspended as town marshal."

"Suspended?" Earp said, clearly astonished. "What the hell for?"

The startled reply brought Clum up short. He stopped pacing. "Wyatt, are you aware that murder warrants have been issued for you and your brothers, and Holliday?"

"No," Earp said flatly. "When did this happen?"

"Sometime this afternoon. I was informed of it at the council meeting."

"Why hasn't Behan served the warrants?"

"According to what I was told," Clum said, "he intends to arrest you tomorrow. He delayed to see what action the council would take with Virgil. He didn't want to be put in the position of arresting the town marshal."

"Behan's clever," Earp said, with a tinge of admiration. "Getting Virg canned lends credibility to the murder charges. He got the town council to convict us before we even have a hearing."

"Good God, that's insidious! I hadn't put it together, but you're absolutely right. Behan planned it to sway public opinion."

"Dirty but effective," Earp noted. "Headlines in the *Nugget* about Virgil's suspension. Then more headlines about the arrests and the hearings. He's running a smear campaign to discredit me in the elections."

Clum looked puzzled. "I must say, you're taking this very well. I thought you would be furious."

"Never lose your temper in a fight, John. If you do, that gives the other fellow a big edge."

"Well, however calmly you take it, we're still in hot water. This could easily cost us the election."

"Or win it."

Earp leaned back in his chair, staring at the wall. His expression was one of deep thought, as though he were wrestling with a complex problem. His gaze finally shifted back to Clum. "Who preferred the murder charges?"

"Ike Clanton and Will Claiborne."

"That means Brocius and Behan are in this together.

Those boys wouldn't make a move without Brocius's permission."

Clum was confused. "What does that have to do with winning the election?"

"Think about it," Earp said. "Brocius must have ordered those boys to prefer charges. So now, Ike and Claiborne will have to get on the witness stand and tell a pack of lies." He paused, a smile at the corner of his mouth. "To support their story, Behan will have to lie, too. After all, he was an eyewitness."

"You're talking about three eyewitnesses with the same story. That sounds scary as hell to me."

"Does it?" Earp said, still smiling. "Imagine the three of them trying to keep their lies straight. How do you think Ike and Claiborne will hold up under cross-examination?"

"Of course!" Clum said with sudden dawning. "They will get confused and trip up one another."

"The one they'll trip up will be our noble sheriff, Johnny Behan. He'll look like a liar or a fool, or both."

"So you believe we can turn the situation around? Make it work against them?"

"Tell you what," Earp said confidently. "I'll wager it never gets past the preliminary hearing. I think it'll be tossed out of court."

"Wouldn't that be something!" Clum laughed. "What an editorial I could write. Behan playing dirty politics and in league with a gang of rascals."

"No need to wait till the end of the hearing. You could plant that thought in tomorrow's paper."

"Indeed I will." Clum hesitated, his features touched by a solemn expression. "You know, of course, that where many people are concerned, you will never be exonerated. No matter what a court decides."

"Difference of opinion," Earp said. "That's what makes horse races. I regret that those boys had to die. But I can live with myself on that score. I did what had to be done."

"I understand that, Wyatt. I wasn't talking about your conscience. I was talking your chances in the election."

"All we need is a simple majority of the vote. I think we've just been handed the leverage we needed."

"You're speaking of these murder charges?"

"John, I can hardly wait to get to court."

Clum went off to write an editorial. When the door closed, Earp's thoughts turned to another matter. Virgil being suspended as town marshal was bad enough. But he would not allow further indignity to be heaped on his brothers. No matter what happened, no matter who got hurt.

Virgil and Morgan would never be arrested.

# Chapter Twenty-Seven

"I'M GOING TO BE ARRESTED."

Lou Rudabaugh stared at him. The mine office opened at eight o'clock and Earp had appeared shortly afterward. Seated at his desk, Rudabaugh didn't offer him a chair. His expression was anything but cordial.

"I assume the charge is murder. How did you find out about it?"

"John Clum tipped me off last night."

Earp went on to relate the gist of the situation. He explained that Virgil had been suspended as town marshal, and that Behan had delayed serving the warrants so as to garner more headlines in the newspaper. When he finished, Rudabaugh was silent a moment.

"No need to say that this is a setback, Wyatt. A very unfortunate situation."

"Bad timing, too," Earp said. "What with the charge being murder, I don't even know if the judge will grant bail. But if he does, I've got all my money tied up in mining stocks."

Rudabaugh looked irritated. "Are you asking me to post the bail?"

"Strictly as a loan, Lou. You can hold my mining stock as collateral."

"How would that make me look? Everyone would believe I'm somehow involved in a murder case."

"You are," Earp said. "Everybody knows you've backed me for sheriff. No way around that."

"On the contrary," Rudabaugh replied. "I could wash

my hands of the whole affair. Issue a public statement withdrawing my support."

"Do that and the Republican ticket will sink like a rock. I'm your only chance to sweep the elections."

"I hardly think our chances are improved with an alleged murderer on the ticket."

"Let's get something straight," Earp said in a hard voice. "I'll walk out of that court a free man. What happened was legal, sworn officers upholding the law."

Rudabaugh cocked his head. "You sound very certain of yourself."

"You're damned right I am. The only choice you've got is whether or not you stick with a winner. I intend to be the next sheriff of Cochise County—with you or without you."

"No need to raise your voice, Wyatt. As I've told you before, a good businessman always weighs the positive against the negative."

"This isn't business," Earp said. "Behan's playing dirty politics, plain and simple."

Rudabaugh was thoughtful. "All right, I'll attend to the matter of posting bail. But take a friendly word of advice, Wyatt. Don't allow these charges to go beyond the preliminary hearing."

"Lou, when it's all over, Johnny Behan will look like the biggest horse's ass in Arizona Territory. That's why I know I'm going to win the election."

"I admire your confidence. But it wouldn't hurt to have a good lawyer representing your case. Have you given any thought to legal counsel?"

"That's my next stop," Earp said. "I'm going to hire Tom Fitch. He's top-notch."

"Excellent choice," Rudabaugh acknowledged. "Do you have any idea when you'll be arrested?"

"Knowing Behan, it'll be before noon. He'll want a court appearance in time for the *Nugget* to crank out another smear job."

"I assume John Clum will counter that with his usual outraged rhetoric."

"That's the safest bet in town. Clum stays up nights thinking of ways to slander Behan."

"Good luck, Wyatt." Rudabaugh rose, extending his hand. "Good luck to us all."

"A man makes his own luck. I'll do just fine, Lou."

Outside the office Earp checked the street in both directions. He was determined that when he was arrested, it would be on his own terms. Whatever happened, he would not allow Behan to accost him on the street like a common criminal. That was one headline he meant to avoid.

Some minutes later he entered the law offices of Thomas Fitch. The attorney was a man of solid reputation, with a practice that included both civil and criminal law. Only a few months before, he'd won acquittal for a miner who had beat another man to death with his fists. Earp outlined the case in some detail and then agreed on a retainer. Fitch promised to be on call throughout the day.

Shortly after nine o'clock Earp stepped outside and turned uptown. His next stop was one he dreaded, for no explanation would satisfy Allie. Early that morning he'd awakened Holliday and arranged to meet him at Virgil's house. By now Holliday would have told them of the pending arrests, and the house would be in a turmoil. Even though he admired Allie, Earp was uneasy with the prospect of facing her. She was a formidable woman when her anger was aroused. Today he expected the worst.

When he walked through the door, they were waiting for him. Holliday, who was seated in a chair, rolled his eyes in warning. Allie was standing by the bedroom door, and Jane came out of the kitchen, drying her hands on a towel. He crossed the parlor, nodding to Allie, who gave him a frosty look. She clearly meant to bar him from the bedroom.

"Morning," Earp said, halting a pace away. "How're Virg and Morg?"

"Alive," she said shortly. "No thanks to you."

Virgil's voice bracketed through the bedroom door. "Allie, goddammit, don't you get started! I told you to leave things be."

"Virgil Earp, I'll have no cursing in my house. You just be still, or I'll tie you down in that bed."

Earp thought she was fully capable of delivering on her word. "Look here, Allie," he said, trying to defuse the situation. "Things aren't as bad as they sound. Give me a chance—"

"You've had your chance!" she broke in hotly. "And where has that gotten us? Virgil and Morgan almost killed, and now they're to be arrested. And for what, Wyatt? For what?"

"You know the answer to that, Allie. The law has to be enforced."

"No!" she said bitterly. "Everything that's happened has happened for only one reason—to get you elected sheriff!"

"Listen to me," he said in a calm voice. "No one could have predicted where this would lead. But once we were into it, what were we supposed to do?"

She eyed him narrowly. "Is that some kind of trick question?"

"Straight question with a straight answer. We could've done our duty and upheld the law. Or we could have backed off and let the crooks have Tombstone. Those were the choices."

"*You* made the choice," she accused. "You always make the choice! Virgil and Morgan just go along."

"Allie, no one forced Virgil to become a lawman. Would you have him tuck tail and run at the first sign of trouble?"

"That's not fair," she said hollowly. "You know very well I'd never ask Virgil to run."

"I would," Jane said, moving to join them. "I've already

asked Morgan to leave Tombstone. Nothing's worth getting killed over."

"And?" Earp said. "What was his answer?"

Jane looked miserable. "He said a man who takes an oath is bound to keep it. Otherwise he couldn't respect himself."

There was a moment of strained silence. When neither of the women spoke, Earp stepped past Allie into the bedroom. Virgil was propped up on one elbow, clearly embarrassed. Morgan smiled weakly, his shoulder swathed in bandages. Earp walked to the bed.

"You boys rest easy," he said. "Behan won't be taking you to jail."

Virgil frowned. "How do you plan to stop him?"

"Leave that to me and Doc. No arrest warrants will be served on you today."

"We're able to be moved," Morgan said gamely. "Don't force his hand on our account."

"I'll tend to it my own way. You just listen to Doc Goodfellow and get well."

Earp started away, then turned back. "Virg, I wish it had worked out different about the town marshal's job. Politics gets dirty sometimes."

"Forget it," Virgil said easily. "Damn job didn't pay enough, anyhow."

"Well, there's better things ahead. Come next spring, I'll make you both deputy sheriffs."

"First things first," Virgil said. "For now, let's clear ourselves on those murder charges."

"I intend to do just that, Virg."

There was a knock at the front door. A pall of silence abruptly fell over the house. Earp moved into the parlor, nodding to Holliday as he crossed the room. Holliday rose from his chair and took a position covering the door. Allie and Jane stood protectively at the entrance to the bedroom.

When Earp opened the door, John Behan was waiting

on the porch. Breakenridge and three deputies, all armed with shotguns, were stationed in the yard. Behan appeared almost jovial, quite pleased with himself. He nodded with a smug expression.

"I tried the hotel. You and Holliday got an early start."

"State your business, Sheriff."

"Why, as you well know, I have murder warrants. I'm here to arrest you, your brothers, and Holliday."

"Not my brothers," Earp said simply. "They're in no condition to be moved."

"That's for me to decide," Behan ordered. "Stand away from the door and I'll check their condition myself."

Earp fixed him with a look. "Doc and I will go along peaceably. Try anything else and you've got trouble."

"Don't be a fool, Earp. The law's on my side, and I've got four men with shotguns. You wouldn't stand a chance."

"Neither would you, Johnny. I'll drop you before those boys know what happened. You wouldn't live to see me dead."

Behan suddenly looked deflated. "How do I know your brothers won't try to escape?"

"Not possible," Earp said. "Virg and Morg aren't able to get out of bed. Doc Goodfellow will confirm that."

"So far as the law's concerned, the warrants are still officially served."

"We have no argument there."

"Well . . ." Behan fidgeted a moment. "I suppose we could consider them under house arrest. Do I have your word they'll stay put?"

Earp nodded. "They're not going anywhere."

"You and Holliday will have to surrender your guns. That's not a matter open to debate."

"We'll hand them over when we get to the courthouse. I wouldn't trust you from here to there with my life."

Behan tried to salvage something. "But you do submit to arrest—right now?"

Earp smiled. "I always obey the law, Johnny."

Holliday joined him at the door, and they moved onto the porch. Once in the yard, Behan ordered his deputies to form a guard around the prisoners. No one bothered to remark that they were still armed. Behan positioned himself at the front, as though he were leading a parade. The contingent marched off toward the courthouse.

An hour later, with Judge Wells Spicer presiding, the court was called to order. Present were Thomas Fitch, counsel for the defense, and Lyle Price, the district attorney for Cochise County. Behan and his deputies stood directly behind the defense table, where Earp and Holliday, now disarmed, were huddled with their attorney. Seated at the rear, on opposite sides of the room, were John Clum and Harry Woods.

District Attorney Price advised the court that defendants Virgil and Morgan Earp, due to physical disability, were being held under house arrest. He then moved for an immediate hearing on murder charges against defendants Wyatt Earp and John Holliday. Tom Fitch asked the court's indulgence, requesting a continuance, based on the fact that he'd had insufficient time to consult with his clients. Judge Spicer, after hearing strenuous objection from Price, granted a continuance of one week.

The subject of bail was then raised. The prosecutor, dwelling on the gravity of the charge, petitioned that the accused be held without bail. Tom Fitch spoke at some length on Earp's record as a lawman and his prominence in the local business community. Though he never mentioned Holliday by name, he requested that the defendants be released on their own recognizance. After argument by both sides, Judge Spicer granted bail in the amount of ten thousand dollars for each defendant. Lou Rudabaugh, who had entered the courtroom only moments before, stepped forward to post bail.

Earp and Holliday agreed to meet with Tom Fitch that afternoon, to prepare for the hearing. Their pistols were returned, and they parted with Rudabaugh outside the courthouse. As they turned uptown, walking toward Virgil's house, Earp appeared lost in thought. At length Holliday gave him a curious look.

"What's got your mind so occupied?"

"Ike Clanton and Will Claiborne. Don't do what you're thinking, Doc."

"Why not?" Holliday said. "No witnesses, no case."

"I want them alive," Earp told him. "I intend to win this one in court."

"Lots of things could go wrong in a courtroom."

In the end, though he thought it a mistake, Holliday agreed. Ike Clanton and Will Claiborne were granted a reprieve.

# Chapter Twenty-Eight

COURT WAS CONVENED THE FIRST WEEK IN NO-vember. The courtroom was packed with spectators and journalists, drawn by the spectacle of what was now known as the Gunfight at the O.K. Corral. There was the added lure of sworn law officers being charged with murder.

Judge Wells Spicer opened the proceedings with a statement. He noted that the purpose of a preliminary hearing was to determine whether sufficient evidence existed for the accused to be bound over for formal trial. The issue at question, he went on, related to an incident that took place on October 26 and resulted in the deaths of three men. The exact nature of their deaths would be the focus of the hearing.

The accused were seated at the defense table with their attorney, Tom Fitch. Virgil, who had recuperated sufficiently to attend the hearing, was seated between Earp and Holliday. He limped noticeably, walking with a cane, but otherwise appeared in good health. The fourth defendant, Morgan Earp, was still confined to bed. The court was advised that he remained under house arrest.

Lyle Price, the district attorney, was seated at the prosecution table. Witnesses for the prosecution and the defense were sequestered in separate rooms elsewhere in the courthouse. Price and Fitch, when queried by the judge, indicated that both sides were ready to proceed with the hearing. Judge Spicer noted for the record that the burden of proof rested on the prosecution. He then instructed Price to call his first witness.

Dr. Horace Matthews, the county coroner, took the stand. After being sworn, he testified as to the cause of death, relating specific gunshot wounds suffered by each of the deceased. Price then led him to agree that certain wounds on William Clanton and Thomas McLaury could have been inflicted while their arms were raised in surrender. On cross-examination Tom Fitch got him to admit that the wounds could just have easily occurred while their arms were lowered.

The next witness was William Allen. A bystander on the day of the shootings, he testified that he had been standing on the opposite side of Fremont Street. From there he had witnessed the entire affair, including the declarations by Ike Clanton and Thomas McLaury, made to Sheriff Behan, that they were unarmed. The witness stumbled on cross-examination by stating that, in his opinion, Doc Holliday had fired the first shot. Fitch was unable to extract admission that Tom McLaury had fired a pistol during the fight. Though certain of other details, the witness pleaded no recollection of McLaury's actions.

Sheriff John Behan then took the stand. Price led him through a recital of his efforts to prevent the shootout. He testified that the Earps, despite his protests, were determined to force the fight. On Fremont Street, when he'd attempted to halt the Earps, he quoted Wyatt Earp as declaring, "The sonsabitches have been looking for a fight and now they'll get one." He went on to state that Wyatt Earp and Doc Holliday had fired the first shots, while the Clantons and McLaurys had their arms in the air. He categorized the shootings as "premeditated murder."

Tom Fitch approached the stand. "Sheriff Behan, you have testified that you were unable to disarm Billy Clanton and Frank McLaury, correct?"

"That's correct."

"Yet, when you met the Earps on Fremont Street, you stated that you had disarmed the so-called 'cowboys.' Isn't that true?"

"No, it's not," Behan said. "I made no such statement."

Fitch smiled. "So if someone else testified to the contrary, the court would have to decide who's lying. Would you agree?"

"Well—yes, I suppose so."

"Where were you when the shooting commenced?"

"Walking toward Fly's Photo Gallery."

"Indeed?" Fitch pinned him with a look. "Sheriff, I suggest you were running, not walking. I further suggest you couldn't have seen who fired the first shot. Or do you have eyes in the back of your head?"

Behan hesitated. "I was looking over my shoulder."

"While running to dive for cover? Come now, Sheriff, are you a contortionist as well?"

"I'm telling—"

"No further questions."

Price next called Will Claiborne to the stand. From the approach of the Earps into the vacant lot, until the time he ran for the photo gallery, his testimony gibed with that of Behan. On cross-examination Fitch asked if he had heard his friends threaten the lives of the Earps. When he denied such threats, Fitch inquired if he had been present at the time Ike Clanton and Tom McLaury purchased pistols in Hamer's Gun Shop. His denial prompted Fitch to ask if he knew the penalty for lying under oath. Claiborne squirmed in his chair, saved only by an objection from Price for badgering the witness. Fitch walked away as the objection was sustained.

The prosecution's final witness was Isaac Clanton. Price guided him through testimony that was remarkably similar to that of Behan and Will Claiborne. Ike reaffirmed that the first shots were fired by the Earps, at the exact moment the deceased were in the act of surrendering. When Price was finished, Ike flicked a nervous glance at the defense table. Tom Fitch moved forward with an expression of disdain and disbelief. His voice was caustic.

"How many times did you threaten the Earps on the day in question?"

"Never threatened them at all."

"How do you explain the fact that there are witnesses to those threats—by you, your brother, and the McLaurys?"

"Don't make no nevermind. I know what I said."

"Do you, indeed?" Fitch countered in an icy tone. "Yet you are on record as stating that the Earps intended to kill you. Isn't that correct?"

"Yeah," Ike admitted. "I said that."

"Then how is it you're still alive?"

"Don't follow you."

"Come, Mr. Clanton." Fitch's voice dripped with scorn. "You deserted your own brother and your closest friends. You ran to Wyatt Earp and clutched desperately at his arm. You begged for your life. True or not?"

Ike grimaced. "Wasn't exactly thataway."

"But you were right on top of him, at point-blank range. If he intended to kill you, Mr. Clanton—why didn't he?"

"I dunno."

"Of course you don't know. You were too terrified to even think about it, weren't you, Mr. Clanton?"

"I was scared, awright. Anybody would've been."

"So tell this court"—Fitch nailed him with a sudden stare—"how do you know who raised their arms? How do you know the exact moment your brother and the McLaurys drew their guns? How did a man that terrified see anything, remember anything? How, Mr. Clanton, when your very soul was focused on the man who spared your life—Wyatt Earp?"

"Objection!" Price shouted. "He's lecturing the witness, Your Honor, not asking questions."

Judge Spicer nodded. "Objection sustained. Try one question at a time, Mr. Fitch."

"No need, Your Honor." Fitch strolled back to the defense table. "I believe Mr. Clanton told us all we need to hear."

Dismissed, Ike hurried from the courtroom with a sheepish look, his head bowed. Lyle Price, still fuming, rested the case for the state. Judge Spicer then consulted the wall clock and noted that it was approaching noontime. He ordered a one-hour recess.

At the defense table, Fitch gave his clients a broad smile. "I never brag until the verdict is in. But I'll tell you this, gentlemen—we've got them on the run."

The courtroom began clearing out. Earp invited Fitch to join them for dinner, but the attorney declined. He stayed behind to prepare for the afternoon session.

When court reconvened, Judge Spicer directed the defense to present its case. In rapid-fire order Tom Fitch called a dizzying array of witnesses. By now it was apparent to everyone that his strategy hinged on proving that the Earps' lives had been threatened. The witnesses he'd uncovered were there to drive the point home.

Julius Kelley, a bartender, testified that Ike Clanton had entered his saloon early the morning of October 26. Armed with a carbine and a pistol, Clanton stated that the "Earp crowd" had insulted him the night before and he intended to "fight them on sight." The next witness was R. J. Campbell, clerk of the municipal court, who testified as to Clanton's threats following his arrest by Virgil Earp for carrying weapons. He was followed to the witness stand by Hobart Sills, the teamster. While asleep in his wagon at the O.K. Corral, Sills related, he'd been awakened by the "cowboys" discussing their plans to "kill all them Earps." He went on to state that he had warned the town marshal, Virgil Earp, of what he'd overheard.

Fitch continued to orchestrate his parade of witnesses. Robert Hatch, a bystander to the shootout, testified that he had heard Sheriff Behan declare, "I have disarmed those men," and Virgil Earp reply, "I don't believe you." Next to take the stand was Mrs. Addie Bourland, a dressmaker whose shop was opposite Fly's Lodging House. From her front window she had seen the fight unfold in the vacant lot across the street. She testified that none of the "cowboys" had raised their arms in surrender, and that the gunfire had commenced in general by both sides. Everything happened so quickly, she stated, that she could not swear as to who fired the first shot.

Lyle Price was like a knife being thrust again and again against stone. As the district attorney cross-examined each of the witnesses, his thrusts were blunted against the firmness of their statements. He was unable to shake their testimony, and disgruntled by his failure to create doubt as to what they had seen and heard. His demeanor went from fierce and feisty to the petulant harangues of a man leading a lost cause. The dressmaker, Addie Bourland, gently hammered him into a fit of frustration. She was unyielding on an issue central to the prosecution's case. The "cowboys" had made not the slightest gesture of surrender.

In a withering salvo, Fitch then called the defendants to the stand. Virgil hobbled across the courtroom, leaning on his cane, and took the oath. His testimony traced the events in precise order, from the night before the gunfight to the bloodbath in the vacant lot. He was followed by Doc Holliday, who verified every detail like a scholar recounting historical fact. Lyle Price attacked Holliday's character, trying to sully the Earps for enlisting the aid of a known "gunman." He went too far by demanding: "Is it not true that you have killed twelve men?"

"Fourteen," Holliday replied equably. "As a point of honor, I allowed them to draw first—including Billy Clanton and the McLaurys."

Price walked away in a daze. Fitch then called his final witness, Wyatt Earp. On the stand, Earp related a series of events that squared in every particular with the testimony of Virgil and Doc Holliday. Fitch at last came to the crux of the hearing, the charge of premeditated murder.

"You made a deal with Ike Clanton for the Wells Fargo reward. Is that correct?"

"It is."

"Clanton later defamed you and provoked trouble. Is that not also correct?"

"Yes, he did."

"At that time, the night of October twenty-fifth, and again the next day, did he not repeatedly threaten your life and the lives of your brothers?"

"On several occasions he made such threats."

"And yet," Fitch said softly, "in the heat of battle, when you could have easily killed him—and been justified in doing so—you spared his life. I ask you now, why did you let him go?"

"I had no choice," Earp said. "Ike never pulled a gun. I had to let him go."

"In other words, you could not bring yourself to shoot a defenseless man. Is that correct?"

"I have never fired on any man unless he pulled first."

"So we have learned here today." Fitch let the statement hang a moment, then walked away. "Your witness, Mr. Price."

"No questions," Price said in a subdued voice.

"In that event"—Fitch turned to face the bench—"the defense rests, Your Honor."

A buzz of conversation swept through the courtroom. Judge Spicer hammered the crowd into silence with his gavel. He stared down at Fitch and Price for a moment, then nodded. His voice was firm but neutral.

"Gentlemen, I will weigh the evidence presented here today. A decision will be rendered at nine o'clock tomorrow morning. Court dismissed."

# Chapter Twenty-Nine

THE MORNING WAS GRAY AND OVERCAST. HEAVY clouds rimmed the Dragoon Mountains to the north, and there was a smell of snow in the air. Shortly before nine, people began streaming into the courthouse. Their opinions on the hearing were sharply divided, as was the general feeling around town. The large turnout reflected a widespread belief that the winner would be their next sheriff.

Ike Clanton stood talking with Will Claiborne near the entrance. He was rolling a last cigarette when he saw the Earps approaching from upstreet with Doc Holliday. A trick of the mind took him back to the vacant lot, where he'd watched them approach with no less terror than he felt today. He dropped the paper and tobacco and nudged Claiborne with an elbow. They hurried into the courthouse.

At the stroke of nine Judge Wells Spicer took his place on the bench. The bailiff called the court to order and everyone resumed their seats. Spicer was a meticulous man, who prided himself on attention to detail, and he spread out several sheets of paper, dense with his handwritten decision. He peered out over the courtroom, satisfying himself that the defendants and their attorney, as well as the prosecutor, were present. Then, ready to proceed, he put on his reading spectacles.

"The case before this court," he read, "has resulted in a volume of testimony and the efforts of eminent legal counsel on both sides. The importance of the case, and the great interest in the community, demands that I should be full and explicit in my conclusions."

Spicer paused to clear his throat. "From the mass of evidence before this court, I have found it necessary for the purposes of this decision to consider only the facts which are established by a large preponderance of the testimony.

"Viewed in this manner," he went on, "I must weigh the claim by the prosecution that the deceased were shot while holding up their hands in obedience to the command of the town marshal."

There was a stir in the courtroom as the crowd realized he was moving swiftly to the pivotal point in the case. "William Clanton," he continued, "was wounded on the wrist of the right hand. This wound was such that it could not be sustained with his hands raised. The shotgun wound received by Thomas McLaury was such that it could not have been sustained with his hands overhead. These circumstances are consistent with the evidence, and cast great doubt upon testimony by witnesses for the prosecution."

Judge Spicer looked up from his sheaf of papers. His eyes searched the courtroom and stopped on Ike Clanton, who was seated with Claiborne and Behan in the first row behind the prosecution table. Then the judge's gaze shifted to Claiborne and Behan momentarily. His mouth pursed in disgust.

"The testimony of Isaac Clanton," he resumed, "that this tragedy was the result of the Earps intent to assassinate him, falls short of the truth. Isaac Clanton suffered no injury at all, and could have been killed first and easiest. But the facts demonstrate that, as Wyatt Earp testified, he was allowed to escape and was not harmed."

The judge paused to shuffle his papers. "I also give great weight to the testimony of Sheriff Behan. A short time before the encounter took place, the sheriff demanded of the Clantons and the McLaurys that they give up their arms.

They refused, and gave as the reason that they would not unless the Earps were also disarmed. I find the demand that the marshal and his deputies should be disarmed is a proposition both monstrous and startling!"

Spicer glanced over his glasses at Behan, then went on. "The evidence further demonstrates that this was not a wanton slaughter of unarmed innocents who were in the act of yielding to officers of the law. Instead, these were armed and defiant men, accepting their wager of battle and succumbing only in death."

A murmur swept through the onlookers, and Spicer gaveled them into silence. "I cannot resist the firm conviction," he said, "that the Earps acted wisely to secure their own self-preservation. I conclude that the defendants were fully justified in committing these homicides—that it was a necessary act, done in the discharge of an official duty."

Spicer removed his spectacles. He looked down at the defense table with a benign expression. "There being no sufficient cause to believe the defendants guilty of the charges before this court, I order them released forthwith."

Shouts of approval as well as murmurs of dissent broke out among the spectators. Earp turned in his chair and looked back at Ike Clanton. Their eyes locked, and for a moment Ike fidgeted in his seat. Then he stood, darting a nervous glance at Claiborne, and they rushed out of the courtroom. Earp shoved back his chair as Virgil and Holliday got to their feet. He extended his hand to Tom Fitch.

"Thanks, Tom," he said genially. "You made them look like a bunch of fools."

Fitch laughed. "Save your thanks until you get my bill."

The attorney collected his briefcase, waved, and moved into the aisle. As he walked away, Behan approached the table. He gave Earp a hangdog look and shrugged.

"No hard feelings, Wyatt. I was just doing my job."

"Do yourself a favor, Behan. Stay away from me. Far away."

Behan flushed, stung by the tone of voice, and walked

off. Earp turned to Virgil and Holliday, who had quietly watched the exchange. "Leave it to Behan to try and mend his fences."

"To hell with him," Virgil said. "We won and that's all that counts. I'd say a celebration is in order."

"What do you think, Doc?" Earp inquired. "Time to celebrate?"

"Why not?" Holliday said with a wry smile. "I suspect we just got you elected to sheriff."

Earp grinned and Holliday fell in beside him as they started up the aisle. Virgil limped along behind them, accepting the congratulations of well-wishers in the crowd. They came out of the courthouse into swirling flurries of snow.


Late that morning, Ike and Claiborne rode into Charleston. The town was hardly more than a crossroads, a handful of adobes sprinkled across a bleak landscape now dusted by powdery snow. Among the few business places were a general store, a cafe, and a saloon.

Ike reined up before the saloon. "How about a drink?"

"Too early for me," Claiborne said. "Think I'll head on home."

"Thought you was comin' out to my place."

"Changed my mind."

"Hell, Will," Ike said crossly. "I need you to help explain things to Curly Bill."

Claiborne looked edgy. "Tell you the truth, I'm moving on. Been thinkin' about it all morning." He made a vague gesture. "I'm quittin' the country."

"You're gonna pull up stakes? What about your place?"

"Won't be leavin' much behind."

Ike couldn't argue the point. Claiborne lived in an abandoned adobe outside town. He subsisted by hiring out as a cowhand, or occasionally rustling cows. Like most saddle tramps, his worldly goods could be packed in a blanket roll.

"You spooked?" Ike asked. "About the Earps gettin' off?"

"Damn right," Claiborne said readily. "Between Holliday and Brocius, we're livin' on borrowed time. It's a toss-up which one gets us first."

"Nothin' to worry about with Brocius. We done everything he wanted."

"What he wanted was the Earps hung. We sorta fell short of the mark."

"Cripes!" Ike snorted. "Wasn't our fault. Gawddamn judge let'em go."

"You tell that to Brocius. I'll be long gone before sundown."

Claiborne rode off without a handshake or a parting word. Feeling somewhat deserted, Ike tromped into the saloon, where he fortified himself with several drinks. Where Brocius was concerned, he wasn't too keen on being the bearer of bad news. He would likely get cursed out and cuffed around before things simmered down. Doc Holliday would hold a grudge and look for a way to settle the score. His life was at risk should they meet again.

An hour or so later Ike dismounted outside the main house. When he walked through the door, Brocius and Ringo were gathered with the others around the dining table. The new gang members—Frank Stilwell, Pete Spence, and Florentino Cruz—had moved into the bunkhouse over the past week. The five men stared at him as though he'd interrupted a festive occasion.

"C'mon in, Ike," Brocius said gruffly. "Join the party."

Ike warily approached the table. "Hate to tell you this, Bill. But there ain't nothin' to celebrate."

"We already heard."

"You did?"

Brocius nodded at Stilwell. "I had Frank stationed at the telegraph office. Figgered they'd get the word soon as the judge handed down a verdict."

"Oh." Ike took a seat, waiting for someone to belt him. "You ain't pissed?"

" 'Course I'm pissed! I oughta beat the daylights out of you. Will Claiborne, too."

"You'd have to hurry with Will. He's headed for parts unknown. Done took off."

"To hell with him," Brocius said. "Had time to get over being mad. What we're talkin' about now is getting even."

"The Earps," Ringo added, "probably bought that goddamn judge. Thing is, that's just the opening round."

Ike slowly accepted the idea that he wasn't to be made the whipping boy. His expression turned eager. "What've you got in mind?"

"Simple," Brocius said with a crooked smile. "We're gonna kill the Earps."

"That'll sure as Christ get my vote! What about Holliday?"

"Him, too," Ringo remarked. "Way past time those high and mighty bastards paid the piper."

"How you figger to do it?"

"Damn sure won't be from the front. You tried that and look what happened."

"We'll ambush'em," Brocius said firmly. "Kill the whole gawddamn bunch and be done with it."

"The whole bunch?" Ike said, slightly baffled. "How you plan to catch'em all together?"

"Why hell, Ike, the sonsabitches are just like anybody else. They're bound to their habits."

"What d'you mean?"

Brocius looked across the table. "Tell him, Pete."

Pete Spence was short and muscular, with a thatch of unruly dark hair. He gave Ike a slow smile. "I got lots of women," he said. "Happens with a man who travels around a lot. One of them lives in Tombstone. Goodlookin' grass widow with her own house."

"Yeah?" Ike said blankly. "So what?"

"So I'm gonna pay her a visit tonight." Spence paused, his smile wider. "She lives across the street from Virgil Earp."

"You're gonna kill Virgil? What about the rest of them?"

"You got it wrong," Spence said. "I'll move in with her for a few days. She'll be happy as a pig in mud. Gives me an excuse to hang around town, keep my eyes open."

Florentino Cruz chuckled. He was a swarthy man, with muddy eyes and a thick mustache. "Pete's real tricky," he observed slyly. "How you say—*espía?*"

"A spy!" Brocius crowed. "Pete's gonna be our spy on the Earps. Watch their every goddamn move."

"Got it all worked out," Ringo noted. "Pete will bird-dog them, find out a regular time they're all together. That's when we pop the bastards."

"Wait a minute," Ike said. "What if they're never all together? You'd have to have all four in the same place at the same time."

"Already thought of that," Brocius said. "Told Pete it's gotta be at least three. Three out of the four."

"Yeah, that'd do it," Ike agreed. "Just make sure one of them three is Doc Holliday."

"Don't worry," Brocius assured him. "Doc Holliday and Wyatt Earp are at the top of the list."

A jug of rotgut was passed around. They sloshed whiskey into battered tin cups. Then they drank a toast to the death of the Earps.

And Doc Holliday.

# Chapter Thirty

VIRGIL WAS A SKILLED POKER PLAYER. HE WAS NOT as crafty as Doc Holliday, nor did he possess the uncanny knack of reading other men's minds. Instead, he was a percentage player, working the mathematical odds. He ground out winners by betting on the laws of probability.

In the past, while serving as town marshal, he'd had little time for poker. But the day after the murder hearing, the town council had officially released him from the post. The firing had nothing to do with justice, and a great deal to do with politics. The vote was four to three despite John Clum's arguments on Virgil's behalf. The town was divided on the issue, and the council took the safe way out.

Four days had passed since the court hearing. With his job gone, Virgil had no choice but to look to another means of livelihood. For three nights now he had been a regular at the poker tables in the Oriental. To avoid any hint of irregularity, he never took a seat in one of Holliday's games. But the other tables were generally packed; there was no scarcity of men eager to test their luck. The money was there to be won.

Though recovered, Virgil still had a gimpy leg. He continued to use a cane, and his leg ached if he was on his feet for an extended period of time. But a poker game, where he was off his feet, allowed him to rest his leg and challenge his mind. Tonight he was seated at a table with four miners, a notions drummer, and Avery Todd, a local merchant. He'd been winning steadily all night.

The game was five-card draw, Western rules prevailing. In some Eastern casinos, the traditional rules of poker had been revised to create even more enticing odds for inveterate gamblers and wealthy high rollers. Introduced into the game were straights, flushes, and the most illusive of all combinations, a straight flush. The highest hand back East was now a royal flush, ten through ace in the same suit. By all reports, the revised rules had infused the game with an almost mystical element.

Poker in the West, however, was still played by the original rules. There were no straights, no flushes, and no straight flushes, royal or otherwise. The game was governed by tenets faithfully observed in earlier times on riverboats and the Creole gaming salons of New Orleans. Whether draw poker or stud poker, there were two unbeatable hands west of the Mississippi. The first was four aces, drawn by most players only once or twice in a lifetime. The other cinch hand was four kings with an ace, which precluded anyone holding four aces. Seasoned players looked upon it as a minor miracle or the work of a skilled cardsharp. Four kings, in combination with one of the aces, surmounted almost incalculable odds.

Shortly before three in the morning Virgil drew an unbeatable hand. The game had weeded out three of the miners and the drummer, their piles of chips depleted. The fourth miner was dealing, and down to his last twenty dollars. By mutual agreement, the game was table stakes with no limit, check and raise. Virgil and the merchant, Avery Todd, were each roughly a hundred dollars ahead. Until now they had butted heads infrequently during the course of the night.

On the first go-round Virgil was dealt three kings. He was under the gun, seated next to the dealer, and he opened the betting for ten dollars. Todd studied his cards a moment then called and raised twenty dollars. The miner, unable to match the bet, dropped out. Virgil called the raise and, with only a slight hesitation, bumped it another twenty. Todd gave him a peculiar look and just called.

When the dealer announced "Cards to the players,"

Virgil drew two cards. He collected them as they were dealt and slipped them beneath the three kings. Without looking at them, he began riffling the cards one over the other, awaiting Todd's call. Todd tossed two cards into the deadwood, silently extending two fingers. The miner slid two cards across the table, and Todd folded them into his hand. He also began riffling his cards, staring now at Virgil.

There was something impenetrable about Virgil in a poker game. His composure was monumental and his expression betrayed nothing of what he was thinking. He held his cards slightly above table level and slowly spread the three kings. Then he inched the fourth card into view, saw the ace of diamonds. Finally, with a flick of his thumb, he spread the fifth card. He sat there a moment, his face unreadable, staring at the case king. He'd drawn an unbeatable hand.

Folding his cards, Virgil pushed a stack of chips into the pot. "Opener bets forty."

Todd squeezed his fifth card into view. He grunted and looked up with a wide peg-toothed grin. "See your forty and raise—fifty."

"Your fifty," Virgil said impassively, "and another hundred." A muscle twitched in Todd's cheek. He scrutinized Virgil a moment, then shook his head. "I think you're bluffing. How much you got in front of you?"

Virgil carefully counted his chips. He glanced up, his features wooden. "Three hundred and change."

"Close enough," Todd said with a terse nod. "I tap you out."

Todd shoved all his remaining chips into the pot. By now a crowd had gathered around the table. They watched intently as Virgil moved stacks of chips to the center of the table.

"You're called," he said in a neutral voice.

Todd laughed, fanning his cards faceup. "Read 'em and weep. Four jacks!"

"Other way 'round," Virgil said, spreading his hand on the table. "I caught the fourth king."

A hush settled over the room. Todd stared down at the cards with shocked disbelief. His face was white and pinched around the mouth.

"Some people—" Todd faltered, slowly sank back in his chair. "Pure outhouse luck, that's all it was!"

"I couldn't agree more, Avery. Tonight was my night."

"Goddamn if it wasn't."

Todd rose and pushed through the crowd. As Virgil sat staring at the mound of chips, a buzz of excitement swept through the onlookers. He wagged his head, finally allowed himself a smile.

"You and me," he said to the miner. "I never quit a game when I'm the big winner. Want another try?"

"Thanks all the same." The miner collected his few remaining chips. "Wouldn't have believed that hand unless I'd dealt it myself. Two of you with four of a kind!"

"Mister, you can deal to me anytime. Cards don't fall any better than that."

The crowd began drifting away as Virgil got to his feet. He scooped the mound of chips into his hat and unhooked his cane off the back of the chair. As he passed by Holliday's table, the gambler nodded to him with a wry smile. He hobbled toward the front of the room.

Earp stood at his usual position, at the end of the bar. His attention was fixed on one of the faro tables when he caught Virgil out of the corner of his eye. He glanced around, then took a second look as he saw the hat overflowing with chips. His mouth split in a grin.

"Looks like your lucky night."

"You should've seen it," Virgil said with a wide smile. "Drew four kings and an ace!"

"Godalmighty," Earp said, astonished. "You couldn't be beat."

"Hell, that's only the half of it. Avery Todd was holding four jacks."

"That must have made some pot. How much did you win?"

"Haven't counted it," Virgil said. "I'd judge pretty close to a thousand dollars."

Earp laughed. "Sounds like you're on a hot streak."

"Maybe so, but I'm still gonna call it a night. I'm plumb tuckered out."

"Your leg bothering you?"

"Not so bad," Virgil said. "Keeping up with you and Doc wears me out. I'm not used to the sporting life anymore."

"Stick around," Earp suggested. "Another hour and things will start to wind down. We'll go get something to eat."

"I'll pass." Virgil dumped the chips on the bar. "Do the tally and credit my account. I'm headed home."

"Whatever you say, lucky. Take it easy on the leg."

"I'll see you tomorrow."

Virgil started toward the door. Earp felt a moment's concern that he would be walking the streets alone. But Virgil would have laughed at the notion and gone ahead anyway. Since the court hearing, calm had prevailed, with no word of Brocius or Clanton. So there was probably nothing to worry about.

Still, had Morgan been there, he would have insisted that Virgil accept an escort home. But Morg's shoulder had sufficiently recovered for him to resume work, and tonight was his night to ride shotgun on the stage to Tucson. Virgil would have laughed at the idea of an escort anyhow, and probably refused. Sometimes Earp wished his brothers weren't so hardheaded.

His attention drifted back to the faro layout.

The night was pitch-black. Streetlamps glowed along the street, casting dim shadows off the buildings. Somewhere in the distance a dog barked. Across the street from the Oriental a structure was being erected. The Huachuca Water Company had torn down the old building and was in the process of constructing new offices. Timbers and scaffolding rose in skeletal outline for the two-story building.

Frank Stilwell stood hidden in the darkness of the construction site. Spread out around him, concealed behind vertical timbers, were Pete Spence, Florentino Cruz, and Ike Clanton. The men wore heavy mackinaws against the cold, and they were all armed with shotguns. They had been waiting since shortly after midnight.

Pete Spence had proved to be an admirable spy. Working out of his lady friend's house, he had scouted the Earps' movements for three days and three nights. The time for an ambush, he'd determined, was in the early morning hours. Around four o'clock, when the Oriental closed down, the Earps and Holliday walked over to the Eagle Lunch Counter. Their late night meal was the only time, night or day, that they were all together.

Brocius had placed Stilwell in charge of the ambush. Stilwell was unconcerned that Brocius and Ringo had stayed behind at the ranch. He saw tonight as a chance to prove himself as a man who could be trusted with a tough job. In particular, he wanted to earn the praise of Ringo, who was clearly the brains of the gang. His one reservation was that he'd been forced to bring Ike Clanton along. He thought Brocius showed weakness by not having killed Ike long ago. A coward with Judas leanings was a bad combination.

Hidden in the darkness, Ike was scared and cold. His nerves were on edge and he felt jittery about the job ahead. No one except himself had seen the Earps and Holliday in action. Though they were armed with shotguns, he wasn't convinced that only four men were equal to the task. He inwardly cursed Brocius and Ringo for playing it safe, again dumping the risk on someone else. The cold and the fear ate at him, and he wondered if he would end the night alive. He fought to keep his teeth from chattering.

The door of the Oriental suddenly opened. A man

stepped outside and crossed the boardwalk. Even in the shadowed light of the streetlamps, there was no mistaking his identity. He leaned heavily on a cane, and as he started across the street, a noticeable limp was apparent in his stride. There was no doubt that it was Virgil Earp.

Ike felt bombarded with questions. Why was he alone? And where were the others? Would they follow him out in the next instant? What the hell was Stilwell waiting on? Like a spring coiled too tight, Ike suddenly snapped. He stepped from behind the timbers, raising the shotgun to his shoulder as he thumbed back the hammers. The sound was crisp and metallic in the still night.

"No!" Stilwell hissed. *"Goddammit!"*

The warning came as Ike fired. He tripped both triggers in a double roar. Spence and Cruz, skittish themselves, were galvanized by the blast. Streaks of flame a yard long spewed from the muzzles of their shotguns. The figure in the street staggered sideways as though struck by a giant fist. Then his arms windmilled wildly as he was hammered again and again by loads of buckshot. His legs collapsed.

"Take off!" Stilwell shouted. "Run!"

The four men scrambled through the framework of the building. At the rear of the structure they sprinted down an alley and turned toward Fremont Street. A block over, in another alley, they reached their horses. A moment later they pounded out of town.

On the still night air acrid gun smoke drifted from the skeletal framing of the Huachuca Water Company. All around town, alerted by roars like thunder, dogs went wild in frenzied barking.

Virgil lay sprawled in the street.

# Chapter Thirty-One

THE HAMMERING ROAR OF GUNFIRE BROUGHT play at the tables to a halt. There were four blasts in rapid succession, and Earp instantly catalogued it as shotgun fire. He rounded the corner of the bar at a run.

Inwardly cursing himself, he rushed toward the door. Some wayward instinct, which he'd ignored, had warned him not to let Virgil walk the streets alone. There was scarcely any doubt in his mind as to what awaited him outside. All the more so since he had heard no return fire from a pistol.

Holliday was only a step behind as he went through the door. Their pistols drawn, they moved out of the spill of light from the door onto the boardwalk. Neither of them needed to say aloud what they were both thinking. The gunmen could still be waiting, knowing they would rush to Virgil's aid.

The glow of a streetlamp bathed Virgil in a spectral light. He lay crumpled on his side, unmoving, his legs twisted at an odd angle. Earp cautiously checked along the street, staring intently at the darkened structure of the Huachuca Water Company. There was no one in sight.

"Cover me," he said. "Keep an eye on the water company."

Holliday brought his pistol to shoulder level, thumbed the hammer. Earp stepped off the boardwalk, scanning the street as he moved forward. He quickly closed the distance and dropped to one knee beside Virgil. In the glow of the streetlamp he saw that the shotguns had done a savage job. The buckshot had blown away part of Virgil's coat, and what lay underneath was thick with blood. His left arm dangled by a thread of bone and flesh at the elbow.

Earp searched for a pulse and found a faint beat. "Get some help out here!" he yelled. "Send somebody for Doc Goodfellow."

Several men were now crowded into the doorway of the Oriental. Holliday waved them forward and sent one to find the surgeon. The others hurried to Earp's side, their faces gone solemn at the sickly sweet scent of blood. Under Earp's direction, careful of the dangling arm, they gently lifted Virgil from the ground. He led them toward the Occidental Hotel.

The desk clerk looked startled when Earp opened the door, pistol still in hand. Then his face blanched as the men carried Virgil into the lobby, blood dripping across the carpet. Earp motioned with the pistol.

"Open the dining room," he ordered. "Have somebody fire the stove and start boiling water."

The men carried Virgil into the dining room. A long serving table was pulled directly underneath an overhead lamp. The table was covered with white cloth and the desk clerk quickly lit the lamp. The clerk moved aside as the men gingerly lowered Virgil onto the table. The white tablecloth almost immediately went red with blood.

Holliday pushed through the men. He stopped at the table and pressed his fingertip to the vein in Virgil's neck. A silence settled over the room as he slowly counted to himself. Several moments slipped past before he looked up at Earp.

"Fairly strong for all the blood he's lost. I think he's got a chance."

Earp nodded. "What about his arm?"

"Looks bad," Holliday said. "We'll just have to wait for Goodfellow."

Virgil's eyes rolled open. He blinked, momentarily blinded by the overhead light. Then he focused on Earp. "What happened?"

"Take it easy," Earp said. "You've been shot."

"Yeah—" His throat went dry and he swallowed. "Out in the street."

"Did you see any of them?"

"No," Virgil said, suddenly lucid. "Where am I?"

"The hotel," Earp replied. "We're waiting on Doc Goodfellow."

"How bad is it?"

The shock wore off and a streak of pain shot through Virgil. His face constricted in agony and his body went rigid. Beads of sweat formed on his forehead and his mouth opened in a low groan. His features were ashen.

"Out of the way! Let me through."

A path cleared as Dr. Goodfellow hurried into the dining room. He placed his black bag on the table beside Virgil's leg. He quickly checked Virgil's eyes and then took his pulse. Finished, he glanced at Holliday.

"Get these men out of here."

Holliday cleared the room. As he closed the door to the lobby, Dr. Goodfellow began his examination. He took surgical scissors from his bag and started cutting the clothing away from Virgil's upper body. With Earp and Holliday assisting, he slowly peeled off the blood-soaked clothing and dropped it on the floor. At last Virgil lay bare above the waist.

"All right," Goodfellow said. "Roll him onto his right side. Be damned easy about it."

While the doctor supported Virgil's left arm, Earp took his shoulders and Holliday grasped his legs. Virgil choked back a scream, then blacked out as they rolled him over. Goodfellow stooped down, clucking softly to himself as he inspected the wounds. The buckshot had ripped through Virgil's left side, slightly above waist level. The slugs had exited at the rear, near the backbone, stripping flesh into a raw mass.

Goodfellow worked swiftly. He cleaned the wounds with warm water, followed by an alcohol-based solution.

While Virgil was unconscious, he began suturing the larger wounds with neat rows of stitches. He was quick and precise, moving along the back and around to the side. After tying off the last suture, he bandaged the wounds with strips of clean bed sheet. Satisfied for the moment, he ordered them to roll Virgil onto his back.

The dining room door burst open. Allie rushed through the entrance, breathing hard. Someone had thought to summon her, and after hurriedly dressing, she'd run all the way from the house. A rictus of horror crossed her face as she approached the table. She stared down at Virgil's inert form, appalled by the sight of so much blood. Huge tears welled up in the corners of her eyes.

"Dear God," she moaned. "Will he live?"

"Too early to say," Goodfellow told her. "Don't you get hysterical on me, Allie. I have to work fast if we're to save him."

"I won't bother you. I promise."

Goodfellow turned his attention to the elbow wound. A load of buckshot had shattered the bones and torn flesh away from the joint. What remained was a bloody pulp flecked through with bone chips. As he completed his inspection, Virgil's eyes opened. Allie moved closer to the table.

"I'm here, honey," she said. "I'm right here."

"Allie." Virgil groaned, blinking against the overhead light. "Jesus, it hurts."

Goodfellow took a spoon and a bottle of laudanum from his bag. He popped the stopper from the bottle with his thumb. "I'll have to knock you out, Virgil."

"Why?"

"Are you alert enough to understand what I'm saying?"

"I guess so."

"Then listen to me," Goodfellow said. "The buckshot passed through your side and back. So far as I can tell, your spine wasn't damaged."

Virgil wet his lips. "I'll be able to walk?"

"Yes, I think so," Goodfellow said cautiously. "But your left elbow is in bad shape. I may have to amputate."

"My arm!"

Virgil craned his head around and looked down at his elbow. His jaw muscles clenched as he stared at his mangled arm. He lay back against the table, staring into the light. "Wyatt?"

Earp bent forward, blocking out the lamplight. "What is it, Virg?"

"Don't let him take my arm," Virgil said weakly. "If I check out, I want both arms with me."

"Come on, Virg, no more talk like that. You'll pull through just fine."

"Wyatt . . ." Virgil held his gaze. "Give me your word."

"Look here," Goodfellow interrupted. "Anything could happen once I start operating. You'll have to leave that decision to me, Wyatt."

"You heard him," Earp said steadily. "Do what you have to do. But don't take his arm."

"For God's sake, that's insanity. I won't be responsible."

Allie looked at the surgeon. "I'll be responsible. Just do what Virgil says."

"Suit yourself," Goodfellow said grudgingly. "Allie, I want you and Wyatt out of the room. Doc, will you assist me?"

Holliday shrugged. "I'm your man."

"Let's get to it, then."

Earp led Allie from the room and closed the door. Holliday began spooning laudanum into Virgil while the surgeon laid out his instruments. Once the opiate took effect, Goodfellow went to work with a scalpel. He first removed damaged flesh and ligaments, and then picked the wound clean of bone chips. That done, he cut deeper into the elbow and removed four inches of bone. Once he'd tied off the blood vessels and sutured the skin flaps, he dropped his instruments in a pan of bloody water. He glanced up at Holliday.

"Waste of time," he said. "Nothing but a broken wing—or worse."

The arm appeared limp and floppy, oddly reduced in size at the elbow. Holliday stared at it a moment, then nodded. "Good thing he's right-handed."

Something more than an hour had passed while the operation was under way. When Allie was again admitted to the room, she went directly to Virgil's side. Goodfellow waited until Earp entered, then closed the door. His expression was grave.

"I've done everything possible. But I have to tell you, that arm should have been amputated."

Earp glanced at the table. "Will he pull through?"

"I wouldn't hazard a guess. Quite frankly, it could go either way."

"How long before we know?"

"All depends," Goodfellow said. "If gangrene sets in, I'll have no choice but to amputate. We'll have a better idea in three or four days."

"I'm obliged," Earp said. "I know you did your best."

"I'm going to wash up. I suggest you get him a room here in the hotel. He shouldn't be moved any distance."

Goodfellow walked toward the rear of the room, where a light burned in the kitchen. Holliday left Allie at the table and joined Earp near the door. His sallow features were set in a grim cast.

"Helluva note," he said. "Even if Virg comes through, he'll be a cripple."

"Goodfellow says he still might have to amputate."

"I've got an idea it won't happen. Virg would rather be dead."

A silence fell between them. They stood for a moment watching Allie bathe Virgil's forehead with a damp cloth. Holliday suppressed a cough, pulling the whiskey flask from inside his jacket. After a long drink, he stoppered the flask and put it away. He nodded toward the table.

"Hate to say I was right," he observed. "Winning in

court didn't solve anything. They're still out to put us under."

"Tell you, Doc," Earp said. "As of tonight, it's the other way 'round."

"How so?"

"You remember, you said we ought to take the fight to them?"

"Yeah?"

"Brocius better be on the lookout. We're headed his way."

# Chapter Thirty-Two

Early THE FOLLOWING MORNING VIRGIL WAS moved to a room on the second floor. With Allie supervising, four men carried him upstairs on a stretcher. He was still heavily dosed on laudanum, and hardly aware of the move. His room was across the hall from Earp and Holliday.

After Virgil was settled, Holliday went off to catch a few hours sleep. Downstairs, in the lobby, Earp arranged with the desk clerk to provide anything needed for the care of his brother. The dining room, still splattered with blood, had been closed to the breakfast trade. Swampers were busily scrubbing the floor in time for a noon opening.

Earp debated whether or not to change clothes. But he finally decided that time, rather than his appearance, was a greater factor. Shortly after seven o'clock he emerged from the hotel and walked uptown to the telegraph office. There, he composed and paid for two telegrams, one to Tucson and the other to Nogales. The telegraph operator gave him a strange look, but wisely made no comment.

On the street again, Earp walked over to the *Epitaph*. The door was locked, and he thought it curious that John Clum had not contacted him about the shooting. Late last night, following Virgil's operation, the new town marshal, Jim Flynn, had stopped by the hotel. Earp's report was short, and sparse on detail, and Flynn's questions were hardly more than a formality. There was small likelihood that either he or John Behan would conduct an investigation. Still, it seemed odd that Clum had not appeared at the hotel.

Downtown, Earp stopped off at the Eagle Lunch Counter. He ordered a breakfast of steak and eggs, with sourdough biscuits and black coffee. Everyone in the cafe had heard of the shooting, and several men inquired about Virgil's condition. As his food was served, Earp saw Lou Rudabaugh pass by the front window. The mine owner seldom ventured downtown, and a lunch counter was not his type of establishment. He entered the door and moved directly to an empty stool beside Earp. His expression was grim.

"I just now heard," he said. "I went by your hotel, but the dining room was closed. They thought you might have come here for breakfast."

"Lost track," Earp said. "Occurred to me a while ago I hadn't eaten since yesterday evening."

The waitress drifted over, but Rudabaugh waved her off. He turned back to Earp. "I understand your brother survived the shooting. How's he doing?"

"Doc Goodfellow thinks he'll make it. Virgil's strong as an ox. That ought to help."

"I'm relieved to hear it," Rudabaugh said with a note of sympathy. "Do you know who's responsible?"

"Brocius," Earp said flatly. "Nobody else had a reason to back-shoot Virgil."

"Are you going to press charges?"

"No."

"Why not?"

"Couple of reasons." Earp took a bite of steak and chewed thoughtfully. "First, Johnny Behan would just go through the motions. Nothing would ever come of it."

"I'm sure you're right," Rudabaugh said. "And the second reason?"

"I prefer to handle it myself."

"You mean—go after Brocius on your own?"

"Who better?" Earp replied. "That's the only way it'll ever be ended."

"Come now, Wyatt," Rudabaugh said uneasily. "You

can't take the law into your own hands. You have no legal
authority."

"There's more than one way to skin a cat."

"What's that supposed to mean?"

"Don't worry about it, Lou. I won't do anything to harm
the election."

Rudabaugh looked offended. "But you won't tell me
your plans?"

"Not yet," Earp said with a cryptic smile. "Maybe later
today."

"Be very careful, Wyatt. We've come too far to upset the
apple cart now."

"Your apples are safe, Lou. Take my word for it."

Rudabaugh clearly wasn't satisfied with the situation.
Yet he saw that Earp had said all he was going to say for
the moment. He reconciled himself to await developments
and hope for the best. After they shook hands, he hurried
off uptown.

Earp finished breakfast with a second cup of coffee. He
was not concerned with Rudabaugh's opinion one way or
another. From a political standpoint, he had come to realize that Rudabaugh needed him far more than he needed
Rudabaugh. For now, his attention centered on Virgil's immediate welfare. And his plans for Curly Bill Brocius.

When he returned to the hotel, he found John Clum
seated in the lobby. The editor looked weary and drawn,
his features somehow troubled. He jumped to his feet as
though jabbed by a sharp stick.

"How's Virgil?" he said nervously. "I understand he's in
a room upstairs."

Earp wagged a hand. "For someone who took four shotgun blasts, he's not too bad. The doc says he's still liable to
lose his left arm."

"It's a wonder he wasn't killed."

"They tried, John. Tried damned hard."

"I know." Clum averted his gaze. "The word's around
town they have a list—a death list."

"Figures," Earp said. "Who'd you hear this from?"

"Everyone's talking about it. They say Virgil's only the first."

"Then Doc, and Morg, and myself. Nothing new there."

"I'm new," Clum said, his features pale. "From what I hear, my name has been added to the list. For all the articles I've written about them."

"Wouldn't discount it," Earp said. "On the other hand, rumors are a dime a dozen. You just never know, John."

"Wyatt, you'll think I'm a coward . . ."

"Coward?"

"I'm leaving town." Clum's voice was an octave too high. "Tonight, on the evening stage. I won't let happen to me"—his voice cracked—"what happened to Virgil."

Earp studied him a moment. "Are you leaving town for good?"

"No, not for good. Just until this blows over. Until the killing stops."

"Where will you go?"

"Anywhere," Clum said softly. "Anywhere that's safe."

"What about the *Epitaph?*" Earp asked. "You're leaving Tombstone to Harry Woods and the *Nugget.*"

"Wyatt, I feel like I'm deserting you. I'm ashamed of myself, more than you can imagine. But not too ashamed to stay here and get killed."

"No apologies needed, John. Hell, in your place, I might do the same thing. I'm just too hardheaded to quit."

They parted on that note. Clum's eyes were moist when they shook hands, and his voice failed him. He walked out the door with a sad smile and an air of defeat. Earp wondered how Lou Rudabaugh, and local Republican leaders, would react to the news. He thought there would be harsh words spoken in Tombstone tonight.

Upstairs, he rapped lightly on the door to Virgil's room. Allie's voice sounded from inside, and he identified himself. She unlocked the door, a pistol in hand, and he entered the room. Her features were haggard, her eyes rimmed with fatigue. Virgil was asleep, tinges of blood dried black on his bandages.

"Any change?" Earp asked.

"Not that I see," Allie said. "Thank God for laudanum, though. He's suffering something terrible."

"When will Doc Goodfellow be back?"

"He said sometime this morning."

"Tell him to stop by my room."

"All right."

Her voice was at once subdued and aggrieved. Earp scrutinized her a moment. "You must be worn-out yourself."

"Don't worry about me," she said. "I'll get along."

"All the same, I'll send someone to fetch Jane. She can spell you looking after Virg."

Her eyes flashed. "You're a great one for looking after people, Wyatt. Why don't you try doing it before they get shot?"

"Fault me all you want," Earp said quietly. "Just remember, I was his brother long before you were his wife. I couldn't feel any worse about what's happened."

"Really?" she said, staring at him. "Then why don't you put an end to it? Get us out of here before it's too late."

"Allie, once a man starts running, he never stops. I'll tend to this in my own way."

"Oh, I never had any doubt about that! The question is, who will get killed before it ends?"

"Head of the list is whoever shot Virg."

Earp walked from the room. As he stepped into the hall, Sadie appeared at the top of the stairwell. She ran forward and took him in her arms, as though to console him. Her oval features were framed in a sorrowful expression.

"One of the girls just woke me," she said. "I can't tell you how terrible I feel about Virgil. How is he?"

"Hurt bad, but still alive. There's a chance he might lose his left arm."

"Omigod, how awful! You must be desolate."

Earp nodded. "I'd sooner it was me than Virg. I'd gladly trade places with him."

"Don't say that," she implored. "You mustn't blame yourself."

"Come on into the room. I have to shave and change clothes."

"Aren't you going to get some rest?"

"Not anytime soon."

They crossed the hall to his room. She had never been there, and she was intrigued by the pervasive masculine sense of his living quarters. A rifle stood propped in one corner, and several pairs of boots lined the wall next to the wardrobe. Shaving gear was arranged on the washstand, and hooked on a nearby wall peg was a woolen robe. A moment later one of the housemen appeared with hot water Earp had ordered before coming upstairs. She took a seat in an easy chair while he began stropping his razor.

"Why are you changing? Are you going somewhere?"

Earp soaped a shaving brush and began lathering his face. "I've got things to arrange," he said. "Morg's scheduled back on the evening stage. We'll be leaving tomorrow."

"Leaving?" she said, concerned. "Leaving for where?"

"Ike Clanton's ranch."

The worry lines around her eyes deepened. Before she could reply, there was a knock at the door. Earp dropped his shaving brush and crossed the room. When he opened the door, a telegraph delivery boy stood in the hallway. The boy's eyes darted between Sadie and Earp's soap-lathered face.

"Telegram for you, Mr. Earp. Two of 'em."

"Here you go, sonny."

Earp gave him a silver dollar and closed the door. He tore open the first telegram and read it. The dateline was Nogales, Mexico.

YOUR   TERMS   ACCEPTABLE   STOP   ARRIVE   TOMBSTONE

TOMORROW LATEST WITH JACK JOHNSON AND JACK VERMILLION
STOP

                                        SHERM MCMASTERS

Folding the slip, Earp opened the second telegram. The
dateline was Tucson.

  REGRET   NEWS   ABOUT   VIRGIL   STOP   FULLY   UNDERSTAND
SITUATION   THERE   STOP   AS   OF   THIS   DATE,   YOU   ARE   HEREBY
APPOINTED DEPUTY U.S. MARSHAL STOP

                                        CRAWLEY P. DAKE
                                        U.S. MARSHAL
                                        ARIZONA TERRITORY

A tight smile touched the corner of Earp's mouth.
Handing the second telegram to Sadie, he moved back to
the washstand. She read it through as he began shaving.
Her eyes suddenly widened.

"You've replaced Virgil?" she asked. "You're the new
marshal?"

"Federal marshal," Earp noted. "Go anywhere, arrest
anybody."

The razor moved swiftly across his jawline. He smiled at
himself in the mirror.

# Chapter Thirty-Three

HALF THE TOWN WAS DUMBFOUNDED. THE OTHER half was fascinated by what had now become a deadly vendetta. The news sent Sheriff John Behan into a snorting rage. Once again he had been reduced to second fiddle.

Earp's commission, being federal, superseded both local and county authority. He was the top lawman in all of southern Arizona, and unlike his brother, there was no question that he would use the badge to force the issue. The balance of power, virtually overnight, had changed hands in Tombstone.

Doc Holliday was almost gleeful. For cool nerve and audacious action, it was a brilliant gambit. With one stroke Earp had risen above personal motives and assumed an enormous advantage over the Brocius gang. Privately, Holliday told himself that dead or alive was no longer an issue. So far as he was concerned, he saw no reason to take prisoners.

Earp convened a war council in his hotel room. Present were Holliday and Morg, who had arrived on the stage from Tucson yesterday evening. There as well were Turkey Creek Jack Johnson, Texas Jack Vermillion, and Sherman McMasters. The three men had ridden straight through from Nogales, arriving at the hotel late last night. The meeting had been put off until morning, so everyone would be rested for the job ahead. After a solid breakfast, they waited now for Earp to lay out the plan.

"First things first," he said. "Everyone raise their right hand."

Looking from one to the other, Earp administered the

oath and swore them in as deputy marshals. Overnight he had commandeered badges from the town marshal's office, and he now passed them out. The badges were stamped DEPUTY MARSHAL, and served well enough for a federal commission. The men pinned them to their shirts without comment.

"Let's get down to business," Earp said. "This morning, the doctor told me he thinks Virgil's out of the woods. So the charge will be attempted murder of a federal officer."

"What about warrants?" Morgan inquired. "How do we get around that?"

"We know who pulled the trigger, but we can't prove it. So our official position is that we're bringing them in for questioning."

"And if they resist arrest?"

Holliday laughed. "Why hell, Morg, they're bound to fight. We're countin' on it."

"Yes and no," Earp said. "Ike turned yellow last time, and he might again. I want it understood that anybody who surrenders gets taken into custody. Everyone clear on that?"

"Whatever you say," Holliday agreed. "But I still think it's a damnfool mistake. If we'd killed him last time, there would be one less to worry about now."

Sherm McMasters, who was seated on the edge of the bed, looked up. "Any idea how many ambushed Virgil?"

"There were four shots," Earp informed him. "That could mean four men, one shot each. Or it could mean two men, with double-barrel shotguns."

"Either way, we're six. I like the odds."

Holliday thought it a practical comment by a practical man. He and Earp had known Sherm McMasters since their Kansas days. Through him, after their move to Tombstone, they had met Johnson and Vermillion. The three men were gamblers and friends, associates of a sort. They were also given to violence at the slightest provocation. South of the border they were known as *pistoleros.*

Watching them now, Holliday thought they were a breed of men uniquely common to the border. At one time or another they had all served as deputy sheriffs or deputy town marshals. Yet they preferred the sporting life, the freedom of vagabond gamblers. In Mexico, where the law was generally whatever a man enforced himself, they had found absolute freedom. Still, when the money was right, they were not above lending their guns to a cause north of the border. Unlike hired assassins, they were not professional killers. They were mercenaries who worked within the law.

Whatever they were being paid, Holliday knew that Earp had got his money's worth. The three men were hardened by time, and experience had made them pragmatic. In particular, their service as lawmen had taught them that an even break was the stuff of dime novelists and dead fools. Whenever possible, a man got the drop on his opponent, and survived by the shoot-first credo. Mc-Masters, Johnson, and Vermillion were, in his opinion, perfect for the job. They would kill anyone who offered resistance.

"Tell you the truth," Earp said now, "we don't know the odds. After the shootout here in town, that left only Brocius, Ringo, and Clanton."

"Some gang!" Vermillion snorted. "Three men."

Holliday was struck by a fit of coughing. The others watched as he pulled out his flask and took a long slug. When he got his breath, he looked at Vermillion. "Ringo's got a reputation for being quick with a gun. Anybody gets the chance, take him first."

McMasters scratched his jaw. "Sounds like you're not real sure what we're up against."

"Nothing hard and fast," Earp admitted. "Brocius laid low after the dustup here in town. We haven't heard anything about him in better than two weeks."

"So we're sorta headed into it blind?"

"Sherm, anything's possible with this bunch. For all we

know, Brocius recruited himself some more men. Just no way to tell."

Morgan shifted around in his chair. His shoulder was still stiff and he slowly rotated his arm. "Tell you what," he said. "I'd be surprised if anybody joined his outfit. Not after we buried three of them."

"On the other hand," Holliday observed, "new men in the gang might've given Brocius some backbone. Maybe that's the reason Virgil got bushwhacked."

Earp motioned for silence. "We'll know how many there are when we find them. Let's leave it at that for now."

"Suits me," Holliday said. "The more, the merrier."

Earp checked his pocket watch. "Sherm, you and the boys get some fresh horses at the livery. Be ready to pull out by noontime."

McMasters nodded. "I'll see to it."

"So what's the plan?" Morg asked. "Are we headed for the Clanton place?"

"Straight as a string," Earp said. "I want to be on the San Pedro by midnight. We'll hit them just after dawn."

"To quote Robert E. Lee . . ." Holliday paused with a wry smile. "Surprise is half the battle."

"Whoever said it, I mean to take them off guard."

"Wyatt, you're finally talkin' my kind of fight."

The dawn sky was metallic, almost colorless. The men were crouched low in an arroyo, their eyes trained on the ranch house. Behind them the San Pedro snaked southward, and the mountains to the east were limned in the first rays of sunrise. Alert, their nerves keyed to a fight, they waited for Earp's signal.

During the night, riding west toward the San Pedro, Earp and Holliday had discussed plans for their raid on the ranch compound. Earp had advanced the argument that a manhunt was not all that different from a cavalry troop chasing hostile Indians. Swift strikes and the element of surprise were everything to an experienced commander.

Time had demonstrated that cavalry tactics, while simple, were deadly effective. Hit fast, hit hard, and strike when the enemy least expected an engagement. A strike at dawn had proved to be the single most effective maneuver in the army's tactical handbook. The trick worked equally well against outlaws, when they were sodden with sleep and unprepared for a fight. The edge for lawmen, no less than soldiers, was the tactical advantage of surprise.

By midnight, when they turned south along the San Pedro, their plan was formulated. An hour before dawn, when they tethered their horses downstream, Earp handed out assignments for storming the compound. McMasters, Johnson, and Vermillion would take the bunkhouse and the attached cook shack. Holliday and Morgan, along with Earp himself, would take the main house. The raid, Earp had informed them, would be carried out as though all the buildings were occupied. Surprise and caution, he'd warned them, were the watchwords.

Soon after dawn the sun crested the distant mountains. Earp waited until the glare of the fireball was at their backs, then he gave the signal. The men scrambled out of the arroyo and rushed across an open stretch of ground. Near the corral they separated into two groups. Johnson hurried toward the cook shack, while McMasters and Vermillion burst through the door of the bunkhouse. Earp, with Holliday and Morgan on his heels, stormed into the main house.

Holliday and Earp quickly checked the bedrooms at the rear of the house. All were empty, and looked as though no one had slept there in several days. Morgan came out of the kitchen as they returned to the front room. He shook his head, indicating he'd found nothing. Walking to the fireplace, Earp bent over and stuck his hand deep into the ashes. He straightened up, affirmation written across his features.

"Stone cold," he said. "Hasn't been used for at least two days."

"Bastards!" Holliday cursed. "They probably cleared out the same night they shot Virgil."

"Left in a hurry, too." Earp gestured at a disarray of clothing and gear scattered about the room. "I'd judge Brocius decided it was time to pull a disappearing act."

Holliday pondered a moment. "Sort of sets you to thinking, doesn't it?"

"Yeah." Earp looked at him as though reading his mind. "They might have been after all of us, not just Virg. Maybe they shot him because he's the only one who showed that night."

"Or by accident," Holliday added. "Somebody might've got jumpy and fired too soon."

Morgan appeared confounded. "What the hell are you two talkin' about?"

"A mix-up," Earp said. "The four of us generally leave the Oriental together every night. But that night, Virg was tired and decided to go home early."

"And you . . ." Holliday motioned at Morgan. "You were on the stage run to Tucson. Starts to sound like an ambush that went wrong."

Earp nodded. "They probably figured to kill all of us in one lick. Something happened to spoil their plan."

"Christ," Holliday said, somewhat startled. "That means they were trailing us, watching our movements. They had us staked out."

"Question is, who?" Earp said with a perplexed look. "We would have spotted Brocius or Ringo, and Clanton for sure. So who was their lookout?"

Holliday grunted. "Goddamn good question."

McMasters appeared in the doorway. He jerked a thumb outside. "Nobody in the bunkhouse," he said. "Way it looks, they hightailed it in a big hurry."

"Same here," Earp remarked. "We were expected."

"What makes you think so?"

"Tell you about it later, Sherm. You boys get the horses."

Some ten minutes later McMasters and his men brought

the horses from downstream. Holliday and Morgan stood by the corral, watching as Earp searched the shoreline west of the river. Suddenly he stopped, dropping to one knee, and studied the ground. He took a smudge of dirt between his fingers, nodding to himself as though the earth possessed some secret knowledge. Then he rose and walked back to the corral.

"A washout," he said. "That last snowfall melted off and ruined the tracks. All I could tell is that they headed west."

"Chapter and verse," Morgan said glumly. "Those stage robbers we chased started out the same way. Then they doubled back into New Mexico."

McMasters tugged at his ear. "Seems pretty clear these boys figured you'd come gunnin' for 'em and they got spooked. You think they skedaddled out of Arizona?"

"Possible," Earp allowed. " 'Course, I'd shy away from second-guessing this bunch. They've fooled us before."

"Amen to that," Holliday affirmed. "Any idea from the tracks how many rode off?"

"The ground turned to mush and then dried out. No way to tell."

"So where do we go from here?"

"We'll try Will Claiborne," Earp said. "I recollect hearing his place is just outside Charleston. Maybe he's got some answers."

"And if he doesn't?"

"Ask me then, Doc."

An hour later Charleston proved to be a washout as well. The saloonkeeper informed them that Will Claiborne had departed town the day their court hearing was concluded. Nor had there been any sign of Brocius, Ringo, or Clanton for the past three days. Other than that, the saloonkeeper volunteered no further information. He seemed a man who believed that lockjaw was the safest course.

Their manhunt suddenly took on all the aspects of a wild-goose chase. Earp saw nothing to be gained by scouring the border or blindly searching the vast countryside. Their quarry had gone to ground, perhaps quit Arizona Territory altogether. Early that evening, they rode back into Tombstone, where Sherm McMasters once again voiced his opinion. He was convinced that the men they sought were long gone.

Neither Earp nor Holliday were persuaded. Though they kept it to themselves, they shared an uneasy hunch. One of their gambler's hunches.

The game had yet to be played out.

# Chapter Thirty-Four

THE WOOD CAMP LAY ON THE WESTERN SLOPE OF the Dragoon Mountains. Some ten miles northeast of Tombstone, it was off the beaten track, tucked away in a remote stretch of wilderness. The owner of record was Pete Spence.

The terrain was heavily forested, climbing steeply eastward into the Dragoons. The camp itself was situated in a small canyon, beside a swift-flowing stream. Surrounding hills were studded with trees, and the site was virtually invisible from a distance. From the southwest, a rocky path into the canyon bordered the stream.

Pete Spence derived a steady profit from the camp. Firewood, the only source of heat during the winter, was in great demand from homes and businesses in Tombstone. The camp was operated by Ramon Vazquez, a Mexican working for Spence, who lived there year-round with his wife Maria and their two children. Vazquez harvested the trees, split them by hand, and hauled the firewood into Tombstone by wagon. There it was delivered to a regular list of customers.

An enterprising man, Spence operated other sidelines as well. He was an accomplished if somewhat occasional horse thief, and the wood camp served as a way station for stolen stock. A split-rail corral held the stock until brands were altered and allowed time to heal. The horses were then sold to a crooked livestock dealer in Bisbee, who falsified the papers. The operation was profitable, yet risky enough that Spence limited his activities. Horse thieves, if caught, were summarily strung from the nearest tree.

Maria Vazquez, Ramon's wife, was the sister of Florentino Cruz. Through them, Spence had met Cruz, and
brought him into the horse stealing operation. Frank
Stilwell, during his short stint as a deputy sheriff, had
stumbled upon their sideline. For a share of the profits,
he'd obligingly kept the information to himself. Later, after
his tenure as a lawman, he had recruited Spence and Cruz
into the business of payroll robbery. The wood camp had
served as their hideout.

The canyon had now become more hideout than wood
camp. Ramon no longer felled trees, but instead assisted
his wife in the kitchen. Their cabin was small and comfortable, sufficient for themselves and their children. Yet
Spence's cabin, a short ways upstream, had become an
overcrowded bunkhouse. Two days ago Spence had ridden
into the canyon with Cruz, Stilwell, and three other men.
They were all quartered in Spence's cabin, with most of
them sleeping on the floor. Ramon and Maria, now reduced to servants, were kept busy preparing meals morning through night.

Tonight, Maria was deeply concerned for her brother.
She could overlook horse stealing, and turn a blind eye to
payroll robbery. But these new men, particularly the ones
named Brocius and Ringo, were clearly dangerous. When
she served their meals, they ignored her, as though she
were deaf or couldn't speak English. From their talk it was
evident that they had botched the job of murdering the
former town marshal, Virgil Earp. Worse, it was plain that
they were planning further violence, the work of *asesinos*.
She feared for her brother's life.

The talk took on a serious note as she began clearing the
dinner dishes. The men were seated around the table in
her cabin, with Ramon in the kitchen and the children
already in bed. The talk centered around the ranch of the
one called Ike Clanton. She gathered that he had somehow
been responsible for spoiling their previous murder attempt. From what she'd overheard, Brocius had given him

a severe beating. His lips were still puffy and one eye was the color of rotten plums.

"One thing's for sure," Ike said peevishly. "We gotta do something or I'll never get my ranch back."

"Had a good thing there," Brocius mused aloud. "Off in nowheres and still close to the border. Place was made to order for rustlin'."

"Forget the ranch," Ringo said bluntly. "Unless we kill Earp, our rustling days are over. Leastways, we're finished in Arizona."

"Earp?" Brocius repeated. "Don't you mean the Earps *and* Holliday?"

"Forget them, too. Wyatt Earp's the only lawman left in the whole bunch. Says so right there."

Ringo gestured to a copy of the *Nugget,* which Ramon had brought from a supply trip to town that afternoon. Brocius stared at the newspaper. "I still say we gotta kill'em all. Whole hog gets the job done."

"C'mon, Bill," Ringo said. "Put your thinkin' cap on. With Earp dead, we're back in business. Holliday wouldn't even stick around for the funeral."

"He's right," Stilwell chimed in. "Holliday's no dummy. Without Earp's badge to hide behind, he'd make tracks muy pronto."

"Don't like it," Brocius grumped. "We set out to get'em all. I say we finish it."

"Business is business," Ringo said. "Kill Earp and we're home free. Why make it difficult?"

Spence bobbed his head. " 'Specially when it ain't that easy to catch'em all together. We done found that out."

"Yeah, the hard way." Brocius glared at Ike. "Wasn't for you, I'd still be sleepin' in a comfy bed back at the ranch. Feel like whipping your ass all over again."

"Chrissake," Ike whined. "Lemme be, won't you, Bill? Done told you I was sorry."

"Sorry won't get it," Ringo said sternly. "We've got to plant Earp six feet under. That's the only answer."

"Awright then!" Brocius conceded, waving his arm. "You're so hot to do it, what's your plan?"

Ringo shrugged. "No sense making another try at the Oriental. They'll be on guard there."

"So what's that leave?"

Ringo considered a moment. His gaze drifted to Pete Spence. "You're sure the Earps never spotted you? When you were spying on them?"

"Never had a clue," Spence said. "I'm real careful that way."

"What about the woman you stayed with? She suspect anything?"

Spence smiled. "She's only got one thing on her mind when I'm around. Damn woman's crazy for me."

Ringo glanced at Brocius. "I say we send Pete back to town. Let him scout things out. Earp's bound to have a weak spot."

"Don't bet on it," Ike said sullenly. "The bastard's got brass balls. Listen close, you'll hear'em ring when he walks."

"Close your trap." Brocius scowled, then looked across the table at Spence. "Don't bring me back no half-baked scheme this time. It's gotta be the straight goods. You savvy?"

"I'll leave now," Spence said. "Warm my toes with that little widder woman tonight."

Spence walked to the door. A deck of cards appeared and a bottle made the rounds at the table. From the kitchen, Maria Vazquez watched them drink and silently crossed herself. She exchanged a look with her husband.

He slowly shook his head.

Marietta Latham threw a filmy housecoat on over her nightgown. The low rapping at the front door caught her just as she was about to crawl into bed. The lamp in the bedroom was still burning, a shaft of light spilling out into the hallway. She hurried toward the door.

The rapping became more insistent. She fluffed her hair, pulling her housecoat tighter. She opened the door and her eyes went round. Spence stood on the front porch.

"Pete!"

"In the flesh."

Spence took her by the waist, lifted her into the air. He kissed her soundly on the mouth, kicking the door closed with his boot heel. She squealed with delight and threw her arms around his neck.

"You're back," she said happily. "So soon."

Spence lowered her to the floor. "Got my business finished up in Bisbee. Rode straight through to get here."

She simpered. "Just to see me?"

"Who else, you little wildcat? Last time left me wantin' more."

Marietta was small and compact, with high, firm breasts and a narrow waist. Her auburn hair was upswept and her china-blue eyes danced with merriment. She almost purred under Spence's touch.

A year ago her husband had dropped dead from a heart attack. The local gossips liked to say that Marietta, who was twelve years younger, had killed him in bed. But she blithely ignored the gossips, for the sale of her departed husband's mercantile store had left her a lady of means. Still, she found that she missed being married.

Of all her beaus in the past year, Pete Spence was the most promising. He was rough around the edges, sometimes uncouth, but a herculean lover. His business as a horse trader kept him on the move and made for infrequent visits. Yet he was on her doorstep again, his second visit within a week. She thought her enticements were working marvelously well. He might be persuaded to stay longer.

Spence unpinned her hair, which cascaded down to her shoulders. A tingle ran through her as she saw the now familiar gleam surface in his eyes. She snuggled against his chest as he lifted her in his arms and carried her toward the bedroom. A moment later his gun belt hit the floor, followed by his boots. Then, as he stepped out of his trousers, she extinguished the lamp.

The next morning Marietta cooked him a large breakfast. Spence was an early riser, and a man of boundless energy. Over the past year, when he'd visited, he had been content to expend that energy in her bed. But today, and during his lengthy visit a week ago, something had changed. She noticed he was curiously on edge, anxious to get out of the house and roam around town. She had no idea where he roamed, or why, but it was no cause for concern. He returned periodically during the day, and always at night, though frequently quite late. His excuse was the press of business, and she thought that encouraging. She hoped it might keep him in Tombstone on a more regular basis.

Yet she noticed something else as well. Last week, and now again today, he went to the front windows, checking the street before leaving the house. She found it odd because it was unusual, as though he was looking for someone on the street. Still, as she'd learned with her late husband, men were often put out of sorts with a woman's curiosity. So long as he returned every night, she was con-.tent to have him there.

Spence was indeed looking for something unusual. On his last trip into Tombstone he had trailed the Earps around town for days. He knew that Earp and Holliday rarely ventured outside their hotel before noon. Holliday, like clockwork, devoted day and night to poker games at the Oriental. Morgan, riding shotgun for Wells Fargo, was on two days, back and forth to Tucson, then off a day. Virgil, confined now to a bed at the hotel, was no longer a factor.

In fact, with the exception of Earp, none of them interested Spence. His assignment was to find a time and place where Earp could be taken off guard. He knew that Earp's afternoons were usually occupied with business affairs, and the evenings split between his lady friend and the Oriental. Daytime was too risky for an ambush, and the Oriental, after the fiasco there, was no longer an option. So in Spence's mind, that left the girl singer at the Birdcage Theater. Earp would have to be trapped with her, at night, either on the street or in her hotel room.

Spence decided to track the girl. Her movements would be the key as to a time and place where Earp might be trapped. While the daytime was out, it was nonetheless important to know her habits. By ten o'clock he was seated in a saloon on Allen Street. Across the way, through the front window, he had a direct view of the Grand Hotel.

Thinking back, he remembered that Earp was an unpredictable lover. Sometimes he spent the night in the girl's room, and other times he stayed at the Oriental until it closed. So a pattern had to be found, a regular time when Earp was in the girl's company. He was still pondering on it when she emerged from the hotel shortly before noon. She was a looker, and it troubled him that she might get caught in the cross fire. A nice piece of fluff like her deserved better.

But then, on second thought, he decided that it was out of his hands. Brocius would kill anybody to get at Earp.

He followed her toward the center of town.

# Chapter Thirty-Five

**S**ADIE FINISHED DRESSING. SHE GLANCED AT THE clock and saw that it was almost five. Moving to the wardrobe, she inspected herself in the mirror. She particularly wanted to look her best tonight.

A good part of her afternoon had been devoted to shopping. She'd bought a new hat, trimmed with colorful feathers, and a velveteen dress in sapphire-blue. Then she had hurried back to the hotel with the boxes, and taken a quick bath. The last step had been her hair and just a touch of makeup.

All the while her mind had been on Wyatt. Late that morning a message had been delivered to her room. He had returned last night and wanted to have dinner with her this evening. Though the message had said nothing more, she knew that his trip had not gone well. Otherwise he would not have returned so soon.

She was torn by mixed emotions. Clearly, he had not found the Brocius gang, and that made her happy. One of her most vivid memories was the terror she had experienced the day of the gunfight beside Fly's boardinghouse. Then, only a few nights ago, Virgil being shot down in the middle of the street: had Wyatt been there, he might have been crippled as well, or worse.

On the other hand, she felt terrible for Wyatt. His ambition to be sheriff was a driving force in his life. Yet he'd been deserted by John Clum, just at the point when he needed newspaper coverage more than ever. No less critical, his political backers were growing increasingly nervous with the continuing violence and death threats. The solution, of course, was to put an end to Brocius and his gang of cutthroats. Which again placed Wyatt in harm's way.

She found no easy answer to her own fear. Or her concern that he would not succeed in his campaign for sheriff. Given a choice, she would have had him leave law enforcement altogether. He was clearly an astute businessman, with a great future in the world of finance and investment. But with his appointment as deputy U.S. Marshal, he'd been drawn even more deeply into the violence and killing. She knew it would be futile to ask him to take off the badge. Not while Virgil's assailants were still at large.

As she turned from the mirror, there was a knock at the door. She squared her shoulders and forced herself to smile. Whatever happened, she was determined not to show her fear. She opened the door, laughing gaily, and pulled him into the room. Her arms went around his neck and she gave him a long, smoldering kiss.

"Well—" he said, taken aback. "I ought to go away more often."

"Don't you dare!" she said, leading him to a small sofa in the sitting area. "I want you right here . . . all the time."

"Suits me," Earp said, still holding her hand. "Fifty miles on horseback gets old real quick."

"Was it bad?"

"Not bad, just a waste of time. Brocius was long gone when we got there."

She felt a kindling of hope. "Maybe he ran off to California, or somewhere."

"Maybe so." Earp looked unconvinced. "Wherever he is, he's gone to ground. I guess he knew Virgil was the last straw."

"I went by the hotel yesterday. Virgil was asleep, but Allie and I talked for a while. She's such a nice woman."

"The woman's a rock, and good thing, too. She's always there when Virg needs her most."

"How is he?" she asked. "Any improvement today?"

"Some," Earp said. "He's still in a lot of pain. But Doc Goodfellow was a little more optimistic. Thinks he might be able to save Virg's arm."

"That's wonderful!" She paused, noting the downcast expression on his face. "Or is it?"

"Not when you think about it. I shouldn't have promised Virg he could keep his arm. Unless he wears a sling, it'll flop like a wet noodle."

"You mean, he won't have any control at all?"

Earp looked away. "There's not enough left of his elbow to do any good. He's a one-armed man."

"But he's alive," she said encouragingly. "From what Allie told me, he's a very lucky man."

"Yeah, I suppose so. A busted wing and a gimpy leg. Not bad for two shootouts."

"Wyatt, honestly! It could have been worse."

"I know," Earp said. "I think about that a lot."

She sensed that his mood had turned morose. His features were wooden, but there was guilt in his voice.

"Be honest," she said. "Are you blaming yourself for what happened to Virgil?"

Earp was silent, as though he'd departed the room a moment. "The night it happened," he said quietly, "I should've made Virg wait. He had no business walking the streets by himself."

"Ask yourself this—could you have stopped him?"

"No, but I could've gone with him. I should have."

"Suppose you had," she said. "Would it have changed anything? Perhaps you wouldn't have been as lucky as Virgil."

Earp laughed, a sardonic sound. "Some men weren't meant to be killed. I'm one of them."

"How can you be so certain?"

"After a while, you get to know somehow. All the times

you should've been killed and you weren't. Maybe it's a sixth sense."

She suddenly realized that he wanted to talk. Not to anyone else, but to her. Her intuition told her that he had never shared such thoughts with his brothers, or Doc Holliday, or anyone. His reserve, the deep reluctance to reveal himself, was now gone. He needed her more than he needed his secrets.

"When you—" she started, then changed directions. "Have you lost your fear of being . . . hurt? Or is it faith in yourself?"

"Little of both," Earp said. "Fear gets put aside, or lost somehow. You concentrate on what has to be done."

"Is it so important to you to be a law officer?"

"When I first came here, it was the last thing on my mind. But with high rollers, the financiers and mine owners, I found out that business and politics go hand in hand. To get ahead in one, I got drawn in by the other."

"Lou Rudabaugh," she said knowingly, "and George Parsons. They convinced you to run for sheriff."

"All part of the bargain," Earp acknowledged. "Not that they're too keen on the way things worked out. I spent most of the afternoon listening to Rudabaugh complain."

"Complain?" she sniffed. "It seems to me that he got the best of the bargain. I don't see anyone shooting at him."

"Lou's a born worrier. He thinks I've let personal matters get in the way of politics."

"Are you talking about Virgil . . . and Brocius?"

"That's his beef," Earp said. "According to him, people think I'm using the law to settle a personal score. He's concerned the governor will try to revoke my U.S. Marshal's appointment."

"Could he?" she asked. "Does the governor have that power?"

"A demand from the governor would carry a lot of weight in Washington. He could probably get me fired."

"Do you think he actually would?"

"I think Rudabaugh's just trying to browbeat me. Not that it makes any difference one way or the other. I'm willing to risk being canned as marshal."

She was concerned. "Wouldn't that hurt your chances of being elected sheriff?"

"Probably," Earp said matter-of-factly. "Rudabaugh made the same point, over and over again. I told him that was the breaks of the game."

She saw now that nothing would dissuade him. He was willing to jeopardize Lou Rudabaugh's support, even the election itself, to avenge his brother. She admired his determination, and at the same time, she feared the price he might have to pay. Yet, given his force of character, she would have expected nothing less of him.

"So you'll continue searching for Brocius?"

"No choice," Earp said. "It's just a matter of who finds who first."

"Are you serious?" she said, alarmed. "You think he's still after you?"

"Brocius and Ringo are back-shooters by nature. But that doesn't make them cowards. They play the odds and try to stack the deck. Sooner or later, they'll try it again."

"Then you don't believe they've left Arizona?"

"Not for a minute," Earp said firmly. "I upset their gravy train, and they want it back. To get it, they'll have to get me."

"But if you get them!" She clapped her hands and laughed. "That means you'll win the election. Doesn't it?"

"I'd say that's a safe prediction."

"Aren't you the clever one, Mr. Earp?"

"I'm glad you think so."

"What I think—" She glanced at the clock. "Omigosh, we have to have supper. I can't be late to the theater."

"Delmonico's or the Maison Doree?"

"Whichever you prefer. Just make very sure you pick me up after the last show. No excuses!"

"Sounds like a winner to me."

Outside the hotel they turned uptown. On the opposite side of the street, Pete Spence trailed them by half a block. He was amused, and envious, at the way the girl clung to Earp. She was animated, talking a blue streak, clearly smitten with the great lawman. He followed them to Delmonico's.

Not quite an hour later they emerged from the restaurant. Spence again trailed a short distance behind, mingling with the crowds on the boardwalk. When they stopped outside the Birdcage Theater, he stepped into Hatch's Saloon & Billiard Parlor. Through the front window, he watched as the girl stood on tiptoe and gave Earp a peck on the cheek. She rushed inside as Earp walked off toward the Oriental.

Spence turned from the window. He moved to the bar and ordered a drink. The saloon offered a perfect vantage point for keeping an eye on the girl. Later tonight, when the Birdcage closed, he would wait to see if Earp called for her or met her at her hotel. In the meantime, he would have a drink and shoot a few games of pool. The click of billiard balls from the back of the room sounded inviting.

Bob Hatch, the saloonkeeper, brought his drink over. "You a pool player?"

"I try my hand every now and then."

"Well, mister, if you like billiards, come around tomorrow night. We've got a big match laid on."

"Yeah?" Spence sipped his whiskey. "What's so special about it?"

Hatch grinned. "Couple of cham-peens, that's what."

"Anybody I ever heard of?"

"George Berry, for one. He's a whiskey drummer out of St. Louis. Slick as an eel with a pool cue."

"Who's he playin'?"

"Morgan Earp," Hatch announced. "Regular goddamn wizard on a pool table."

Spence spilled his drink. "We talkin' about the same Earp? One of the Earp brothers?"

"None other," Hatch said. "Last time Berry was through here, Earp beat him out of three hundred simoleons."

"And Berry's here now?"

"Arrives tomorrow on the noon stage. Wired ahead by telegraph and challenged Earp to a match for five hundred dollars."

"No joke?" Spence tried to appear casual. "I heard Earp got busted up in that shootout last month. That gonna slow him down?"

"Not that you'd notice," Hatch remarked. "We're giving even odds on the match, take your pick."

"Think Wyatt Earp's gonna bet on his brother?"

"Already has," Hatch said. "Him and Doc Holliday both. Got reserved seats for'em tomorrow night."

"You must be expectin' a big turnout."

"Mister, you'd better get here early. It'll be standing room only."

Hatch moved away to serve another customer. Spence looked beyond the bar to the billiard room. There were two pool tables and a snooker table, end to end in an attachment built onto the back of the saloon. His eye was drawn to a side door, opposite the center pool table. The upper half of the door was framed in glass.

The setup, Spence told himself, was made to order. Tomorrow night the two Earps and Doc Holliday would be in the same place at the same time. Which was the exact thing Brocius had been clamoring for all along. Spence downed his drink, the plan already forming in his mind.

He hurried out of the saloon.

# Chapter Thirty-Six

"TEN BALL IN THE CORNER POCKET."

Morgan leaned over the pool table. He stroked the cue stick with a practiced hand and cleanly sank the ten ball. The cue ball magically reversed itself, spinning backward on the green felt, then rolled to a stop near the left-hand side pocket. The angle was perfect for his next shot, on the eleven ball.

"Would you look at that position? Talk about blind luck!"

George Berry's tone was bantering, slightly envious. Standing nearby, he watched as Morgan eyed the eleven ball. Earp and Holliday, who were seated on a bench along the far wall, exchanged a knowing glance. Spectators, and hecklers, they were having a good laugh at Berry's expense. No one spoke as Morgan sliced the eleven into the side pocket. Quickly, calling his shots without hesitation, he cleaned the table. When the fifteen ball dropped, he looked up with a wide grin. He winked at Earp, then glanced across the table at Berry.

"Tough break," he said with mock sympathy. "You had it sewed up till you missed the ten ball."

"We're not done yet," Berry said confidently. "Before it's over, I'll still trim your wick. Another fifty says it's so."

"You're on!" Morgan mugged, playing to the spectators. "Like taking candy from a baby."

The onlookers laughed appreciatively at Morgan's gibe. Hatch's Saloon & Billiard Parlor was packed, the crowd pulling for the hometown player. To make room for spectators, the front pool table and the snooker table at the rear had been closed to play. Crammed shoulder to shoulder on benches, men lined the walls around the center table.

The score was eight to five, Morgan's favor. They were playing rotation pool, a game in which the balls were pocketed in consecutive number. By mutual agreement, every ball had to be called in a designated pocket. The winner of the match would be the first man to win fifteen games. The stakes were now $550, winner take all.

"Don't get too cocky," Earp said, gesturing with his cigar at Morgan. "Do your strutting after you win."

Morgan cracked a wiseacre grin. "Just call me bull-of-the-woods. I can't be beat."

"Tall talk," Berry said in a jesting voice. "We'll see who has the last laugh."

"C'mon, George," Morgan rejoined, waving his cue stick like a wand. "Rack the balls and watch my stuff."

Berry shook his head, walking to the end of the table. He was a heavyset man, on the sundown side of thirty, with the florid features of a drinker. His line was fine spirits, but west of St. Louis he was universally known as a whiskey drummer. His skill at pool was a lucrative supplement to his regular income. Having lost to Morgan the last time he was in town, he was determined to win tonight's match. The crowd was just as determined to see him lose.

While Berry racked the balls, Morgan chalked his cue and prepared to break. The pool table was ornate, hand-carved oak, with ivory inlay on the rails, and an overhead lamp bathed the table in brilliant light. The side door, with glass in the upper panel, led to the alleyway. Up front, a crowd was ranged along the bar. It was nearing midnight, and the murmur of their conversation was sportive, well-laced with liquor.

Morgan dropped the four and the nine on the break. Talking and shooting, he then ran the one through the seven. The eight ball lay flush against the rail, offering a difficult bank shot. He took a moment to study the angle, and finally addressed the cue ball with a great show of confidence. The eight ball zipped across the table, caught the corner of the pocket, and bounced erratically to the far rail. His grin faded and he gave the eight a look of raw disbelief. Berry laughed out loud, moving into position.

"Stand back, my good man! Gimme room!"

Stepping aside, Morgan halted beside Earp and Holliday. They immediately began razzing Berry, who returned their gibes with vulgar good humor. No slouch on a pool table, he pocketed the eight ball with a double bank shot. The cue ball rolled into perfect position, and he took a vaudevillian bow. Then, calling his shots, he began running the table with methodical precision.

Watching him, Holliday reflected on the vagaries of gambling, and to a larger extent, life itself. In a swift flight of mind, he realized that only three days had passed since Virgil had been gunned down. Somehow it seemed much longer, and far more wearing than he might have expected. The general consensus around town was that Brocius and his band had quit Arizona Territory. There was speculation that they had retired to less hazardous pursuits after the failed attempt on Virgil's life. The most common theory was that they had taken refuge somewhere in Old Mexico. On either side of the border all was peaceful, uncommonly quiet. Which convinced many people that the bloodshed had at last ended.

Holliday thought their assessment of Brocius was far too optimistic. An outlaw might tuck tail and run for cover, but that made him no less dangerous. In Holliday's experience, a back-shooter was the most tenacious of all mankillers. Some perverted sense of pride, harnessed with an obsession for revenge, gave them extraordinary patience. He knew of instances where such men had waited for years, nursing a long-forgotten grievance, before they struck. He considered it very probable that Curly Bill Brocius was just such a man.

A murmur from the crowd intruded on Holliday's wool

gathering. Berry had cleaned the table swiftly, demonstrating his skill with several difficult shots. While Morgan racked the balls, Berry marched around the room, encouraging the spectators to greater appreciation. The response was a scattering of catcalls and joshful boos. The crowd, for the most part, had their money on Morgan.

Berry broke the balls with a resounding crack. The six, nine, and twelve were blasted into pockets, and the others spread out in a favorable pattern across the table. Working quickly, he then proceeded to run the table with a steady click-click-click. Pocketing the fourteen, he drew the cue ball the length of the table for perfect position on the fifteen. He tapped it in with a broad smile.

The score now stood at eight to seven.

The riders crossed Toughnut Street at the east end of town. They rode four abreast, their features cloaked in shadow where the streetlamps ended. Farther upstreet, miners wandered in and out of whorehouses lining the red-light district. The sound of a rinky-dink piano drifted on the still air.

A pale sickle moon lighted the sky. The riders held their horses to a walk, forming into single file as they moved through a passageway separating darkened buildings. On the other side they emerged into an alley that bisected the block between Toughnut and Allen streets. Directly across the alley was the rear of Hatch's Saloon & Billiard Parlor.

Frank Stilwell signaled a halt. He had again been selected to ramrod the operation. With him were Pete Spence, Florentino Cruz, and Ike Clanton. He was cautious tonight, his nerves considerably more on edge than last time. Brocius had made it clear that failure would not be brooked, no excuses accepted. His orders, stated in no uncertain terms, were to kill Wyatt Earp. Nothing less would do.

Yet, for all his wariness, Stilwell was nonetheless confident. The report delivered by Pete Spence had set everyone's spirits to soaring. By sheer happenstance, the Earps and Holliday would be gathered in the same place at the same time. A pool game, perhaps the last thing any of them would have expected, was the magnet for the gathering. Given any luck at all, there would be three funerals tomorrow.

The riders dismounted. Stilwell had elected to bring their horses closer to their work. With the saloon full, and a risk of pursuit, he meant to ensure a speedy escape. The men stood for a moment, staring across the alley, where the billiard room jutted out from the surrounding buildings. A shaft of light streamed from the window in the back door.

"Ike," Stilwell said in a low, raspy voice, "you hold the horses. Make gawddamn sure you're here when we get back."

"Well, hell," Ike said peevishly. "Where would I go?"

"Listen to me, you little sonovabitch! You mess up again and I'll personally cut your nuts off."

Stilwell turned to Cruz. "You stay here and give us covering fire. Anybody comes out of there when Pete and me head back this way, you blast his ass good. Got it?"

"*Si*," Cruz mumbled. "Nobody follow you."

"Awright, Pete," Stilwell said. "Let's get it done."

Spence and Stilwell started across the alley. Ike collected the reins of all four horses and turned them heading back toward Toughnut Street. Cruz positioned himself for a clear field of fire on the billiard room.

He watched as Stilwell and Spence approached the back door.

Morgan was at the table. The score was now nine to seven, his favor, and he was about to run out. George Berry, who had missed a tough shot in the last game, was nursing a beer. His attention was focused on the table, and the crowd waited expectantly. Their man was about to make it ten to seven.

Morg dropped the fourteen ball and stood back to survey the last shot. He was directly across the table, facing Earp and Holliday, on line with the side door. As he chalked his cue, one of the saloon regulars, Butch Corbin, walked back to have a look. Wobbling slightly, Corbin appeared to be feeling no pain. He listed to a stop beside Holliday and focused a bloodshot gaze on the pool table.

"I got four bits says Morg makes it."

"Four bits!" Morgan laughed. "Bet your whole backroll, Butch. It's a lead-pipe cinch!"

"No, make it four bits," Berry said humorously. "I'll cover it, and I wouldn't want your friend to go away busted."

"That's a helluva note," Morgan said with a mocking smile. "Sounds like you're trying to shark me."

"Totally unnecessary," Berry needled him. "You're getting ready to miss that shot. I can see it in your eyes."

"Good try, but you just lost four bits. I couldn't miss that shot if my hands were tied! You hide and watch."

Morgan chuckled and stepped in behind the cue ball. The fifteen ball was opposite him, almost directly in line with the side pocket. He dabbed chalk on the tip of his cue stick and checked the angle one last time. Then he leaned forward over the table.

The upper panel in the alley door suddenly erupted in a sheet of flame and shattered glass. The roar of gunfire swept through the room like a drumroll. Morgan screamed and dropped the cue stick. His hands clawed at empty air, then he fell on top of the pool table and slowly crumpled to the floor.

Shots snicked across the room in a hailstorm of lead. Earp and Holliday, miraculously unscathed, flung themselves off the bench. All around them slugs thunked into the walls and exploded the bench in a shower of splinters. George Berry staggered, struck by a wayward bullet, and collapsed as though his legs had been chopped off. In the same instant, Earp rolled across the floor toward the end of the pool table. A split second later he rose to one knee, drawing the Colt. He leveled his arm and thumbed three quick shots through the alley door.

Then, as suddenly as it began, the firing ceased. A haze of gun smoke hung over the pool table and a tomblike stillness descended on the room. For a moment, frozen in the eerie quiet, no one moved.

Holliday broke the spell. Circling the pool table, he crossed the room and flattened himself against the wall. Then he jerked open the door and moved swiftly into the alleyway. He crouched low, his Colt extended and cocked.

Ahead he saw dark figures sprinting away. Before he could fire, the night blossomed with the muzzle flash of a pistol from the opposite side of the alley. A slug fried the air around his ears, and three more shots hammered out in rapid succession. The door, standing open behind him, rocked backward under the impact of lead. He got off one shot, then jumped through the doorway. A moment later he heard the pounding thud of hooves fade into the distance.

Turning into the billiard room, Holliday found Earp kneeling beside Morgan. His gaze dropped to the youngster, and he saw immediately that it was hopeless. Morgan had been hit several times, one of the slugs drilling through his back and exiting high on his chest. His shirtfront was splotched with blood.

Morgan groaned, his breathing rapid and uneven. His eyes focused on Earp and a trickle of blood seeped down his chin. The corners of his mouth lifted in a ghastly smile.

"Looks like my last game."

"Hang on," Earp muttered softly. "The doc's on his way."

"Funny." Morgan blinked, casting his eyes about, "I can't see a damn thing."

A shudder swept over him and his mouth opened in a long sigh. One boot heel drummed the floor in a spasm of afterdeath. Then he lay still.

Several moments passed in stunned silence. All the color leeched out of Earp's face and he stared stonily down at his brother. His face was blank, but his jaw muscles ticked as though he were trying to say something. At last Holliday bent forward and placed a hand on his shoulder.

"He's gone, Wyatt."

Earp might have been deaf, for there was no response. His face became congested and the veins in his temple knotted into purple ropes. He couldn't look away from the body.

"Wyatt." Holliday gently shook him. "It's no use. He's dead."

Earp seemed to awaken. He shrugged off Holliday's hand, took a deep breath and blew it out heavily. Almost tenderly, he reached down and closed Morgan's sightless eyes. Then he climbed to his feet.

"Somebody get the undertaker. I want him looked after proper."

The night lay gripped in a mealy, weblike darkness. A clot of men stood watching from the saloon door. The undertaker and his assistant had already loaded Morgan into the hearse. Now, carrying the shroud-wrapped body of George Berry, they crossed the boardwalk.

Some moments later, their task completed, they closed and latched the rear doors. Walking forward, they mounted the driver's seat from opposite sides. The undertaker gathered the reins and clucked to his team of matched coal-black geldings. The hearse moved off upstreet and slowly disappeared into the night.

Under a nearby streetlamp Earp stared after the hearse until it vanished. Then his gaze shifted to the men crowded in the doorway, and he waited as they moved back inside the saloon. Finally he glanced at Holliday.

"Find Sherm McMasters and the boys. They're likely in a poker game somewhere."

Holliday nodded. "What do I tell them?"

"Tell them we ride tomorrow. We won't be back till we've found Brocius."

"Where are you going?"

"To the hotel."

Earp stepped off the boardwalk. His shoulders were slumped as he started across the street. A sense of desolation seemed to match him stride for stride.

He wondered how he was going to tell Virgil.

# Chapter Thirty-Seven

"ARE YOU SURE ABOUT THIS?"

"Not absolutely certain. I just think it's very strange."

Allie studied the woman a moment. She had known Marietta Latham since moving to Tombstone. Their houses were across the street from one another, and they often exchanged pleasantries on the street. The gossip about her was something Allie had chosen to ignore. Until now, it was none of her business.

The hour was early, and Allie was still in her housecoat. The Latham woman had appeared at the hotel only moments before, and proceeded to spill out her suspicions. The story sounded oddly plausible, and the woman's physical appearance somehow made it even more credible. A dark bruise, now turning purple, covered her left cheek.

Allie turned, glancing back at the bed. Virgil was still asleep, and she was fearful of waking him. Last night, his face sagging with grief, he had cried when told of Morgan's death. After Earp left, she'd held him, trying to console him. But he seemed to have lost the spark of life, the will to fight. He had finally drifted off into a troubled sleep.

"Come with me, Marietta."

Allie led the way across the hall. She knocked on Earp's door, and heard the creak of floorboards as he crossed the room. She knew he would have a gun in his hand.

"Who's there?"

"Wyatt, it's Allie. Let me in."

The door opened and Earp stepped back. He was fully dressed, having already paid a visit to the funeral parlor earlier that morning. Holstering his pistol, he looked from one to the other. His features were drawn, a grim visage.

"What is it, Allie?"

"Wyatt, this is Mrs. Marietta Latham. She lives across the street from me."

Earp nodded. "I've got no time for talk, Allie."

"You will have," she said plainly. "Mrs. Latham thinks she knows who killed Morgan."

"How would she know that?"

"Let her tell you herself. I don't want to leave Virgil alone."

Allie started away, but Earp's voice stopped her. "Go knock on Doc's door. Tell him to come in here."

She turned away, and Earp waved Marietta Latham into the room. "Have a seat, Mrs. Latham."

"Thank you." She seated herself in one of the chairs. "I'm so sorry about your brother, Mr. Earp."

"How'd you hear of it?"

"One of the neighbor women dropped by early this morning. Her husband was at Hatch's last night . . . when it happened."

"So you came to Allie," Earp observed. "Why not come to me? Didn't you know I'm a U.S. Marshal?"

"Yes, I knew," she said. "But we've never met. I thought it best to start with Allie."

Earp looked her over carefully. She was attractive, with a trim figure, and dressed with some taste. Her most distinctive feature today was the ugly bruise on her cheek.

Holliday appeared in the doorway. Earp motioned him inside, waiting until he'd closed the door. He then performed the introductions, waving Holliday to the other easy chair. He took a seat on the edge of the bed.

"Doc, I want you to hear this. Mrs. Latham claims to know who killed Morgan."

Holliday's eyes narrowed. "That's a serious accusation. How did you come by the information?"

She blushed, then recovered herself. "I suppose there's

.no need for modesty. I'm a widow and I have a gentleman friend. At least, I thought he was a gentleman . . . until yesterday."

"What happened yesterday?" Earp asked.

"Well, he went out early and stayed gone all day. Then he came rushing in and began collecting his things."

"Does he live with you?"

"Only when he's in town," she said. "He's a horse trader and he travels a lot."

"What's his name?"

"Spence. Pete Spence."

Earp and Holliday exchanged a look. The name meant nothing to either of them. "Go on," Earp prompted her. "What happened next?"

"I tried to stop him," she said. "He was stuffing things in his saddlebags, and he wouldn't tell me why he was leaving. He was in a terrible hurry."

"How long had he been staying with you?"

"Just the one night. That's why I got so upset. A lady doesn't like to be treated like . . ."

Her voice trailed off and Earp nodded. "I understand," he said gently. "Tell it in your own way."

"Well, I became insistent, and he got madder and madder. Then he hit me—with his fist."

Her hand went to the discolored splotch on her cheek. Earp and Holliday were smooth interrogators, having worked together many times in the past. Holliday adopted a skeptical tone. "That's it?" he said. "Spence hit you, and that makes him a murderer?"

"Of course not," she said, clearly offended. "There were other things, lots of things."

"Such as?"

"For one, the way he was always hovering around the front windows. I didn't put it together until I remembered the last time he was here."

"When was that?"

She looked at Earp. "Don't you see, that's what made

me suspicious. I thought back, and he ran out on me the same way last time. The night before your other brother was shot."

"Virgil?" Earp said. "He was in town then?"

"For three days," she replied. "And he kept hanging around the windows then, too. I think he was watching your brothers. From my window, you can see both their houses."

"What did he do during the daytime? At night?"

"It was always the same. He'd be gone most of the day and return late at night. Sometimes not until four or five in the morning."

Earp and Holliday stared at her with deadpan expressions. Yet the same thought took root in their minds. Someone knew their habits, which meant they were being followed. They had suspected it when Virgil had been ambushed. After last night, with the attempt made on all their lives, their suspicion had turned to certainty. Someone was trailing them, and that someone might be Pete Spence.

"Out of curiosity," Earp said in an offhand manner, "does Spence have any friends here in town—besides you?"

"I often wondered about that," she said guilelessly. "Gone all day and out to all hours of the night. Where did he go?"

"Did he ever mention anyone by name?"

She considered a moment. "Yes, now that you ask, there were a couple of men. Pete owns a wood camp in the Dragoon Mountains. He likes to brag about his business ventures." She paused, thinking about it. "He sometimes joked about a half-breed who works for him. I believe the name was Cruz. Florentino Cruz."

The name meant nothing to Earp. He shrugged, holding her gaze. "And the other man?"

"Oh, that's easy. Everyone knows Frank Stilwell. After all, he was a deputy sheriff. Pete said they'd gone into the horse-trading business together."

Earp and Holliday swapped a quick glance. "This wood camp?" Earp inquired. "Do you know where it's located?"

"As a matter of fact," she said brightly, "Pete told me it's near the headwaters of San Palo Creek. He once bragged that he'd homesteaded the land."

"Anyone else?" Earp said. "Did he ever mention the names Brocius, or Ringo?"

"No, not that I recall."

Earp rose to his feet. "I want to thank you, Mrs. Latham. You've been a great help."

"Then you believe Pete's responsible—for your brothers?"

"When we find him, we'll have a better idea."

"Well, box his ears for me," she said, rising from her chair. "Imagine, hitting a woman!"

Earp showed her to the door. "We'll take care of it, Mrs. Latham."

"You know," she said on her way out, "I think he stayed with me just to spy on your brothers. I hope he ends up on the gallows!"

"Whew," Holliday said as the door closed. "Talk about a woman scorned. Given the chance, she'd probably shoot Spence herself."

"I think he's our man," Earp commented. "It explains how they knew we'd all be in Hatch's last night."

"Way I figure it, there were at least three, maybe four men. Definitely two men at the door doing the shooting. Then a third who covered them from across the alley."

"Their getaway was timed to the second. So it's likely a fourth man held their horses."

"Question is," Holliday mused, "who were the shooters?"

"They're all guilty," Earp said tightly. "The horse holder as much as whoever pulled the trigger."

"Yeah, but how does that explain Spence? Until today, we never heard of him."

"Doc, it's like links in a chain. Spence was tied in with

Frank Stilwell, and Stilwell used to work for Behan. Add one more link and you come to Brocius."

"Dovetails in another way, too. You'll recall the rumor that Stilwell had gone into robbing payrolls. Word was, he had two partners."

"Spence and Cruz," Earp said. "Which further explains why Spence was spying on us. Likely as not, Brocius recruited the three of them into his gang."

"All hangs together," Holliday agreed. "Spence already had a thing going with the Latham woman. So Brocius got himself a ready-made spy in the deal."

"One we didn't know and had no reason to suspect. That made it easy for Spence to trail us around town."

"Like we figured, they were after the four of us the night they got Virgil. No question about last night, of course. You and me were targets the same as Morg."

A shadow crossed Earp's face. The mention of Morgan's name was like salt poured into a wound. For a moment his mind flashed back to last night, the gunfire and the blood. Then he shook it off.

"Way I tally it," he said, "three and three makes six. Brocius, Ringo, and Clanton from the original bunch. Then, however the connection was made, they recruited Stilwell, Spence, and Cruz."

Holliday nodded, thoughtful. "You think Johnny Behan knew anything about it?"

"Doc, I wish to hell we could prove it. I'd add his name to the list."

"So where do we go from here?"

"The courthouse," Earp said. "I'm going to have a talk with Judge Spicer. Tell him what we learned from the Latham woman."

Holliday smiled. "I assume you'll ask him to issue arrest warrants?"

"Once he hears the story, I think he'll go along. We'll make it nice and legal this time."

"Want me to go with you?"

"Got another job for you," Earp said. "Get Sherm and the boys ready to move out. Extra cartridges all around, and whatever foodstuffs they can cram in their saddlebags."

Holliday looked at him. "Sounds like you're planning a long campaign."

"We'll travel fast and light. Wherever they run, we'll follow."

"You figure to hit Spence's wood camp first?"

"This afternoon," Earp told him. "I just suspect that's their new hideout. Probably been there since Virgil was shot."

"Maybe we'll get lucky," Holliday said. "We might catch the whole bunch with their pants down."

"We'll take it as it comes. Either way, we don't quit until the job's done."

"Are we taking prisoners?"

"We'll see that justice gets its day, Doc. Morg deserves that much, at least."

Earp left for the courthouse. Holliday went to gather McMasters and the other men. There was little question in his mind as to how it would end. Brocius and his gang would get justice, summary justice.

At the end of a gun.

# Chapter Thirty-Eight

$F$LORENTINO CRUZ REMINDED HIMSELF TO LIGHT
a candle to the Virgin. A swarthy man of mixed blood, he
treated religion with the superstition of one who believes
that all gods are whimsical and must be constantly ap-
peased. He thought it would be a serious error not to offer
thanks for his good fortune.

A horse thief, and more recently an assassin, he had
taken refuge with his sister and her husband. Cruz's
brother-in-law, who operated the wood camp for Pete
Spence, tolerated his presence. His sister spent the day
crossing herself and saying her beads. They were all too
aware that he had taken part in a murder last night. Their
fear was that he would bring death to their doorstep. Neither of them believed he was long for this world.

Only this morning, the gang had ridden off on fresh
mounts. He had elected to remain behind, certain in the
knowledge that Brocius would draw pursuit. He considered it unfortunate, almost an omen, that Earp had not
been killed at the billiard hall last night. He also considered himself a wise man for having separated from his
gringo *companeros*. No one knew of his connection with
the gang or his part in the murder. Here, with his sister
and her husband, he was out of harm's way. He was just
another Mexican in baggy trousers.

Last night, on their return from Tombstone, Brocius had
been furious. Stilwell, albeit reluctantly, had reported that
only Morgan Earp had been killed. Holliday, and their
main target, Wyatt Earp, had escaped without a scratch.
Brocius had vented his fury on Stilwell and Spence, curs-

ing them roundly. But Ringo, the quiet one, had voiced the opinion that they needed a new hideout. While no one knew of the wood camp, Ringo still felt it was time to move on. Everyone agreed, with the exception of Cruz and Spence, who saw no reason to run.

Overnight, after considerable discussion, Spence had finally been persuaded. The argument then turned to the selection of a hideout, somewhere the law would never think to look. Cruz was not involved in the debate, for he'd decided to stay on at the wood camp. No one paid him any attention, figuring he was free to stay or go as he chose. That morning, when they rode out, he had half-heartedly agreed to join them in a day or so. The moment they were gone, he'd changed into the loose-fitting trousers and shirt of a peon.

Late that afternoon, Cruz and his brother-in-law, Ramon, were splitting wood outside the cabin. Maria appeared in the doorway and tossed a pan of dirty water into the yard. She wiped her hand on her dress and stood for a moment watching the men. Then, on the verge of turning back into the house, she suddenly stiffened. She stared west, shielding her eyes against the dying flare of sunset. Some distance away she saw five riders approaching through the canyon. Their features were indistinct, but their clothing immediately identified them as gringos.

The men, following her gaze, stopped splitting wood. The riders moved toward them at a slow trot, silhouetted against the last rays of daylight. Then, emerging into the silty dusk, their features became visible. Cruz instantly recognized Wyatt Earp and Doc Holliday. He dropped his axe, jerked a pistol from the waistband of his trousers. His eyes flicked to the cabin, then he quickly changed his mind. He ran toward the corral.

As he rounded the corner of the house, Cruz broke stride and skidded to an abrupt halt. Three of the riders, one of them Doc Holliday, were circling the corral from the west. Behind him, he heard the thud of hoofbeats as the others spurred their horses to a gallop. Trapped and desperate, he sprinted toward a wooded outcropping north of the corral. Before he could reach the knoll, Holliday and two men he'd never seen cut him off. A moment later Earp and his companion closed in from the rear.

Cruz flung his six-gun on the ground and raised his hands. He watched with a doglike stare as the riders joined ranks in a loose, half-moon formation. No one spoke, but he felt Earp's gaze boring into him with the intensity of fire. The horses advanced, crowding ever closer, and he scuttled backward to avoid being trampled. Slowly, relentlessly, the riders forced him up the knoll. At the crest, still backing away, he lost his balance and tumbled head over heels down the reverse slope. The horsemen kneed their mounts into the defile and reined to a halt before him. Dazed and shaken, he hauled himself to his feet.

"What do you think?" Holliday said. "Looks like his name ought to be Florentino Cruz."

Earp merely nodded, then turned to Vermillion. "Ask him if he knows who I am."

Vermillion leaned forward. *"Conoces este hombre?"*

*"Si, este hombre se llama Earp."*

"Tell him"—Earp's voice dropped—"I came here to kill him for what he did to my brother."

Vermillion ducked his chin at Earp. *"Este hombre esta aqui para matarte. Por la cosa tu hiciste a su hermano."*

*"Madre Dios!"* Cruz clasped his hands like a man offering prayer. *"Por favor yo soy innocente! Yo no quiero morir!"*

Vermillion spat tobacco juice on the ground. "Says he didn't do it."

"Gutless bastard!" Earp made a quick, savage gesture. "Tell him he's got one chance to live. I'll let him go if he tells us where to find Brocius."

*"Dile a ellos donde esta Brocius y este hombre no le mata."*

Cruz blanched at the mention of Brocius's name. He darted an imploring look at the other men, only to be met

by grim stares. After a moment Earp pulled his carbine
from the saddle boot and slowly cocked the hammer.
Kneeing his horse to the right, he laid the carbine over the
saddle horn and lowered the muzzle until it was centered
on Cruz's head. The half-breed's eyes went round as sau-
cers. His gaze was riveted on the muzzle.

Earp wagged the tip of the barrel. "Tell him he's got five
seconds to talk or he'll be shakin' hands with his maker."

*"Usted tiene cinco segundos para hablar o usted va con
Jesus Cristo muy pronto."*

Cruz swallowed, his voice choked with terror. *"Brocius y
siete de los hombres estan en Iron Springs."*

"We got it," Vermillion said, easing back in his saddle.
"He says Brocius and the rest of the gang are holed up at
Iron Springs. Near as I recollect, that's over in the Whet-
stone Mountains."

Earp lowered the hammer. He returned the carbine to
the saddle boot and glanced at Holliday. "Toss him your
gun, Doc."

"What?" Holliday croaked. "Don't be a damn fool."

"Just do it."

Holliday frowned, pulling his pistol, and arched it
through the air. Cruz caught the gun and held it cupped
in both hands. He stood immobile, staring at them.

"Mr. Cruz, I have to break my word," Earp said. "Let's
see if you understand English. My friend is going to count
to three. You can use that gun any time after he starts
counting. *Comprender?*"

Cruz hesitated, then nodded. *"Si,"* he managed. "And if
I kill you, senor?"

"Then you're a free man," Earp said. "Go ahead, Doc
. . . start counting."

Holliday sighed heavily. "One—"

Cruz broke the count. He fumbled the pistol into his
right hand and thumbed the hammer. As he raised it, Earp
drew his Colt and fired in a fluid motion. The slug struck
Cruz in the chest and he lowered the gun, a surprised

expression on his face. Then he slowly folded to the ground.

Holliday stepped down from the saddle. He reclaimed his pistol and looked at the other men. "For the record, Cruz was shot resisting arrest."

"Game little bastard," McMasters said. "He gave it a good try."

Earp reined his horse around and rode off. The others trailed him over the knoll and down past the corral. Out front of the cabin, the Mexican and the half-breed woman were standing with their heads bowed. Earp signaled a halt, and the men reined in their mounts directly behind him. When the dust settled, he turned his gaze on the couple. His eyes were cold and impassive, his mouth razored in a tight line. He motioned to Vermillion.

"Tell'em Cruz is dead." He dug out a gold coin and tossed it in the dirt at their feet. "Twenty dollars ought to buy him an impressive mass."

*"Su amigo esta muerto."*

The man removed his sombrero, looking down at the coin, and bobbed his head. The woman stood stock-still, her eyes frozen on the patch of ground at her feet. Earp brought his horse sharply around and spurred off into the gathering darkness.

The men kicked their mounts into a lope and rode after him. The thud of hoofbeats slowly diminished, and within moments the riders were lost to sight.

The sister of Florentino Cruz crossed herself and slowly collapsed in the doorway. Her husband stooped down, wiping dust off the coin, and stuck it in his pocket. He went inside the cabin, returned a moment later with a lighted lantern and a shovel. He walked in the direction of the knoll.

Late the next afternoon, deep in the Whetstone Mountains, they rounded a curve in the trail. Earp was in the lead, followed by Holliday, with the others strung out in single file. The trail, used for centuries by the Apache, seemed to end where an escarpment dropped off into space.

The sun sank lower, smothering in a bed of copper beyond the mountains. The ragged crests jutted skyward like sentinels guarding a cruel and lifeless land. Far below, bordered by a grove of trees, the springs lay hidden in purple shadow. There was no sound, only the foreboding silence of oncoming night.

The men reined to a halt on a craggy ridge overlooking the spring. A narrow trail led downward to the wooded gorge, winding around a rocky spur near the bottom. McMasters dismounted, quickly inspecting the trail where it sloped steeply off the ridge. He grunted to himself, spotting marks left by shod horses in the hard-packed ground. After closer examination he turned and indicated the tracks with a sweeping motion of his arm.

Earp told the other men to stay with the horses. He walked forward and joined McMasters at the edge of the escarpment. They went belly down, removing their hats, and began a systematic inspection of the basin below. The springs was plainly visible, a cool water hole freshened from deep within the earth's core. The shelter belt of trees, thick with undergrowth and obscured by shadow, curved in a gentle arc beyond the springs. There was no movement, no picket line of horses, no sign of man. To all appearances, only wilderness creatures came to drink at Iron Springs.

Earp looked perplexed. "What do you make of that?"

"Beats me," McMasters said, studying the springs intently. "Looks dead as a doornail down there."

"No way they could've known we're on their trail."

"You reckon they're camped back in those trees?"

"Got me," Earp confessed. "If they are, why don't we see smoke from a fire? They'd have no reason to pitch a cold camp."

"Well, I know one thing," McMasters said with conviction. "Those tracks were made yesterday. Somebody went down that trail before nightfall."

"Then where the hell are they?"

"Is there another way out of here?"

"Could be," Earp allowed, pointing south along the gorge. "The ground seems to drop off in that direction. Maybe something spooked them and they've hightailed it."

"I guess there's only one way to find out."

"You're right, Sherm. Let's go have a look."

In the deepening twilight, the men gathered their horses. Earp led the way, followed by Holliday, then Mc-Masters, with Vermillion and Johnson bringing up the rear. They went down the narrow trail single file, the jangle of saddle gear chiming musically in the stillness. No one spoke, for the men were weary, their senses dulled after nearly two days in the saddle. They had come here prepared for a fight, and there was a natural letdown now that it appeared Brocius had once again slipped away.

The trail bottomed out and Earp reined toward the springs. One by one the men rode forward, loosely grouped behind him. The gorge was rapidly turning dark, and ahead the grove of trees was cloaked in inky shadow. Then, like blinking fireflies, a row of guns spat flame all along the tree line.

Earp's saddle horn disintegrated and his hat flew off his head. He kicked free of the stirrups, grabbing his carbine, and dove headlong from the saddle. He landed on his side and rolled over, thumbing back the hammer as he came to rest on his stomach. Across the water hole the trees were now alive with the fiery blast of gunshots. He slammed the carbine into his shoulder and centered on a muzzle flash. When he pulled the trigger, the carbine misfired and he jerked his pistol.

Behind him, the men had quit their horses and hit the ground. With the exception of Holliday's horse, they had survived the first volley unscathed. Veterans of countless

shootouts, they reacted almost instinctively after the initial
shock of the ambush. The gunfire swelled in intensity as
they quickly joined the fight. Bellied down, they made
poor targets despite the storm of lead whistling across the
water hole. The crack of the outlaws' rifles was punctuated
by the dull boom of their own six-guns. Unlike the outlaws, however, they were not scattering their shots in a
random barrage. Instead, making each bullet count, they
fixed on a muzzle flash and aimed slightly to the right.
Accuracy under darkened conditions was difficult, but
their fire had a telling effect. A howl indicated that at least
one of the gang had been wounded, and another fell
thrashing at the edge of the tree line. Yet the fight quickened in tempo, and the sound of gunfire rose to a staccato
roar. A patchwork of snarling lead hissed back and forth
across the springs.

From his position at the front, Earp hugged the ground
and poured a steady fire into the trees. He was aware of
Holliday, who was shooting from behind the fallen horse,
and he heard the bark of guns off to one side. But he was
too busy to count, and he had no idea who might have
been wounded or killed. When he emptied the Colt, he
rolled to a new position and reloaded all six chambers. His
next shot drew return fire, two quick rounds. One slug
kicked dirt in his face and the other whizzed past his
head. Beside a tree, momentarily revealed in the muzzle
flash, he saw the bare outlines of a man's face. He dropped
his sights a notch and thumbed off three shots, rapid fire.
Almost instantly there was a downward flash as the rifle
fired into the ground and the man pitched sideways into
the undergrowth. Then, too sudden to comprehend, all
firing from the tree line abruptly ceased.

Several more shots were fired by McMasters and the
others before they realized the fight was over. A stillness
settled across the spring, and moments later the rumble of
hooves filtered through the trees. A blur of horses, almost

invisible in the darkness, suddenly bolted from the far end of the grove. The riders whipped their mounts into a gallop and were quickly gone, clattering south through the gorge. Within seconds even the thud of hoofbeats faded to nothing.

Earp ordered a fire built, and it soon became clear that Holliday's horse was the only casualty. McMasters had been grazed along the cheekbone, and Vermillion had suffered a flesh wound, but Johnson was untouched. By the light of the fire it was also apparent that Earp enjoyed a state of grace almost beyond belief. His clothes hung in tatters. There were three holes through his coat, another drilled through his hat, and a slug was embedded in the heel of his boot. Not one had drawn blood.

In the light of the fire it was revealed that two outlaws had answered the call. One of them was the man Earp had shot, three neat holes stitched beneath his breastbone. His identity was unknown, but papers in his wallet revealed him to be Pete Spence. The second man was instantly recognizable. Curly Bill Brocius had taken two slugs directly above his belt buckle. His shirtfront was a starburst of blood and gore.

Earp seemed to derive no satisfaction from the outlaw leader's death. His expression betrayed no hint of vindication. He stared down at the body, slowly shook his head.

"Two down," he said. "Three to go."

Holliday looked at him. "I'd say Brocius is a pretty good start."

"The others are just as guilty, Doc. Nothing's settled till we get them."

"Without Brocius, they might split up. What if they take off for who-knows-where?"

"Doesn't matter," Earp said coldly. "I'll still hunt them down."

Holliday nodded. "Might take a while."

"I've got time, Doc. A whole lifetime."

\* \* \*

Some miles from the springs, the outlaws reined to a halt. Their horses were lathered and blowing hard, almost spent. They dismounted, allowing the animals a needed breather.

"Let's be quick," Ike said in a wild voice. "Them bastards might be right on our heels."

"Not in the dark," Stilwell replied, stamping his feet against the cold. "They'll hole up till mornin'."

"Dark doesn't seem to bother them all that much. Tracked us to the springs, didn't they?"

"Did they?" Ringo said doubtfully. "I've got an idea Cruz tipped them off. Wonder if they let him go?"

Stilwell grunted. "I'd tend to doubt it. Way things shape up, they're lookin' to take scalps."

"Hell's fire!" Ike waved off into the dark. "They got Curly Bill and Pete back there. You'd think that was enough."

"You'd think wrong," Stilwell said. "Earp won't quit till we're all dead. Not after we killed his brother."

"Sonovabitch better have himself a good horse. He'll have to chase me to hell and gone!"

"We're through running," Ringo said quietly. "Otherwise we'll be looking over our shoulders the rest of our lives."

Ike suddenly went still. "What d'you mean—we're through running?"

"I mean that's what Earp expects. So we're gonna do the exact opposite."

"Johnny's right," Stilwell added. "Only chance we've got is to take the fight to them."

"Jesus Christ!" Ike wailed. "You'll just get us killed quicker."

Ringo laughed. "You've got it bassackward, Ike. Earp and Holliday are the ones that get killed this time."

"You'll recollect we tried that a couple of times already. You aim to pull a rabbit out of the hat?"

"Maybe I will. I'll have to think about it."

Ringo stared off into the dark. He was struck by a sudden fatalistic sense of what it meant to turn and fight. Then, amused by the thought, he laughed at himself.

One way or another, any man could be killed. All he needed was a hat trick, and Earp was dead.

He put his mind to work on it.

# Chapter Thirty-Nine

THREE DAYS LATER THEY RODE INTO TOMBSTONE. Their search had taken them south from Iron Springs into the wastelands along the border. Then, after the trail doubled back in a northerly direction, a hard, cold rain had wiped out the tracks. Yet their hunt, though temporarily suspended, had confirmed what Earp suspected. Johnny Ringo, Ike Clanton, and Frank Stilwell were still riding together.

A brisk afternoon wind whipped down Allen Street. The men dropped their horses off at the livery stable and walked up to the hotel. On the street people stopped to stare as they trooped past. Everyone in town knew they had gone off in pursuit of Brocius and his gang. Watching them now, passersby were gripped by a certain ghoulish curiosity. But none dared ask the question on all their minds. Earp looked in no mood to talk.

The men were grungy with trail dust, their faces unshaven. At the hotel, Earp left them and continued on to Dr. Goodfellow's office. He had to wait several minutes while the physician finished with a patient. When he was shown into the examining room, Goodfellow wisely suppressed his own curiosity about the manhunt. Earp was there to talk about Virgil, and he demanded hard answers to hard questions. Somewhat reluctantly, Goodfellow gave him the reassurance he sought.

On the street again, Earp turned back toward the hotel. As he was crossing Fourth and Allen, Harry Woods, editor of the *Nugget*, intercepted him. Woods was out of breath, whoofing puffs of frost in the cold air. He appeared to have run all the way from his office.

"Mr. Earp," he said, trying to catch his wind. "I just heard you'd returned to town."

Earp kept walking. "News travels fast."

"I'd like to ask you some questions."

"Why should I give you the time of day? All you'll do is misquote me."

Woods trotted along to keep pace. "For one thing, I'm the only newspaper in town. John Clum hasn't returned."

"Try again," Earp said. "Where you're concerned, the only good news is no news."

"I'll give you my word as a gentleman. Anything you say will be quoted verbatim."

"For your sake, your word better be good. Go ahead, fire away."

Woods pulled out a pad and pencil. "First, I understand you obtained warrants for William Brocius and five other men. Were you able to apprehend any of them?"

"No," Earp said shortly. "Brocius, Spence, and Cruz were killed resisting arrest. The other three are still at large."

"What does that mean—resisting arrest?"

"What it means, Harry, is that they fired guns at us. We fired back."

Woods tried to write while he walked. "Were any of your men hurt?"

"No."

"Where did this encounter take place?"

"Two places," Earp said. "Cruz bought it over in the Dragoons. We tracked the others to Iron Springs."

"Where you killed Brocius and Spence?"

"After they opened fire on sworn law officers."

Woods jotted it down. "What are your plans now?"

Earp stopped, and the newspaperman skidded to a halt. "Write this down word for word, Harry. I intend to bring these fugitives to justice, however long it takes. When I do"—he paused with a tight smile—"the criminal alliance between Sheriff John Behan and the outlaw element of Cochise County will be ended. Got all that?"

Woods scribbled furiously. "Isn't that just a touch too slanderous?"

"You can quote me as saying it's the God's honest truth."

"Let me ask you—"

"The interview's ended, Harry. See you around."

Earp left him standing on the boardwalk. Downstreet, he entered the hotel, ignoring an inquisitive look from the desk clerk. He ordered pails of hot water sent to his room, enough for a bath. Upstairs, he knocked gently on Virgil's door. Allie's voice sounded from inside, and he identified himself. She opened the door, a pistol hidden beneath the folds of her skirt.

"Come in, Wyatt," she said. "You look like you've been to hell and back."

"That's about the size of it, Allie."

Virgil was propped up in bed, resting against a bank of pillows. His color was good, though his left arm was bound in a sling, and his eyes appeared alert. A gun was near at hand on the bedside table.

"Well, now," Earp said, grinning. "Bright-eyed and bushy-tailed, aren't you?"

"Wouldn't say that," Virgil replied. "But I'm a helluva lot better than I was when you left."

"That's easy to see."

"Doc stopped by a while ago. He told me you got Brocius and a couple of others."

"Which leaves three," Earp said crisply. "Ringo, Clanton, and Frank Stilwell."

"Any ideas?" Virgil asked. "Doc says you think they doubled back in this direction."

"One thing about Ringo, he's no quitter. I figure he's still looking to even the score."

"You think he'll come after you, then?"

"I'm betting on it," Earp said. "But you and Allie won't be here when he does. I'm sending you to California."

"Hold on," Virgil said hotly. "I can still pull my own weight."

"Not anytime soon, Virg. You'd be better off with Ma and Pa till you're in the pink. That California sunshine ought to be just the ticket."

Allie moved to the bedside. Her eyes fastened on Earp. "You think Ringo will come after Virgil, don't you?"

"Yeah, I do," Earp admitted. "Just now, Ringo probably figures Virg for an easy mark. He'll take any payback he can get."

"We'll have to ask Dr. Goodfellow if Virgil's in any condition to travel."

"I went by there before I came here. The doc says he's fit enough for the train ride to California."

"Then it's settled." She glanced at Virgil. "No argument out of you, either. We're going to see your folks."

Virgil surrendered with his good arm. "You two are a caution when you get started. So when do we leave?"

"Tomorrow," Earp said. "I'll make the arrangements."

"What about Morgan?"

"I planned to send him on to California, anyway. I think Ma and Pa would want him buried there."

"Yeah," Virgil said sadly. "It's for the best."

Earp stayed a few minutes longer. Then, pressed for time, he went on to his room. The hot water he'd ordered was waiting, and he treated himself to a bath. Afterward, he shaved and selected a vested suit from the wardrobe. Dressed, he made his way downstairs, still ignoring the clerk's inquisitive look. Outside, he turned downstreet.

"Earp! Wyatt Earp!"

Behan, flanked by a deputy, hurried along the boardwalk. He halted a few paces away, thumbs hooked in his gun belt. His features were flushed with anger.

"I want to see you, Earp."

"Behan, if you're not careful, you'll see me once too often."

"Harry Woods says you told him I'm involved in some kind of criminal deal. Is that true?"

"On both counts," Earp said. "I told him, and you are. Too bad Brocius decided to fight. He could've sent you to prison."

"Says you!" Behan darted a nervous glance at passersby on the street. "I'm going to look into these so-called 'killed while resisting arrest' shootings. Just one irregularity, and I'll come for you with a warrant."

"Don't come for me at all, Behan. Never again."

"I plan to sue you for slander, too."

"Good. That's certain to get me elected."

Behan opened his mouth, but nothing came out. His jaw quivered and his face mottled with rage. Then, unhooking his thumbs from his gun belt, he turned and stalked away. The deputy trailed along behind.

The exchange improved Earp's spirits. Apart from putting Behan in jail, winning at the polls would be the next best thing. He continued down the street and entered the Grand Hotel. Upstairs, when Sadie opened her door, her eyes went round with joy. She threw her arms around his neck.

"Oh, Wyatt!" She kissed him, pulling him into the room. "I've been worried sick about you!"

Earp dropped his hat on a chair. "Told you, I always come back. You can bank on it."

She hugged him fiercely. "What happened? Is it over?"

"Not quite yet."

Earp gave her a quick version of the last several days. Then he explained why he was sending Virgil to California. Her eyes suddenly went misty.

"So it's not over."

"Soon," Earp said. "Trust me on that."

"I do," she told him. "You know I do. I just can't help worrying . . ."

"Then put on your best dress and a big smile. We'll order champagne with supper tonight. I want you in a good mood."

"Why, Mr. Earp! You don't have to ply me with champagne."

"Never know," Earp said, mock serious. "I might have to get you tipsy tonight."

"Oh, really?" She caught something different in his voice. "What's so different about tonight?"

"Lots of things. Leastways, I hope so. I'll tell you at supper."

"What?" Her eyes were bright and wide. "Tell me now!"

Earp grinned. "One time in Dodge City, there was this Chinaman who used to do my laundry. Wise old bird, regular Confucius. Know what he used to say?"

"No, what?"

"Anticipation is half the joy."

"That's not—" She stopped, caught her breath. "Omigod! Are you serious?"

"Send a message over to the theater. Tell them you won't be there tonight."

"You are serious!"

"See you for supper."

Earp kissed her lightly on the mouth. Before she could respond, he collected his hat and went out the door. Halfway down the stairs his smile faded into a somber expression. He remembered that he had still another stop to make. On the street he turned uptown. His face was now stony.

He walked toward the funeral parlor.

In the early morning hours, with the sky still dark, the evacuation got under way. Everyone had an assignment, and there was a sense of foreboding about the preparations. Earp and Holliday, assisted by Vermillion, took one of the buckboards to the funeral parlor. There, Morgan's coffin was loaded aboard and lashed down with rope. Mc-

Masters and Johnson, meanwhile, got the rest of the family ready to travel. Virgil and Allie, along with Jane, Morgan's widow, were dressed and waiting when Earp returned. The women were allowed only one trunk apiece, and even then the buckboards were cramped and overcrowded. As false dawn lighted the horizon, the little caravan rolled north out of Tombstone.

Their immediate destination was Contention. A railway junction, the small settlement lay some twelve miles north along the banks of the San Pedro. While the distance was not that great, it was a remote stretch of road, well-suited to ambush. Earp, heedful of his own warning about Ringo, treated the operation somewhat like a military withdrawal. Outriders were assigned to the cardinal points. With himself and Holliday in the vanguard, Vermillion and Johnson rode on the flanks. McMasters brought up the rear.

Around mid-morning, after an uneventful journey, their caravan pulled into Contention. At the train station Earp stepped down from his saddle and took a position by the buckboard with Virgil and Allie. He signaled Vermillion and Johnson to the other buckboard, driven by Jane, which bore Morgan's casket. McMasters went to make arrangements with a livery stable. Their horses, as well as the buckboards, would be left behind.

Holliday circled the depot. Apart from the usual loafers, there was no one around. Still, the loafers were intrigued by the caravan with a coffin and five heavily armed men. Holliday inspected the waiting room, ignoring the stares, and finally walked to the ticket window. There, he bought eight tickets, and baggage car space for the coffin, to Tucson. The stationmaster came outside for a better look as he walked back to the buckboards.

Earp was determined that Virgil would leave Arizona alive. He and Holliday stood guard while the coffin was moved to the station platform. When McMasters went off with the horses, the other men were posted around the depot. The coffin, bathed in the pewter light from an overcast sky, reminded them that three of the killers were still at large. Vigilance seemed entirely in order.

They waited for the noon train to Tucson.

# Chapter Forty

THE STORM BROKE SHORTLY AFTER NIGHTFALL. A blue-white bolt of lightning seared the sky, and an instant later a thunderclap shook the depot. Then a torrent of rain struck the earth in a rattling deluge.

Already an hour overdue, the westbound pulled into Tucson just as the storm unleashed its fury. A groaning squeal racketed back over the coaches as the engineer throttled down and set the brakes. The engine rolled past the depot and ground to a halt, showering fiery sparks in a final burst of power. The station agent, dressed in a rain slicker, walked forward as the conductor stepped down from the lead coach.

When the train stopped alongside the platform, Earp emerged from underneath the depot's overhanging roof. He carried a double-barrel shotgun, and the shadowy figures ranged behind him edged forward. He slowly inspected the platform, watching intently as several passengers alighted from the train and hurried into the station house. Then he turned his head and nodded.

McMasters moved forward and took a position near the express car. A row of lanterns, strung along the front of the station house, gave him a commanding view in either direction. Vermillion and Johnson appeared from beneath the overhang, pulling a baggage cart that contained Morgan's coffin and the women's trunks. They trundled the cart across the platform and jockeyed it into position before the express car. A messenger threw the door open, motioning with his hand. The men scrambled onto the cart, one on either end of the coffin, and carried it inside.

The trunks went next, and within moments they returned, jumping from the cart to the platform. They moved past Earp and took up positions near the station-house door.

Late that afternoon their train from Contention had arrived in Tucson. Stepping onto the depot platform, Earp carried a shotgun he'd previously stored with the luggage. A short conversation convinced the stationmaster that he was a federal marshal and there on official business. While Earp and the others stood guard, Holliday had then checked out the station house. Finally, satisfied that all was clear, Virgil had been carried into the waiting room by Vermillion and Johnson. Holliday, trailed by the women, had escorted them inside. He'd been assigned to watch them until the westbound train arrived.

Morgan's coffin had then been transferred from the express car onto a baggage cart. Under dark skies threatening rain, the baggage cart had been rolled beneath the depot's overhanging roof. McMasters, Vermillion, and Johnson had taken positions spread out along the platform. Earp, cradling the shotgun over one arm, had posted himself outside the door of the waiting room. Still concerned, even though they had made it safely to Tucson, he'd watched silently as the train got under way for Phoenix. Some sixth sense had told him not to relax his vigilance until Virgil was aboard the train for California. Beneath the storm clouds, he'd settled in to wait.

The wait was now over, the westbound huffing steam in a steady downpour. Nodding to the other men, Earp walked directly to the station-house door. Opening it, he stuck his head inside, then turned and moved back onto the platform. Holliday stepped outside, trailed closely by the women, and splashed through the rain to the middle passenger car. Vermillion and Johnson carried Virgil from the waiting room and took him aboard the train. A moment later Holliday reappeared, halting beside Earp and McMasters. Vermillion and Johnson, emerging onto the platform, assumed positions in front of the coach.

"Christ," Holliday said, water dripping off his hat. "It's pouring cats and dogs."

"Lower elevation here," McMasters noted. "Probably snowin' like hell in Tombstone."

Earp seemed oblivious to the rain. "Get everybody settled?"

"All set," Holliday replied. "Virgil and Allie are in the compartment just ahead of Jane."

"I'm going aboard. Keep a sharp lookout."

Earp took a last look around, then moved inside the coach. Holliday's coat was now soaked, the rain drumming harder. Through the car windows he saw Earp enter Jane's compartment. Watching them, he was aware that his friend now faced the worst of the ordeal. All evening Earp had roamed the station, avoiding conversation, curiously withdrawn. But with time running out, there was no way to avoid it any longer. The moment for parting was at hand.

On the train, Jane turned from the window as Earp stopped in the doorway of her compartment. She was dressed entirely in black, a widow in mourning. Upon leaving Tombstone, she had bravely insisted on driving the buckboard with Morgan's coffin. Yet now, thinking of him consigned to the baggage car, she felt separated by more than distance. She looked drained of courage.

"Jane—" Earp hesitated, his features grim. "I'm not all that good with words. But I wanted you to know—"

"You don't have to say it, Wyatt. I know how much you loved Morgan. And he worshiped you—"

Her voice broke, tears spilling down her cheeks. Earp moved forward, took her in his arms. She sobbed quietly, her head pressed to his chest. He ran a hand gently over her hair.

"You made Morg happy," he said. "Think of it that way, and maybe things won't be so hard. He thought he was the luckiest man in the world."

"I miss him." She shuddered, caught her breath. "I miss him so much."

Earp stroked her hair. Then he hugged her tightly and stepped into the passageway. Allie and Virgil were waiting for him in their compartment. The bed was turned down and Virgil was resting against a bank of pillows. He appeared tired, somehow older.

"Guess it's time," Earp said. "Anything you need?"

"No," Virgil assured him. "We're fine."

Earp was silent a moment. Then, his voice low, he looked at Virgil. "I wish things had worked out different. For you and Morg."

Virgil smiled. "Don't worry yourself about me. Just finish what we started in Tombstone."

Earp leaned forward, shook his hand. "Tell Ma and Pa I'll be out for a visit one of these days."

Watching them, Allie realized that two strong men were saying good-bye in the only way they knew how. Nothing maudlin, their emotions reined tight, telling one another without words. She thought it was the saddest parting anyone could imagine.

Earp turned toward the door, squeezed her arm. "Take care of yourself, Allie."

She pulled his face down, kissed him on the cheek. "God be with you, Wyatt."

Earp found no way to reply. He nodded, moving into the passageway, and a moment later stepped out the coach door. His features were somber, almost stark in the glow of lamps from the depot. He glanced around the platform, then looked at Holliday.

"Everything all right out here?"

"So far." Holliday extracted a telegram from his inside coat pocket. "This came over the wire just before you called us out of the waiting room. Figured it could wait till we got Virgil boarded."

Earp opened the telegram. He scanned it quickly, then grunted. "It's from Sadie. Word's out that Frank Stilwell was sighted here in Tucson this afternoon. The marshal here wired Behan, and word somehow leaked out."

"No secret there. The telegraph operator in Tombstone has the biggest mouth in town."

"I'll have to give him a medal. If Stilwell's here, that means Ringo and Clanton aren't far behind."

Holliday knuckled his mustache. "You think they know we're here?"

"Probably," Earp said. "Lots of people knew we were sending Virg to California. Doc Goodfellow and Lou Ruda-baugh, just to name two."

"Talk spreads fast," Holliday observed. "Ringo and those boys would've had plenty of time to get here."

"Especially if they'd been tipped off yesterday. I wouldn't put it past Johnny Behan."

"Hell, I'd lay odds on it!"

Earp's eyes strayed to the front of the train. A lightning bolt illuminated the sky and he suddenly stiffened. The figure of a man darted from behind a stack of railroad ties and ran across the tracks, disappearing around the front of the engine. Earp rapped out a sharp command.

"Sherm, you and the boys stay here! Don't let anyone else on board. Doc, you come with me."

McMasters motioned for Vermillion and Johnson to hold their positions. Earp, followed by Holliday, led the way down the platform. At the rear of the caboose they crossed the tracks onto the opposite side of the train. Ahead they saw what appeared to be two men moving toward them, rising every few steps to peer in the coach windows. Then, glancing in their direction, the men spotted them and whirled to run. Earp threw the shotgun to his shoulder.

"Halt or I'll fire!"

The men stopped, eased around with their arms in the air. As Earp and Holliday approached them, light from the coaches clearly outlined their features. Johnny Ringo and Frank Stilwell stared at them with a mixture of fear and bravado. Holliday was on the left, his pistol out and cocked. Earp held the shotgun extended at waist level. He halted facing Ringo.

"Glad you boys showed up. Saves the trouble of running you down."

Ringo faked a smile. "I never argue with a shotgun."

"Where's Ike Clanton?"

"Wouldn't have the least notion."

"How long have you been here?"

"Long enough."

Earp wagged the shotgun at the coaches. "What was your plan? Get Virgil and then catch me coming around the train?"

"Just walkin' the tracks," Ringo said. "No law against that."

"There's a law against murder. I have a warrant for your arrest."

"So take me to jail. You've got nothin' on me."

"Yeah, I do," Earp told him. "All we need is one witness who's willing to talk. Frank's our man."

Ringo glanced at Stilwell, then back at Earp. "What makes you think he'll talk?"

"Hell, Ringo, he was just following orders. When he swings, he'll want you there beside him."

"I don't get it. Why are you tellin' me all this?"

Earp shifted the shotgun to his left hand. "I'll give you an even break with pistols. Kill me and you walk away."

"What about Frank?"

"That's between him and Doc. Holster your gun, Doc."

Holliday lowered the hammer, then holstered his Colt. The train jolted forward and the first passenger car slowly rolled past them. Out of the corner of his eye, Earp saw the conductor and several passengers peering out the coach window. Ringo used the momentary distraction to lower his arms. His hand suddenly darted to his side.

Earp was a beat faster. He fired as Ringo's gun cleared leather, vaguely aware of Stilwell clawing at his holster. Then Holliday's Colt belched flame, and Stilwell collapsed at the knees. Ringo dropped his pistol, clutching at his chest, blood seeping through his fingers. His expression was one of amazement, shocked disbelief. He slowly folded to the ground.

The train gathered speed. Intermittent light from the coach windows framed the faces of Ringo and Stilwell in a flickering death mask. Abruptly, from the direction of the depot, there was a single shot followed by a volley of gunfire. The express car rattled by as echoes from the gunshots faded away. A moment later the taillights of the caboose swept past.

Across the tracks Earp saw McMasters and the other men walking toward the far end of the depot. They stopped where a body lay sprawled on the platform, halfway between the stack of railroad ties and the station house. Vermillion knelt down, inspecting the body, and said something over his shoulder. McMasters turned back toward Earp and Holliday.

"Ike Clanton," he shouted. "Winged a shot at us and took off running. He's dead."

Earp motioned down at the tracks. "We got Ringo and Stilwell."

"Good," McMasters called out. "What now?"

"Send one of the boys to find Crawley Dake, the U.S. Marshal. You'll probably catch him at home this time of evening. Tell him to come down here."

McMasters signaled, turning toward the depot. Holliday was staring down at the bodies beside the tracks. He shook his head. "What made you think Ringo would go for it?"

"Wouldn't you?" Earp said. "A roll of the dice beats a hangman's knot."

"Guess it does at that."

Holliday looked across at the depot. He watched a moment as the other men stood talking. Finally, with a nod in their direction, he glanced at Earp.

"Three down and none to go. Ike was the last one."

"Not quite."

"What do you mean?"

"John Behan's the last one. When I whip him in the election, then it's over."

Holliday laughed. "Wyatt, if you're not careful, you'll wind up owning Tombstone."

"That's not a bad idea either, Doc."

Earp turned so abruptly that he caught Holliday by surprise. A pace behind, Holliday trailed him across the platform.

"Slow down," Holliday said. "What's the big rush?"

"Got to send Sadie a telegram."

"What for?"

Earp grinned. "Tell her I'm coming home. Home to stay."

"Hell, that'll be the day! I'll lay seven to three she never gets you to the altar."

"Doc, you just lost yourself a bet."

They walked toward the depot.

# Afterword

WYATT EARP MARRIED JOSEPHINE SARAH MARCUS. Yet the wanderlust that had governed his life continued to draw him onward. After leaving Tombstone, he and Sadie spent parts of 1882 in San Francisco and Gunnison, Colorado. Thus began a western odyssey that took them from boom town to boom town for more than twenty years.

The greater part of 1883 was spent in Colorado. In 1884, Wyatt and Sadie traveled to Idaho, joining the gold rush at Coeur d'Alene. The next year saw them in Cripple Creek, Colorado, followed by jaunts to Wyoming and Texas. Wyatt never again wore a badge, devoting himself instead to business ventures. He operated gambling halls and saloons, and speculated in mining properties.

From 1886 to 1890, Wyatt operated a saloon in San Francisco. He was joined by Virgil at various times in his business enterprises. In 1887, he traveled to Glenwood Springs, Colorado, for a last visit with Doc Holliday, who died shortly afterward, at age thirty-five, in a sanatorium. During the period 1891–1896, he and Virgil operated a gambling hall in San Diego. On the side, Wyatt raised thoroughbred horses.

In 1897, Wyatt and Sadie joined the gold rush to Alaska. Locating in Nome, they remained there until 1901, with Wyatt engaged in the operation of a saloon and gaming parlor. Late in 1901, they joined Virgil in Nevada, where a new gold rush was under way. For the next five years, Wyatt and Virgil ran businesses in Goldfield and Tonopah. Then, in 1906, Virgil died of pneumonia.

Wyatt and Sadie quit the boom camps and settled permanently in Los Angeles. Devoted solely to business, Wyatt invested in gold and silver mines, as well as newly developed oil fields. By the 1920s, with motion pictures all the rage, Wyatt was sought out by Hollywood producers for research on the Old West. Among his many friends were the cowboy movie stars William S. Hart and Tom Mix.

Wyatt Earp died a natural death at the age of eighty in 1929. He was survived by Sadie, who worked to perpetuate his memory as a frontier lawman until her own death nearly twenty years later. His biography, written by a young journalist, was published in 1931. The title, in only four words, provided a summation of the legend. *Wyatt Earp: Frontier Marshal.*

In 1889, Bill Tilghman joined the historic land rush that transformed a raw frontier into Oklahoma Territory. A lawman by trade, he set aside his badge to make his fortune in the boom-towns. Yet Tilghman was called into service once more, on a bold, relentless journey that would make his name a legend for all time—in an epic confrontation with outlaw Bill Doolin.

# OUTLAW KINGDOM

# MATT BRAUN

**OUTLAW KINGDOM**
Matt Braun
_____ 95618-5  $5.99 U.S./$6.99 CAN.

For decades the Texas plains ran with the blood of natives and settlers, as pioneers carved out ranch land from ancient Indian hunting grounds and the U.S. Army turned the tide of battle. Now the Civil War has begun, and the Army is pulling out of Fort Belknap—giving the Comanches a new chance for victory and revenge.

Led by the remarkable warrior, Little Buffalo, the Comanche and Kiowa are united in a campaign to wipe out the settlers forever. But in their way stand two remarkable men...

Allan Johnson is a former plantation owner. Britt Johnson was once his family slave, now a freed man facing a new kind of hatred on the frontier. Together, with a rag-tag volunteer army, they'll stand up for their hopes and dreams in a journey of courage and conscience that will lead to victory...or death.

# BLACK FOX

## A Novel by
## MATT BRAUN

### Bestselling author of *Wyatt Earp*